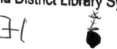

The Trail to
CRAZY MAN

Center Point
Large Print

Also by Louis L'Amour and available from Center Point Large Print:

Borden Chantry
Glory Riders
Riding for the Brand

This Large Print Book carries the Seal of Approval of N.A.V.H.

The Trail to CRAZY MAN

A Western Duo

Louis L'Amour

CENTER POINT LARGE PRINT
THORNDIKE, MAINE

This Circle Ⓥ Western is published by
Center Point Large Print in the year 2016 in
co-operation with Golden West Literary Agency.

First Edition
March, 2016

Printed in the United States of America
on permanent paper.
Set in 16-point Times New Roman type.

ISBN: 978-1-62899-908-2

Library of Congress Cataloging-in-Publication Data

Names: L'Amour, Louis, 1908-1988. | L'Amour, Louis, 1908–1988.
Trail to Peach Meadow Cañon. | L'Amour, Louis, 1908–1988. Trail to
Crazy Man.
Title: The trail to crazy man : a western duo / Louis L'Amour.
Description: First edition. | Thorndike, Maine : Center Point Large Print,
2016. | Series: A Circle V western
Identifiers: LCCN 2015037597 | ISBN 9781628999082
   (hardcover : alk. paper)
Subjects: LCSH: Western stories.
Classification: LCC PS3523.A446 A6 2016 | DDC 813/.52—dc23
LC record available at http://lccn.loc.gov/2015037597

The Trail to
CRAZY MAN

Editor's Note

by Jon Tuska

Very early in his career as a pulp writer, in the period just prior to the outbreak of the Second World War, Louis L'Amour created a series character named Pongo Jim Mayo, the master of a tramp steamer in Far Eastern waters, in L'Amour's words "an Irish-American who had served his first five years at sea sailing out of Liverpool and along the west coast of Africa's Pongo River, where he picked up his nickname. He's a character I created from having gotten to know men just like him while I was a seaman in my yondering days." After the war, when L'Amour began to specialize in Western fiction, he wrote most frequently under the pseudonym Jim Mayo, taking it from this early fictional character. "The Trail to Peach Meadow Cañon" by Jim Mayo appeared in *Giant Western* (10/49). It was subsequently reprinted under this same title and byline in *Triple Western* (Fall, 56). The text was expanded and substantially changed when it subsequently was published as an original paperback titled *Son of a Wanted Man* in 1984.

"The Trail to Crazy Man" by Jim Mayo was published in *West* (7/48) and was later expanded into a paperback original by Louis L'Amour first published by Ace Books in 1954 as *Crossfire Trail*. This version was subsequently filmed as *Crossfire Trail* (TNT, 2001), starring Tom Selleck.

There is a special magic in these original short novels as they first appeared in their magazine versions, and the texts of both have been scrupulously restored. It has been a pleasure for me to gather these two fine Western stories in book form.

The Trail to Peach Meadow Cañon

I

Winter snows were melting in the forests of the Kaibab, and the red-and-orange hue of the 1,000-foot Vermilion Cliffs was streaked with the dampness of melting frost. Deer were feeding in the forest glades among the stands of ponderosa and fir, and the trout were leaping in the streams. Where sunlight trailed through the webbed overhang of the leaves, the water danced and sparkled.

Five deer were feeding on the grass along a mountain stream back of Finger Butte, their coats mottled by the light and shadow of the sun shining through the trees. A vague something moved in the woods behind them, and the five-pronged buck lifted his regal head and stared curiously about. He turned his nose into the wind, reading it cautiously. But his trust was betrayal, for the movement was downwind of him.

The movement came again, and a young man stepped from concealment behind a huge fir not twenty feet from the nearest deer. He was straight and tall in gray, fringed buckskins, and he wore no hat. His hair was thick, black, and wavy, growing fully over the temples, and his face was lean and brown. Smiling, he walked toward the deer with quick, lithe strides, and had taken three

11

full steps before some tiny sound betrayed him.

The buck's head came up and swung around, and then with a startled snort it sprang away, the others following.

Mike Bastian stood grinning, his hands on his hips.

"Well, what do you think now, Roundy?" he called. "Could your Apache beat that? I could have touched him if I had jumped after him!"

Rance Roundy came out of the trees—a lean, wiry old man with a gray mustache and blue eyes that were still bright with an alert awareness.

"No, I'll be darned if any Apache ever lived as could beat that!" he chortled. "Not a mite of it! An' I never seen the day I could beat it, either. You're a caution, Mike, you sure are. I'm glad you're not sneakin' up after *my* hair!" He drew his pipe from his pocket and started stoking it with tobacco. "We're goin' back to Toadstool Cañon, Mike. Your dad sent for us."

Bastian looked up quickly. "Is there trouble, is that it?"

"No, only he wants to talk with you. Maybe"—Roundy was cautious—"he figures it's time you went out on a job. On one of those rides."

"I think that's it." Mike nodded. "He said in the spring, and it's about time for the first ride. I wonder where they'll go this time."

"No tellin'. The deal will be well planned, though. That dad of yours would have made a fine general, Mike. He's got the head for it, he sure has. Never forgets a thing, that one."

"You've been with him a long time, haven't you?"

"Sure . . . since before he found you. I knowed him in Mexico in the war, and that was longer ago than I like to think. I was a boy then, my own self. Son," Roundy said suddenly, "look!"

He tossed a huge pine cone into the air, a big one at least nine inches long.

With a flash of movement, Mike Bastian palmed his gun, and almost as soon as it hit his hand it belched flame—and again. The second shot spattered the cone into a bunch of flying brown chips.

"Not bad!" Roundy nodded. "You still shoot too quick, though. You got to get over that, Mike. Sometimes, one shot is all you'll ever get."

Side-by-side the two walked through the trees, the earth spongy with a thick blanket of pine needles. Roundy was not as tall as Mike, but he walked with the long, springy stride of the woodsman. He smoked in silence for some distance, and then he spoke up.

"Mike, if Ben's ready for you to go out, what will you do?"

For two steps, Bastian said nothing. Then he spoke slowly. "Why, go, I guess. What else?"

"You're sure? You're sure you want to be an outlaw?"

"That's what I was raised for, isn't it?" There was some bitterness in Mike's voice. "Somebody to take over what Ben Curry started?"

"Yeah, that's what you were raised for, all right. But this you want to remember, Mike. It's your life. Ben Curry, for all his power, can't live it for you. Moreover, times have changed since Ben and me rode into this country. It ain't free and wild like it was, because folks are comin' in, settlin' it up, makin' homes. Gettin' away won't be so easy, and your pards will change, too. In fact, they have already changed. When Ben and me come into this country, it was every man for himself. More than one harum-scarum fella, who was otherwise all right, got himself the name of an outlaw. Nobody figured much about it, then. We rustled cows, but so did half the big ranchers of the West. And if a cowpoke got hard up and stopped a stage, nobody made much fuss unless he killed somebody. They figured it was just high spirits. But the last few years, it ain't like that no more. And it ain't only that the country is growin' up . . . it's partly Ben Curry himself."

"You mean he's grown too big?" Mike put in.

"What else? Why, your dad controls more land than there is in New York State. Got it right under his thumb. And he's feared over half the West by those who knows about him, although not many do.

"Outside of this country around us, nobody

ain't seen Ben Curry in years, not leastwise to know him. But they've heard his name, and they know that somewhere an outlaw lives who rules a gang of almost a thousand men. That he robs and rustles where he will, and nobody has nerve enough to chase him.

"He's been smart, just plenty smart," old Roundy went on. "Men ride out and they meet at a given point. The whole job is planned in every detail . . . it's rehearsed, and then they pull it and scatter and meet again here. For a long time folks laid it to driftin' cowpunchers or to gangs passin' through. The way he's set up, one of the gangs he sends out might pull somethin' anywhere from San Antone to Los Angeles, or from Canada to Mexico, although usually he handles it close around.

"He's been the brains, all right, but don't ever forget it was those guns of his that kept things in line. Lately he hasn't used his guns. Kerb Perrin and Rigger Molina or some of their boys handle the discipline. He's become too big, Ben Curry has. He's like a king, and the king isn't gettin' any younger. How do you suppose Perrin will take it when he hears about you takin' over? You think he'll like it?"

"I don't imagine he will," Mike replied thoughtfully. "He's probably done some figuring of his own."

"You bet he has. So has Molina, and neither of

them will stop short of murder to get what they want. Your dad still has them buffaloed, I think, but that isn't going to matter when the showdown comes. And I think it's here."

"You do?" Mike said, surprise in his voice.

"Yeah, I sure do. . . ." Roundy hesitated. "You know, Mike, I never told you this, but Ben Curry has a family."

"A *family?*" Despite himself, Mike Bastian was startled.

"Yes, he has a wife and two daughters, and they don't have any idea he's an outlaw. They live down near Tucson somewhere. Occasionally they come to a ranch he owns in Red Wall Cañon, a ranch supposedly owned by Voyle Ragan. He visits them there."

"Does anybody else know this?"

"Not a soul. And don't you be tellin' anybody. You see, Ben always wanted a son, and he never had one. When your real dad was killed down in Mesilla, he took you along with him, and later he told me he was goin' to raise you to take over whatever he left. That was a long time ago, and since then he's spent a sight of time and money on you.

"You can track like an Apache," Roundy said, looking at the tall lad beside him. "In the woods you're a ghost, and I doubt if old Ben Curry himself can throw a gun any faster than you. I'd say you could ride anything that wore hair, and what you don't know about cards, dice, and roulette wheels ain't in it. You can handle a knife and fight with your fists, and you can open anything a man ever made in the way of safes and locks. Along with that, you've had a good education, and you could take care of yourself in any company. I don't reckon there ever was a boy had the kind of education you got, and I think Ben's ready to retire."

"You mean . . . to join his wife and daughters?" Mike questioned.

"That's it. He's gettin' no younger, and he wants it easy-like for the last years. He was always scared of only one thing, and he had a lot of it as a youngster. That's poverty. Well, he's made his pile, and now he wants to step out. Still and all, he knows he can't get out alive unless he leaves somebody behind him that's strong enough and smart enough to keep things under control. That's where you come in."

"Why don't he let Perrin have it?"

"Mike, you know Perrin. He's dangerous, that one. He's poison mean and power crazy. He'd have gone off the deep end a long time ago if it wasn't for Ben Curry. And Rigger Molina is kill crazy. He would have killed fifty men if it hadn't been that he knew Ben Curry would kill him when he got back. No, neither of them could handle this outfit. The whole shebang would go to pieces in ninety days if they had it."

Mike Bastian walked along in silence. There was little that was new in what Roundy was saying, but he was faintly curious as to the old man's purpose. The pair had been much together, and they knew each other as few men ever did. They had gone through storm and hunger and thirst together, living in the desert, mountains, and forest, only rarely returning to the rendezvous in Toadstool Cañon.

Roundy had a purpose in his talking, and Bastian waited, listening. Yet even as he walked, he was conscious of everything that went on around him. A quail had moved back into the tall grass near the stream, and there was a squirrel up ahead in the crotch of a tree. Not far back a gray wolf had crossed the path only minutes ahead of them.

It was as Roundy had said. Mike was a woodsman, and the thought of taking over the outlaw band filled him with unease. Always, he had been aware this time would come, that he had been schooled for it. But before, it had seemed remote and far off. Now, suddenly, it was at hand; it was facing him.

"Mike," Roundy went on, "the country is growin' up. Last spring some of our raids raised merry hell, and some of the boys had a bad time gettin' away. When they start again, there will be trouble and lots of it. Another thing, folks don't look at an outlaw like they used to. He isn't just a wild young cowhand full of liquor, nor a fellow who needs a poke, nor somebody buildin' a spread of his own. Now, he'll be like a wolf, with every man huntin' him. Before you decide to go into this, you think it over, make up your own mind.

"You know Ben Curry, and I know you like him. Well, you should. Nevertheless, Ben had no right to raise you for an outlaw. He went his way of his own free will, and, if he saw it that way, that was his own doin'. But no man has a right to say to another . . . 'This you must do . . . this you must be.' No man has a right to train another, startin' before he has a chance to make up his mind, and school him in any particular way."

The old man stopped to relight his pipe, and Mike kept a silence, would let Roundy talk out what seemed to bother him.

"I think every man should have the right to decide his own destiny, insofar as he can," Roundy said, continuing his trend of thought. "That goes for you, Mike, and you've got the decision ahead of you. I don't know which you'll do. But if you decide to step out of this gang, then I don't relish bein' around when it happens, for old Ben will be fit to be tied.

"Right now, you're an honest man. You're clean as a whistle. Once you become an outlaw, a lot of things will change. You'll have to kill, too . . . don't forget that. It's one thing to kill in defense of your home, your family, or your country. It's another thing when you kill for money or for power."

"You think I'd have to kill Perrin and Molina?" Mike Bastian asked.

"If they didn't get you first!" Roundy spat. "Don't forget this, Mike, you're fast. You're one of the finest and, aside from Ben Curry, probably the finest shot I ever saw. But that ain't shootin' at a man who's shootin' at you. There's a powerful lot of difference, as you'll see.

"Take Billy the Kid, this Lincoln County gunman we hear about. Frank and George Coe, Dick Brewer, Jesse Evans . . . any one of them can shoot as good as him. The difference is that the part down inside of him where the nerves should be was left out. When he starts shootin' and when he's bein' shot at, he's like ice! Kerb Perrin's that way, too. Perrin's the cold type, steady as a rock. Rigger Molina's another kind of cat . . . he explodes all over the place. He's white-hot, but he's deadly as a rattler."

Mike was listening intently as Roundy continued his description: "Five of them cornered him one time at a stage station out of Julesburg. When the shootin' was over, four of them were down and the fifth was holdin' a gunshot arm. Molina, he rode off under his own power. He's a shaggy wolf, that one. Wild and uncurried and big as a bear."

Far more than Roundy realized did Mike

20

Bastian know the facts about Ben Curry's empire of crime. For three years now, Curry had been leading his foster son through all the intricate maze of his planning. There were spies and agents in nearly every town in the Southwest, and small groups of outlaws quartered here and there on ranches who could be called upon for help at a moment's notice.

Also, there were ranches where fresh horses could be had, and changes of clothing, and where the horses the band had ridden could be lost. At Toadstool Cañon were less than 200 of the total number of outlaws, and many of those, while living under Curry's protection, were not of his band.

Also, the point Roundy raised had been in Mike's mind, festering there, an abscess of doubt and dismay. The Ben Curry he knew was a huge, kindly man, even if grim and forbidding at times. He had taken the homeless boy and given him kindness and care, had, indeed, trained him as a son. Today, however, was the first inkling Mike had of the existence of that other family. Ben Curry had planned and acted with shrewdness and care.

Mike Bastian had a decision to make, a decision that would change his entire life, whether for better or worse.

Here in the country around the Vermilion Cliffs was the only world he knew. Beyond it? Well, he supposed he could punch cows. He was trained to do many things, and probably there were jobs awaiting such a man as himself.

He could become a gambler, but he had seen and known a good many gamblers and did not relish the idea. Somewhere beyond this wilderness was a larger, newer, wealthier land—a land where honest men lived and reared their families.

II

In the massive stone house at the head of Toadstool Cañon, so called because of the gigantic toadstool-like stone near the entrance, Ben Curry leaned his great weight back in his chair and stared broodingly out the door over the valley below.

His big face was blunt and unlined as rock, but the shock of hair above his leonine face was turning to gray. He was growing old. Even spring did not bring the old fire to his veins again, and it had been long since he had ridden out on one of the jobs he planned so shrewdly. It was time he quit.

Yet this man, who had made decisions sharply and quickly, was for the first time in his life uncertain. For six years he had ruled supreme in this remote corner north of the Colorado. For twenty years he had been an outlaw, and for fifteen of those twenty years he had ruled a gang that had grown and extended its ramifications until it was an empire in itself.

Six years ago he had moved to this remote country and created the stronghold where he now lived. Across the southern limit rolled the Colorado River, with its long cañons and maze of rocky wilderness, a bar to any pursuit from the country south of the river, where he operated.

As far as other men were concerned, only at Lee's Ferry was there a crossing, and, in a cabin nearby, his men watched it night and day. In fact, there were two more crossings—one that the gang used in going to and from their raids, and the other known only to himself. It was his ace in the hole, even if not his only one.

One law of the gang, never transgressed, was that there was to be no lawless activity in the Mormon country to the north of them. The Mormons and the Indians were left strictly alone and were their friends. So were the few ranchers who lived in the area. These few traded at the stores run by the gang, buying their supplies closer to home and at cheaper prices than they could have managed elsewhere.

Ben Curry had never quite made up his mind about Kerb Perrin. He knew that Perrin was growing restive, that he was aware that Curry was aging and was eager for the power of leadership. Yet the one factor Curry couldn't be certain about was whether Perrin would stand for the taking over of the band by Mike Bastian.

Well, Mike had been well trained; it would be his problem. Ben smiled grimly. He was the old bull of the herd, and Perrin was pawing the dirt, but what would he say when a young bull stepped in? One who had not won his spurs with the gang?

That was why Curry had sent for him, for it was time Mike be groomed for leadership, time he moved out on his first job. And he had just the one. It was big, it was sudden, and it was dramatic. It would have an excellent effect on the gang if it was brought off smoothly, and he was going to let Mike plan the whole job himself.

There was a sharp knock outside, and Curry smiled a little, recognizing it.

"Come in!" he bellowed.

He watched Perrin stride into the room with his quick, nervous steps, his eyes scanning the room.

"Chief," Perrin said, "the boys are gettin' restless. It's spring, you know, and most of them are broke. Have you got anything in mind?"

"Sure, several things. But one that's good and tough. Struck me it might be a good one to break the kid in on."

"Oh?" Perrin's eyes veiled. "You mean he'll go along?"

"No, I'm going to let him run it. The whole show. It will be good for him."

Kerb Perrin absorbed that. For the first time, he

felt worry. For the first time, an element of doubt entered his mind. He had wondered before about Bastian and what his part would be in all this.

For years, Perrin had looked forward to the time when he could take over. He knew there would be trouble with Rigger Molina, but he had thought out that phase of it. He knew he could handle it. But what if Curry was planning to jump young Bastian into leadership?

Quick, hot passion surged through Perrin, and, when he looked up, it was all he could do to keep his voice calm.

"You think that's wise?" he questioned. "How will the boys feel about goin' out with a green kid?"

"He knows what to do," Curry said. "They'll find he's smart as any of them, and he knows plenty. This is a big job, and a tough one."

"Who goes with him?"

"Maybe I'll let him pick them," Curry said thoughtfully. "Good practice for him."

"What's the job?" Perrin asked, voice sullen.

"The gold train."

Perrin's fingers tightened, digging into his palms. This was the job *he* wanted! The shipment from the mines! It would be enormous, rich beyond anything they had done!

Months before, in talking of this job, he had laid out his plan for it before Curry. But it had been vetoed. He had recommended the killing of every man jack of them, and burial of them all, so the train would vanish completely.

"You sound like Molina," Curry had said, chuckling. "Too bloody."

"Dead men don't talk," he had replied grimly.

Yet, even as he spoke, he was thinking of something else. He was thinking of the effect of this upon the men of the outfit. He knew many of them liked Mike Bastian, and more than one of them had helped train him. In a way, many of the older men were as proud of Mike as if he had been their own son. If he stepped out now and brought off this job, he would acquire power and prestige in the gang equal to Perrin's own.

Fury engulfed Perrin. Curry had no right to do this to him! Sidetracking him for an untried kid. Shoving Bastian down all their throats.

Suddenly the rage died, and in its place came resolution. It was time he acted on his own. He would swing his own job, the one he had had in mind for so long, and that would counteract the effect of the gold-train steal. Moreover, he would be throwing the challenge into Ben Curry's teeth, for he would plan this job without consulting him. If there was going to be a struggle for leadership, it could begin here and now.

"He'll handle the job, all right," Curry said confidently. "He has been trained, and he has the mind for it. He plans well. I hadn't spoken of it before, but I asked his advice on a few things without letting him know why, and he always came through with the right answers."

Kerb Perrin left the stone house filled with burning resentment but also something of triumph. At last, after years of taking orders, he was going on his own. Yet the still, small voice of fear was in him, too. *What would Ben Curry do?*

The thought made him quail. He had seen the cold fury of Curry when it was aroused, and he had seen him use a gun. He himself was fast, but was he as fast as Ben Curry? In his heart, he doubted it. He dismissed the thought, although storing it in his mind. Something would have to be done about Ben Curry. . . .

Mike Bastian stood before Ben Curry's table, and the two men stared at each other.

Ben Curry, the old outlaw chief, was huge, bear-like, and mighty, his eyes fierce yet glowing with a kindly light now, and something of pride, too. Facing him, tall and lithe, his shoulders broad and mighty, was Mike Bastian, child of the frontier, grown to manhood and trained in every art of the wilds, every dishonest practice in the books, every skill with weapons. Yet educated, too, a man who could conduct himself well in any company.

"You take four men and look over the ground yourself, Mike," Ben Curry was saying. "I want you to plan this one. The gold train leaves the mines on the Twentieth. There will be five wagons, the gold distributed among them, although there won't be a lot of it as far as quantity is concerned. That gold train will be worth roughly five hundred thousand dollars.

"When that job is done," he continued, "I'm going to step down and leave you in command. You knew I was planning that. I'm old, and I want to live quietly for a while, and this outfit takes a strong hand to run it. Think you can handle it?"

"I think so," Mike Bastian said softly.

"I think so, too. Watch Perrin . . . he's the snaky one. Rigger is dangerous, but whatever he does will be out in the open. Not so Perrin. He's a conniver. He never got far with me because I was always one jump ahead of him. And I still am."

The old man was silent for a few minutes as he stared out the window.

"Mike," he said then, doubt entering his voice, "maybe I've done wrong. I meant to raise you the way I have. I ain't so sure what is right and wrong, and never was. Never gave it much thought, though.

"When I come West, it was dog eat dog, and your teeth had to be big. I got knocked down and kicked around some, and then I started taking big bites myself. I organized, and then I got bigger. In all these years nobody has ever touched me. If *you've* got a strong hand, you can do the same. Sometimes you'll have to buy men, sometimes you'll have to frighten them, and sometimes you'll have to kill."

He shook his head as if clearing it of memories past, and then glanced up.

"Who will you take with you?" he asked. "I mean, in scouting this layout?"

Ben Curry waited, for it was judgment of men that Bastian would need most. It pleased him that Mike did not hesitate.

"Roundy, Doc Sawyer, Colley, and Garlin."

Curry glanced at him, his eyes hard and curious. "Why?"

"Roundy has an eye for terrain like no man in this world," Mike said. "He says mine's as good, but I'll take him along to verify or correct my judgment. Doc Sawyer is completely honest. If he thinks I'm wrong, he'll say so. As for Colley and Garlin, they are two of the best men in the whole outfit. They will be pleased that I ask their help, which puts them on my side in a measure, and they can see how I work."

Curry nodded. "Smart . . . and you're right. Colley and Garlin are two of the best men, and absolutely fearless." He smiled a little. "If you have trouble with Perrin or Molina, it won't hurt to have them on your side."

Despite himself, Mike Bastian was excited. He was twenty-two years old and by frontier standards had been a man for several years. But in all that time, aside from a few trips into the Mormon country and one to Salt Lake, he had never been out of the maze of cañons and mountains north of the Colorado.

Roundy led the way, for the trail was an old one to him. They were taking the secret route south used by the gang on their raids, and, as they rode toward it, Mike stared at the country. He was always astonished by its ruggedness.

Snow still lay in some of the darker places of the forest, but as they neared the cañon, the high cliffs towered even higher and the trail dipped down through a narrow gorge of rock. Countless centuries of erosion had carved the rock into grotesque figures resembling those of men and animals, colored with shades of brown, pink, gray, and red, and tapering off into a pale yellow. There were shadowed pools among the rocks, some from snow water and others from natural springs, and there were scattered clumps of oak and piñon.

In the bottom of the gorge the sun did not penetrate except at high noon and there the trail wound along between great jumbled heaps of boulders, cracked and broken from their fall off the higher cliffs.

Mike Bastian followed Roundy, who rode hump-shouldered on a ragged, gray horse that seemed as old as he himself but also as sure-footed and mountain-wise. Mike was wearing a black hat now, but his same buckskins. He had substituted boots for the moccasins he usually wore, although they reposed in his saddlebags, ready at hand.

Behind them rode Doc Sawyer, his lean, saturnine face quiet, his eyes faintly curious and interested as he scanned the massive walls of the cañon. Tubby Colley was short and thick-chested, and very confident—a hard-jawed man who had been a first-rate ranch foreman before he shot two men and hit the outlaw trail.

Tex Garlin was tall, rangy, and quiet. He was a Texan, and little else was known of his background, although it was said he could carve a dozen notches on his guns if he had wished.

Suddenly Roundy turned the gray horse and rode abruptly at the face of the cliff, but when he came close up, the sand and boulders broke and a path showed along the under-scoured rock. Following this for several hundred yards, they found a cañon that cut back into the cliff itself and then turned to head toward the river.

The roar of the Colorado, high with spring freshets, was loud in their ears before they reached it. Finally they came out on a sandy bank littered with driftwood.

Nearby was a small cabin and a plot of garden. The door of the house opened, and a tall old man came out.

"Howdy!" he said. "I been expectin' somebody." His shrewd old eyes glanced from face to face, and then hesitated at sight of Mike. "Ain't seen you before," he said pointedly.

"It's all right, Bill," Roundy said. "This is Mike Bastian."

"Ben Curry's boy?" Bill stared. "I heard a sight of you, son. I sure have! Can you shoot like they say?"

Mike flushed. "I don't know what they say," he said, grinning. "But I'll bet a lot of money I can hit the side of that mountain if it holds still."

Garlin stared at him thoughtfully, and Colley smiled a little.

"Don't take no funnin' from him," Roundy said. "That boy can shoot."

"Let's see some shootin', son," Bill suggested. "I always did like to see a man who could shoot."

Bastian shook his head. "There's no reason for shootin'," he protested. "A man's a fool to shoot unless he's got cause. Ben Curry always told me never to draw a gun unless I meant to use it."

"Go ahead," Colley said. "Show him."

Old Bill pointed. "See that black stick end juttin' up over there? It's about fifty, maybe sixty paces. Can you hit it?"

"You mean that one?" Mike palmed his gun and fired, and the black stick pulverized.

It was a movement so smooth and practiced that no one of the men even guessed he had intended to shoot. Garlin's jaws stopped their calm chewing, and he stared with his mouth open for as long as it took to draw a breath. Then he glanced at Colley.

"Wonder what Kerb would say to that?" he said, astonished. "This kid can shoot."

"Yeah," Colley agreed, "but the stick didn't have a gun."

Old Bill worked the ferry out of a cave under the cliff and freighted them across the swollen river in one hair-raising trip. With the river behind, they wound up through the rocks and started south.

III

The mining and cow town of Weaver was backed up near a large hill on the banks of a small creek. Colley and Garlin rode into the place at sundown, and an hour later Doc Sawyer and Roundy rode in.

Garlin and Colley were leaning on the bar having a drink, and they ignored the newcomers. Mike Bastian followed not long afterward and walked to the bar alone.

All the others in the saloon were Mexicans, except for three tough-looking white men lounging against the bar nearby. They glanced at Mike and his buckskins, and one of them whispered something to the others, at which they all laughed.

Doc Sawyer was sitting in a poker game, and his eyes lifted. Mike leaned nonchalantly against the bar, avoiding the stares of the three toughs who stood near him. One of them moved over closer.

"Hi, stranger," he said. "That's a right purty suit you got. Where could I get one like it?"

Garlin looked up and his face stiffened. He nudged Colley. "Look," Garlin said quickly. "Corbus and Fletcher. An' trouble huntin'. We'd better get into this."

Colley shook his head. "No. Let's see what the kid does."

Mike looked around, his expression mild. "You want a suit like this?" he inquired of the stranger. His eyes were innocent, but he could see the sort of man he had to deal with. These three were toughs, and dangerous. " 'Most any Navajo could make one for you."

"Just like that?" Corbus sneered.

He was drinking and in a nagging, quarrelsome mood. Mike looked altogether too neat for his taste.

"Sure. Just like this," Mike agreed. "But I don't know what you'd want with it, though. This suit would be pretty big for you to fill."

"Huh?" Corbus's face flamed. Then his mouth tightened. "You gettin' smart with me, kid?"

"No." Mike Bastian turned, and his voice cracked like a whip in the suddenly silent room. "Neither am I being hurrahed by any lame-brained, liquor-guzzling saddle tramp. You made a remark about my suit, and I answered it. Now, you can have a drink on me, all three of you, and

I'm suggesting you drink up." His voice suddenly became soft. "I want you to drink up because I want to be very, very sure we're friends, see?"

Corbus stared at Bastian, a cold hint of danger filtering through the normal stubbornness of his brain. Something told him this was perilous going, yet he was stubborn, too stubborn. He smiled slowly. "Kid," he drawled, "supposin' I don't want to drink with no tenderfoot brat?"

Corbus never saw what happened. His brain warned him as Mike's left hand moved, but he never saw the right. The left stabbed his lips and the right cracked on the angle of his jaw, and he lifted from his feet and hit the floor on his shoulder blades, out cold.

Fletcher and the third tough stared from Corbus to Mike. Bastian was not smiling. "You boys want to drink?" he asked. "Or do we go on from here?"

Fletcher stared at him. "What if a man drawed a gun instead of usin' his fists?" he demanded.

"I'd kill him," Bastian replied quietly.

Fletcher blinked. "I reckon you would," he agreed. He turned and said: "Let's have a drink. That Boot Hill out there's already got twenty graves in it."

Garlin glanced at Colley, his eyebrows lifted. Colley shrugged.

"I wonder what Corbus will do when he gets up?" he said.

Garlin chuckled. "Nothin' today. He won't be feelin' like it."

Colley nodded. "Reckon you're right, an' I reckon the old man raised him a wildcat. I can hardly wait to see Kerb Perrin's face when we tell him."

"You reckon," Garlin asked, "that what we heard is true? That Ben Curry figures to put this youngster into his place when he steps out?"

"Yep, that's the talk," Colley answered.

"Well, maybe he's got it. We'll sure know before this trip is over."

Noise of the stagecoach rolling down the street drifted into the saloon, and Mike Bastian strolled outside and started toward the stage station. The passengers were getting down to stretch their legs and to eat. Three of them were women.

One of them noticed Mike standing there and walked toward him. She was a pale, pretty girl with large gray eyes.

"How much farther to Red Wall Cañon?" she inquired.

Mike Bastian stiffened. "Why, not far. That is, you'll make it by morning if you stick with the stage. There is a cross-country way if you had you a buckboard, though."

"Could you tell us where we could hire one? My mother is not feeling well."

He stepped down off the boardwalk and headed toward the livery stable with her. As they drew alongside the stage, Mike looked up. An older woman and a girl were standing near the stage, but he was scarcely aware of anything but the girl. Her hair was blonde, but darker than that of the girl who walked beside him, and her eyes, too, were gray. There the resemblance ended, for where this girl beside him was quiet and sweet, the other was vivid.

She looked at him, and their eyes met. He swept off his hat. The girl beside him spoke.

"This is my mother, Missus Ragan, and my sister Drusilla." She looked up at him quickly. "My name is Juliana."

Mike bowed. He had eyes only for Drusilla, who was staring at him.

"I am Mike Bastian," he said.

"He said he could hire us a rig to drive across country to Red Wall Cañon," Juliana explained. "It will be quicker that way."

"Yes," Mike agreed, "much quicker. I'll see what I can do. Just where in Red Wall did you wish to go?"

"To Voyle Ragan's ranch," Drusilla said. "The V Bar." He had turned away, but he stopped in mid-stride. "Did you say . . . Voyle Ragan's?"

"Yes. Is there anything wrong?" Drusilla stared at him. "What's the matter?"

He regained his composure swiftly. "Nothing. Only, I'd heard the name, and . . ."—he smiled— "I sort of wanted to know for sure, so if I came calling . . ."

Juliana laughed. "Why, of course. We'd be glad to see you."

He walked swiftly away. These, then, were Ben Curry's daughters! That older woman would be his wife! He was their foster brother, yet obviously his name had meant nothing to them. Neither, he reflected, would their names have meant anything to him, nor the destination, had it not been for what Roundy had told him only the previous day.

Drusilla her name was. His heart pounded at the memory of her, and he glanced back through the gathering dusk at the three women standing there by the stage station.

Hiring the rig was a matter of minutes. He liked the look of the driver, a lean man, tall and white-haired. "No danger on that road this time of year," the driver said. "I can have them there in no time by takin' the cañon road."

Drusilla was waiting for him when Mike walked back. "Did you find one?" she asked, and then listened to his explanation and thanked him.

"Would it be all right with you," Mike said, "if I call at the V Bar?"

She looked at him, her face grave, but a dancing light in her eyes. "Why, my sister invited you, did she not?"

"Yes, but I'd like you to invite me, too."

"I?" She studied him for a minute. "Of course, we'd be glad to see you. My mother likes visitors as well as Julie and I, so won't you ask her, too?"

"I'll take the invitation from you and your sister as being enough." He grinned. "If I ask your mother, I might have to ask your father."

"Father isn't with us." She laughed. "We'll see him at Ragan's. He's a rancher somewhere up north in the wilds. His name is Ben Ragan. Have you heard of him?"

"Seems to me I have," he admitted, "but I wouldn't say for sure."

After they had gone, Mike wandered around and stopped in the saloon, after another short talk with a man at the livery stable. Listening and asking an occasional question, he gathered the information he wanted on the gold shipment. Even as he asked the questions, it seemed somehow fantastic that he, of all people, should be planning such a thing.

Never before had he thought of it seriously, but now he did. And it was not only because the thought went against his own grain, but because he was thinking of Drusilla Ragan.

What a girl she was! He sobered suddenly. Yet, for all of that, she was the daughter of an outlaw. Did she know it? From her question, he doubted it very much.

Doc Sawyer cashed in his chips and left the poker game to join Mike at the bar.

"The Twentieth, all right," he said softly. "And five of them are going to carry shotguns. There will be twelve guards in all, which looks mighty tough. The big fellow at the poker table is one of the guards, and all of them are picked men."

Staring at his drink, Mike puzzled over his problem. What Roundy had said was of course true. This was a turning point for him. He was still an honest man; yet, when he stepped over the boundary, it would make a difference. It might make a lot of difference to a girl like Dru Ragan, for instance.

The fact that her father, also, was an outlaw would make little difference. Listening to Sawyer made him wonder. Why had such a man, brilliant, intelligent, and well-educated, ever become a criminal?

Sawyer was a gambler and a very skillful one, yet he was a doctor, too, and a fine surgeon. His education was as good as study and money could make it, and it had been under his guidance that Mike Bastian had studied.

"Doc," he said suddenly, "whatever made you ride a crooked trail?"

Sawyer glanced at him suddenly, a new expression in his eyes. "What do you mean, Mike? Do you have doubts?"

"Doubts? That seems to be all I do have these last few days."

"I wondered about that," Doc said. "You have been so quiet that I never doubted but what you were perfectly willing to go on with Ben Curry's plans for you. It means power and money,

Mike . . . all a man could want. If it is doubt about the future for outlaws that disturbs you, don't let it. From now on it will be political connections and bribes, but with the money you'll have to work with, that should be easy."

"It should be," Mike said slowly. "Only maybe . . . just maybe . . . I don't want to."

"Conscience rears its ugly head." Sawyer smiled ironically. "Can it be that Ben Curry's instructions have fallen on fallow ground? What started this sudden feeling? The approach of a problem? Fear?" Doc had turned toward Mike and was staring at him with aroused interest. "Or," he added, "is there a woman? A girl?"

"Would that be so strange?"

"Strange? No. I've wondered it hasn't happened before, but then you've lived like a recluse these past years. Who is she?"

"It doesn't matter," Mike answered. "I was thinking of this before I saw her. Wondering what I should do."

"Don't ask me," Sawyer said. "I made a mess of my own life. Partly a woman and partly the desire for what I thought was easy money. Well, there's no such a thing as easy money, but I found that out too late. You make your own decision. What was it Matthew Arnold said? I think you learned the quotation."

" 'No man can save his brother's soul, or pay his brother's debt.' "

41

"Right. So you save your own and pay your own. There's one thing to remember, Mike. No matter which way you go, there will be killing. If you take over Ben Curry's job, you'll have to kill Perrin and Molina, if you can. And you may have to kill them, and even Ben Curry, if you step out."

"Not Dad," Mike said.

"Don't be so sure. It isn't only what he thinks that matters, Mike. No man is a complete ruler or dictator. His name is only the symbol. He is the mouthpiece for the wishes of his followers, and, as long as he expresses those wishes, he leads them. When he fails, he falls. Ben Curry is the boss not only because he has power in him, but also because he has organization, because he has made them money, because he has offered them safety. If you left, there would be a chink in the armor. No outlaw ever trusts another outlaw who turns honest, for he always fears betrayal."

Bastian tossed off his drink. "Let's check with Roundy. He's been on the prowl."

Roundy came to them hastily. "We've got to get out of town quick," he said. "Ducrow and Fernandez just blew in, and they are drunk and raisin' the devil. Both of them are talkin', too, and, if they see us, they will spill everything."

"All right." Mike straightened. "Get our horses. Get theirs, too. We'll take them with us."

Garlin and Colley had come to the bar. Garlin

shook his head. "Ducrow's poison mean when he's drunk, and Fernandez sides him in everything," Garlin informed. "When Ducrow gets drunk, he always pops off too much. The boss forbade him weeks ago to come down here."

"He's a pal of Perrin's," Colley said, "so he thinks he can get away with it."

"Here they come now!" Roundy exclaimed.

"All right . . . drift," Bastian ordered. "Make it quick with the horses."

IV

Saloon doors slammed open, and the two men came in. One look, and Mike could see there was cause for worry. Tom Ducrow was drunk and ugly, and behind him was Snake Fernandez. They were an unpleasant pair, and they had made their share of trouble in Ben Curry's organization, although always protected by Perrin.

Bastian started forward, but he had scarcely taken a step when Ducrow saw him.

"There he is!" he bellowed loudly. "The pet! The boss' pet!" He stared around at the people in the barroom. "You know who this man is? He's . . ."

"Ducrow!" Mike snapped. "Shut up and go home. Now!"

"Look who's givin' orders!" Ducrow sneered. "Gettin' big for your britches, ain't you?"

"Your horses will be outside in a minute," Mike said. "Get on them and start back, fast!"

"Suppose," Ducrow sneered, "you make me!"

Mike had been moving toward him, and now with a panther-like leap he was beside the outlaw and, with a quick slash from his pistol barrel, floored him.

With an oath, Snake Fernandez reached for a gun, and Mike had no choice. He shot him in the shoulder. Fernandez staggered, the gun dropping from his fingers. Mouthing curses, he reached for his left-hand gun.

But even as he reached, Garlin—who had stayed behind when the others went for the horses—stepped up behind him. Jerking the gun from the man's holster, he spun him about and shoved him through the door.

Mike pulled the groggy Ducrow to his feet and pushed him outside after Fernandez.

A big man got up hastily from the back of the room. Mike took one quick glimpse at the star on his chest. "What goes on here?" the sheriff demanded.

"Nothing at all," Mike said affably. "Just a couple of the boys from our ranch feeling their oats a little. We'll take them out and off your hands."

The sheriff stared from Mike to Doc Sawyer and Colley, who had just come through the door.

"Who are you?" he demanded. "I don't believe I know you *hombres*."

"That's right, sir, you don't," Mike said. "We're from the Mogollons, riding back after driving some cattle through to California. It was a rough trip, and this liquor here got to a couple of the boys."

The sheriff hesitated, looking sharply from one to the other.

"*You* may be a cowhand," he said, "but that *hombre*"—he pointed to Sawyer—"looks like a gambler."

Mike chuckled. "That's a joke on you, boy!" he said to Doc. Then he turned back to the sheriff. "He's a doctor, sir, and quite a good one. A friend of my boss'."

A gray-haired man got up and strolled alongside the sheriff. His eyes were alive with suspicion.

"From the Mogollons?" he queried. "That's where I'm from. Who did you say your boss was?"

Doc Sawyer felt his scalp tighten, but Mike smiled.

"Jack McCardle," he said, "of the Flying M. We aren't his regular hands, just a bunch passing through. Doc, here, he being an old friend of Jack's, handled the sale of the beef."

The sheriff looked around.

"That right, Joe?" he asked the gray-haired man. "There's a Flying M over there?"

"Yes, there is." Joe was obviously puzzled. "Good man, too, but I had no idea he was shipping beef."

The sheriff studied Bastian thoughtfully. "Guess you're all right," he said finally. "But you sure don't *talk* like a cowhand."

"As a matter of fact," Mike said, swallowing hard, "I was studying for the ministry, but my interests began to lead me in more profane directions, so I am afraid I backslid. It seems," he said gravely, "that a leaning toward poker isn't conducive to the correct manner in the pulpit."

"I should say not." The sheriff chuckled. "All right, son, you take your pardners with you. Let 'em sleep it off."

Mike turned, and his men followed him. Ducrow and Fernandez had disappeared. They rode swiftly out of town and took the trail for Toadstool Cañon. It wasn't until they were several miles on the road that Sawyer glanced at Mike.

"You'll do," he said. "I was never so sure of a fight in my life."

"That's right, boss," Garlin said. "I was bettin' we'd have to shoot our way out of town. You sure smooth-talked 'em. Never heard it done prettier."

"Sure did," Colley agreed. "I don't envy you havin' Ducrow an' Fernandez for enemies, though."

Kerb Perrin and Rigger Molina were both in conference with Ben Curry when Mike Bastian came up the stone steps and through the door. They both looked up sharply.

46

"Perrin," Bastian said, "what were Ducrow and Fernandez doing in Weaver?"

"In Weaver?" Perrin straightened up slowly, nettled by Mike's tone, but puzzled, too.

"Yes, in Weaver. We nearly had to shoot our way out of town because of them. They were down there, drunk and talking too much. When I told them to get on their horses and go home, they made trouble."

Kerb Perrin was on dangerous ground. He well knew how harsh Ben Curry was about talkative outlaws, and, while he had no idea what the two were doing in Weaver, he knew they were trouble-makers. He also knew they were supporters of his. Ben Curry knew it, and so did Rigger Molina.

"They made trouble?" Perrin questioned now. "How?"

"Ducrow started to tell who I was."

"What happened?"

Mike was aware that Ben Curry had tipped back in his chair and was watching him with interest.

"I knocked him down with a pistol barrel," he said.

"You *what?*" Perrin stared. Ducrow was a bad man to tangle with. "What about Fernandez?"

"He tried to draw on me, and I put a bullet in his shoulder."

"You should've killed him," Molina said. "You'll have to, sooner or later."

Kerb Perrin was stumped. He had not expected

this, or that Mike Bastian was capable of handling such a situation. He was suddenly aware that Doc Sawyer had come into the room.

Bastian faced Ben Curry. "We got what we went after," he said, "but another bad break like Ducrow and Fernandez, and we'd walk into a trap."

"There won't be another." Curry said harshly.

When Mike had gone out, Doc Sawyer looked at Ben Curry and smiled.

"You should have seen him and heard him," he said as Molina and Perrin were leaving. "It would have done your heart good. He had a run-in with Corbus and Fletcher, too. Knocked Corbus out with a punch and backed Fletcher down. Oh, he'll do, that boy of yours, he'll do. The way he talked that sheriff out of it was one of the smoothest things I've seen."

Ben Curry nodded with satisfaction. "I knew it. I knew he had it."

Doc Sawyer smiled, and looked up at the chief from under his sunburned eyebrows. "He met a girl, too."

"A girl? Good for him. It's about time."

"This was a very particular girl, chief," Sawyer continued. "I thought you'd like to know. If I'm any judge of men, he fell for her and fell hard. And I'm not so sure it didn't happen both ways. He told me something about it, but I had already seen for myself."

Something in Sawyer's tone made Curry sit up a little. "Who was the girl?" he demanded.

"A girl who came in on the stage." Doc spoke carefully, avoiding Curry's eyes now. "He got the girl and her family a rig to drive them out to a ranch. Out to the V Bar."

Ben Curry's face went white. So Doc knew! It was in every line of him, every tone of his voice. The one thing he had tried to keep secret, the thing known only to himself and Roundy, was known to Doc! And to how many others?

"The girl's name," Doc continued, "was Drusilla Ragan. She's a beautiful girl."

"Well, I won't have it," Curry said in a strained voice.

Doc Sawyer looked up, faintly curious. "You mean the foster son you raised isn't good enough for your daughter?"

"Don't say that word here!" Curry snapped, his face hard. "Who knows besides you?"

"Nobody of whom I am aware," Doc said with a shrug. "I only know by accident. You will remember the time you were laid up with that bullet wound. You were delirious, and that's why I took care of you myself . . . because you talked too much." Doc lighted his pipe. "They made a nice-looking pair," he said. "And I think she invited him to Red Wall Cañon."

"He won't go! I won't have any of this crowd going there!"

"Chief, that boy's what you made him, but he's not an outlaw yet," Doc said, puffing contentedly on his pipe. "He could be, and he might be, but if he does become one, the crime will lie on your shoulders."

Curry shook himself and stared out the window.

"I said it, chief, the boy has it in him," Sawyer went on. "You should have seen him throw that gun on Fernandez. The kid's fast as lightning. He thinks, too. If he takes over this gang, he'll run this country like you never ran it. I say *if.* . . ."

"He'll do it," Curry said confidently, "you know he will. He always does what I tell him."

Doc chuckled. "He may, and again he may not. Mike Bastian has a mind of his own, and he's doing some thinking. He may decide he doesn't want to take over. What will you do then?"

"Nobody has ever quit this gang. Nobody ever will!"

"You'd order him killed?"

Ben Curry hesitated. This was something he had never dreamed of, something . . . "He'll do what he's told," he repeated, but he was no longer sure.

A tiny voice of doubt was arising within him, a voice that made him remember the Mike Bastian who was a quiet, determined little boy who would not cry, a boy who listened and obeyed. Yet now Curry knew, and admitted it for the first time, that Mike Bastian always had a mind of his own.

Never before had the thought occurred to him

that Mike might disobey, that he might refuse. And if he did, what then? It was a rule of the outlaw pack that no man could leave it and live. It was a rule essential to their security. A few had tried, and their bodies now lay in Boot Hill. But Mike, his son? No, not Mike!

Within him, there was a deeper knowledge, an awareness that here his interests and those of the pack would divide. Even if he said no, they would say yes.

"Who would kill him, chief? Kerb Perrin? Rigger Molina? You?" Doc Sawyer shook his head slowly. "You *might* be able to do it, maybe one of the others, but I doubt it. You've created the man who may destroy you, chief, unless you join him."

Long after Doc Sawyer was gone, Ben Curry sat there staring out over the shadowed valley. He was getting old. For the first time he was beginning to doubt his rightness, beginning to wonder if he had not wronged Mike Bastian.

And what of Mike and Dru, his beloved, gray-eyed daughter? The girl with dash and spirit? But why not? Slowly he thought over Mike Bastian's life. Where was the boy wrong? Where was he unfitted for Dru? By the teachings given him by Curry's own suggestion? His own order? Or was there yet time?

Ben Curry heaved himself to his feet and began to pace the carpeted floor. He would have to decide. He would have to make up his mind, for a man's life and future lay in his hands, to make or break.

What if Dru wanted him anyway, outlaw or not? Ben Curry stopped and stared into the fireplace. If it had been Julie now, he might forbid it. But Dru? He chuckled. She would laugh at him. Dru had too much of his own nature, and she had a mind of her own.

Mike Bastian was restless the day after the excitement in Weaver. He rolled out of his bunk and walked out on the terrace. Only he and Doc Sawyer slept in the stone house where Ben Curry lived. Roundy was down in town with the rest of them, but tonight Mike wanted to walk, to think.

There had been a thrill of excitement in outtalking the sheriff, in facing down Fletcher, in flattening Corbus. And there had been more of it in facing Ducrow and Fernandez. Yet, was that what he wanted? Or did he want something more stable, more worthwhile? The something he might find with Drusilla Ragan?

Already he had won a place with the gang. He knew the story would be all over the outlaw camp now.

Walking slowly down the street of the settlement, he turned at right angles and drifted down a side road. He wanted to get away from things for a little while, to think things out. He turned again and stared back into the pines, and then he heard a voice coming from a nearby house. The words halted him.

". . . at Red Wall," Mike heard the ending.

Swiftly he glided to the house and flattened against the side. Kerb Perrin was speaking.

"It's a cinch, and we'll do it on our own without anybody's say-so. There's about two thousand cattle in the herd, and I've got a buyer for them. We can hit the place just about sunup. Right now, they have only four hands on the place, but about the first of next month they will start hiring. It's now or not at all."

"How many men will we take?" That was Ducrow speaking.

"A dozen. That will keep the divvy large enough, and they can swing it. Hell, that Ragan Ranch is easy. The boss won't hear about it until too late, and the chances are he will never guess it was us."

"I wouldn't want him to," Fernandez said.

"To hell with him!" Ducrow was irritated. "I'd like a crack at that Bastian again."

"Stick with me," Perrin said, "and I'll set him up for you. Curry is about to turn things over to him. Well, we'll beat him to it."

"You said there were girls?" Ducrow suggested.

"There's Curry's two girls and a couple of Mexican girls who work there. One older woman. I want one of those girls myself . . . the youngest of the Ragan sisters. What happens to the others is none of my business."

Mike Bastian's hand dropped to his gun, and his lips tightened. The tone of Perrin's voice filled him with fury, and Ducrow was as bad as Perrin.

"What happens if Curry does find out?" Ducrow demanded.

"What would happen?" Perrin said fiercely. "I'll kill him like I've wanted to all these years. I've hated that man like I never hated anyone in my life."

"What about that Bastian?" Ducrow demanded.

Perrin laughed. "That's your problem. If you and Fernandez can't figure to handle him, then I don't know you."

"He knocked out Corbus, too," Ducrow said. "We might get him to throw in with us, if this crowd is all afraid of old Ben Curry."

"I ain't so sure about him my own self," said another voice, which Mike placed as belonging to an outlaw named Bayless. "He may not be so young any more, but he's hell on wheels with a gun."

"Forget him!" Perrin snapped. Then: "You three, and Clatt, Panelli, Monson, Kiefer and a few others, will go with us. All good men. There's a lot of dissatisfaction, anyway. Molina wants to raid the Mormons. They've a lot of rich stock, and there's no reason why we can't sell it south of the river and the other stock north of it. We can get rich."

V

Mike Bastian waited no longer, but eased away from the wall. He was tempted to wait for Perrin and brace him when he came out. His first thought was to go to Ben Curry, but he might betray his interest in Drusilla, and the time was not yet ripe for that. What would her father say if he found the foster son he had raised to be an outlaw was in love with his daughter?

It was foolish to think of it, yet he couldn't help it. There was time between now and the Twentieth for him to get back to Red Wall and see her.

A new thought occurred to him. Ben Curry would know the girls and their mother were there and would be going to see them. That would be his chance to learn of Ben's secret pass to the riverbank and how he crossed the Colorado.

Recalling other trips, Bastian knew the route must be a much quicker one than any he knew of, and was probably farther west and south, toward the cañon country. Already he was eager to see the girl again, and all he could think of was her trim figure, the laughter in her eyes, the soft curve of her lips.

There were other things to be considered. If there was as much unrest in the gang as Perrin said, things might be nearing a definite break.

Certainly outlaws were not the men to stand hitched for long, and Ben Curry had commanded them for longer than anyone would believe. Their loyalty was due partly to the returns from their ventures under his guidance, and partly to fear of his far-reaching power. But he was growing old, and there were those among them who feared he was losing his grip.

Mike felt a sudden urge to saddle his horse and be gone, to get away from all this potential cruelty, the conniving and hatred that lay dormant here, or was seething and ready to explode. He could ride out now by the Kaibab trail through the forest, skirt the mountains, and find his own way through the cañon. It was a question whether he could escape, whether Ben Curry would let him go. To run now meant to abandon all hope of seeing Dru again, and Mike knew he could not do that.

Returning to his quarters in the big stone house, he stopped in front of a mirror. With deadly, flashing speed, he began to practice quick draws of his guns. Each night he did this twenty times as swiftly as his darting hands could move.

Finally he sat down on his bed thinking. Roundy first, and today Doc Sawyer. Each seemed to be hoping he would throw in the sponge and escape this outlaw life before it was too late. Doc said it was his life, but was it?

There was a light tap on the door. Gun in hand,

he reached for the latch. Roundy stepped in. He glanced at the gun.

"Gettin' scary, Mike?" he queried. "Things are happenin'!"

"I know."

Mike went on to explain what he had overheard, and Roundy's face turned serious. "Mike, did you ever hear of Dave Lenaker?"

Bastian looked up. "You mean the Colorado gunman?"

"That's the one. He's headed this way. Ben Curry just got word that Lenaker's on his way to take over the Curry gang!"

"I thought he was one of Curry's ablest lieutenants?"

Roundy shrugged. "He was, Mike, but the word has gone out that the old man is losing his grip, and outlaws are quick to sense a thing like that. Lenaker never had any use for Perrin, and he's most likely afraid that Perrin will climb into the saddle. Dave Lenaker's a holy terror, too."

"Does Dad Curry know?" Mike said.

"Yeah. He's some wrought up, too," Roundy answered. "He was figurin' on bein' away for a few days, one of those trips he takes to Red Wall. Now he can't go."

Morning came cool and clear. Mike Bastian could feel disaster in the air, and he dressed hurriedly and headed for the bunkhouse. Few of the men were eating, and those few were silent. He knew they were all aware of impending change. He was finishing his coffee when Kerb Perrin came in.

Instantly Mike was on guard. Perrin walked with a strut, and his eyes were bright and confident. He glanced at Bastian, faintly amused, and then sat down at the table and began to eat.

Roundy came in, and then Doc Sawyer. Mike dallied over his coffee, and a few minutes later was rewarded by seeing Ducrow come in with Kiefer, followed in a few minutes by Rocky Clatt, Monson, and Panelli.

Suddenly, with the cup half to his mouth, Mike recalled with a shock that this was the group Perrin planned to use on his raid on the Ragan Ranch. That could mean the raid would come off today!

He looked up to see Roundy suddenly push back his chair and leave his breakfast unfinished. The old woodsman hurried outside and vanished.

Mike put down his own cup and got up. Then he stopped, motionless. The hard muzzle of a gun was prodding him in the back, and a voice was saying: "Don't move."

The voice was that of Fernandez, and Mike saw Perrin smiling.

"Sorry to surprise you, Bastian," Perrin said. "But with Lenaker on the road we had to move fast. By the time he gets here, I'll be in the saddle. Some of the boys wanted to kill you, but I figured you'd be a good talkin' point with the old man. He'd be a hard kernel to dig out of that stone shell of his without you. But with you for an argument, he'll come out all right."

"Have you gone crazy, Perrin? You can't get away with this."

"I am, though. You see, Rigger Molina left this morning with ten of his boys to work a little job they heard of. In fact, they are on their way to knock over the gold train."

"The gold train?" Bastian exclaimed. "Why, that was *my* job! He doesn't even know the plan made for it. Or the information I got."

Perrin smiled triumphantly. "I traded with him. I told him to give me a free hand here, and he could have the gold train. I neglected to tell him about the twelve guards riding with it, or the number with shotguns. In fact, I told him only five guards would be along. I think that will take care of Rigger for me." Perrin turned abruptly. "Take his guns and tie his hands behind his back, then shove him out into the street. I want the old man to see him."

"What about *him?*" Kiefer demanded, pointing a gun at Doc Sawyer.

"Leave him alone. We may need a doctor, and he knows where his bread is buttered."

Confused and angry, Mike Bastian was shoved out into the warm morning sun, then jerked around to face up the cañon toward the stone house.

Suddenly fierce triumph came over him. Perrin would have a time getting the old man out of that place. The sunlight was shining down the road from over the house, fully into their faces. The only approach to the house was up thirty steps of stone, overlooked by an upper window of the house. From that window and the doorway, the entire settlement could be commanded by an expert rifleman.

Ben Curry had thought of everything. The front and back doors of every building in the settlement could be commanded easily from his stronghold.

Perrin crouched behind a pile of sandbags hastily thrown up near the door of the store.

"Come on down, Curry!" he shouted. "Give yourself up or we'll kill Bastian!"

There was no answer from up the hill. Mike felt cold and sick in his stomach. Wind touched his hair and blew a strand down over his face. He stared up at the stone house and could see no movement, hear no response.

"Come on out!" Perrin roared again. "We know you're there! Come out or we'll kill your son!"

Still no reply.

"He don't hear you," Clatt said. "Maybe he's still asleep. Let's rush the place."

"You rush it," Kiefer said. "Let me watch!"

Despite his helplessness, Mike felt a sudden glow of satisfaction. Old Ben Curry was a wily fighter. He knew that once he showed himself or spoke, their threat would take force. It was useless to kill Bastian unless they knew Curry was watching them.

Perrin had been so sure Curry would come out rather than sacrifice Mike, and now they were not even sure he was hearing them! Nor, Mike knew suddenly, was anybody sure Ben would come out even if they did warn him Mike would be killed.

"Come on out!" Perrin roared. "Give yourself up and we'll give you and Bastian each a horse and a half mile start! Otherwise, you both die! We've got dynamite!"

Mike chuckled. Dynamite wasn't going to do them much good. There was no way to get close to that stone house, backed up against the mountain as it was.

"Perrin," he said, "you've played the fool. Curry doesn't care whether I live or die. He won't come out of there, and there's no way you can get at him. All he's got to do is sit tight and wait until Dave Lenaker gets here. He will make a deal with Dave then, and where will you be?"

"Shut up!" Perrin bellowed. But for the first time he seemed to be aware that his plan was not working. "He'll come out, all right."

"Let's open fire on the place," Ducrow suggested. "Or rush it like Clatt suggested."

"Hell!" Kiefer was disgusted. "Let's take what we can lay hands on and get out! There's two thousand head of cattle down in those bottoms.

Rigger's gone and Lenaker ain't here yet, so let's take what we can an' get out."

"Take pennies when there's millions up there in that stone house?" Perrin demanded. His face swelled in anger and the veins stood out on his forehead. "That strong room has gold in it! Stacks of money! I know it's there. With all that at hand, would you run off with a few cattle?"

Kiefer was silent but unconvinced.

Standing in the dusty street, Mike looked up at the stone house. All the loyalty and love he felt for the old man up there in that house came back with a rush. Whatever he was, good or bad, he owed to Ben Curry. Perhaps Curry had reared him for a life of crime, for outlawry, but to Ben Curry it was not a bad life. He lived like a feudal lord and had respect for no law he did not make himself.

Wrong he might be, but he had given the man that was Mike Bastian a start. Suddenly Mike knew that he could never have been an outlaw, that it was not in him to steal and rob and kill. But that did not mean he could be disloyal to the old man who had reared him and given him a home when he had none.

He was suddenly, fiercely proud of the old man up there alone. Like a cornered grizzly, he would fight to the death. He, Mike Bastian, might die here in the street, but he hoped old Ben Curry would stay in his stone shell and defeat them all.

Kerb Perrin was stumped. He had made his plan quickly when he'd heard Dave Lenaker was on his way here, for he knew that, if Lenaker arrived, it might well turn into a bloody four-cornered fight. But with Molina out of the way, he might take over from Ben Curry before Lenaker arrived, and kill Lenaker and the men he brought with him in an ambush.

He had been sure that Ben Curry would reply, that he might give himself up or at least show himself, and Perrin had a sniper concealed to pick him off if he moved into the open. That he would get nothing but silence, he could not believe.

Mike Bastian stood alone in the center of the street. There was simply nothing he could do. At any moment Perrin might decide to have him killed where he stood. With his hands tied behind him, he was helpless. Mike wondered what had happened to Roundy? The old mountain man had risen suddenly from the table and vanished. Could he be in league with Perrin?

That was impossible. Roundy had always been Ben Curry's friend and had never liked anything about Kerb Perrin.

"All right," Perrin said suddenly, "we'll hold Bastian. He's still a good argument. Some men will stay here, and the rest of us will make that raid on the Ragan outfit. I've an idea that when we come back, Curry will be ready to talk business."

VI

Bastian was led back from the street and thrown into a room in the rear of the store. There his feet were tied and he was left in darkness.

His mind was in a turmoil. If Perrin's men hit the ranch now, they would take Drusilla and Juliana! He well knew how swiftly they would strike and how helpless any ordinary ranch would be against them. And here he was tied hand and foot, helpless to do anything!

He heaved his body around and fought the ropes that bound him, until sweat streamed from his body. Even then, with his wrists torn by his struggles against the rawhide thongs that made him fast, he did not stop. There was nothing to aid him—no nail, no sharp corner, nothing at all.

The room was built of thin boards nailed to two-by-fours. He rolled himself around until he could get his back against the boards, trying to remember where the nails were. Bracing himself as best he could, he pushed his back against the wall. He bumped against it until his back was sore. But with no effect.

Outside, all was still. Whether they had gone, he did not know. Yet, if Perrin had not gone on his raid, he would be soon leaving. However, if Mike could escape and find Curry's private route across the river, he might beat them to it.

He wondered where Doc Sawyer was. Perhaps he was afraid of what Perrin might do if he tried to help. Where was Roundy?

Just when he had all but given up, he had an idea—a solution so simple that he cursed himself for not thinking of it before. Mike rolled over and got up on his knees and reached back with his bound hands for his spurs. Fortunately he was wearing boots instead of the moccasins he wore in the woods. By wedging one spur against the other, he succeeded in holding the rowel almost immovable, and then he began to chafe the rawhide with the prongs of the rowel.

Desperately he sawed, until every muscle was crying for relief. As he stopped, he heard the rattle of horses' hoofs. They were just going! Then he had a fighting chance if he could get free and get his hands on a gun!

He knew he was making headway, for he could feel the notch he had already cut in the rawhide. Suddenly footsteps sounded outside. Fearful whoever was there would guess what he was doing, Mike rolled over on his side.

The door opened and Snake Fernandez came in, and in his hand he held a knife. His shoulder was bandaged crudely but tightly, and the knife was held in his left hand. He came in and closed the door.

Mike stared, horror mounting within him. Perrin

was gone, and Snake Fernandez was moving toward him, smiling wickedly.

"You think you shoot Pablo Fernandez, eh?" the outlaw said, leering. "Now, we see who shoots. I am going to cut you to little pieces. I am going to cut you very slowly."

Bastian lay on his shoulder and stared at Fernandez. There was murder in the outlaw's eyes, and all the savagery in him was coming to the fore. The man stooped over him and pricked him with the knife. Clamping his jaws, Mike held himself tense.

Rage mounted in the man. He leaned closer. "You do not jump, eh? I make you jump."

He stabbed down hard with the knife, and Mike whipped over on his shoulder blades and kicked out wickedly with his bound feet. The movement caught the killer by surprise. Mike's feet hit him in the knees and knocked him rolling. With a lunge, Mike rolled over and jerked at the ropes that bound him.

Something snapped, and he jerked again. Like a cat the killer was on his feet now, circling warily. Desperately Mike pulled at the ropes, turning on his shoulders to keep his feet toward Fernandez. Suddenly he rolled over and hurled himself at the Mexican's legs, but Fernandez jerked back and stabbed.

Mike felt a sliver of pain run along his arms, and then he rolled to his feet and jerked wildly at the thongs. His hands came loose suddenly and he hurled himself at Fernandez's legs, grabbing one ankle.

Fernandez came down hard, and Bastian jerked at the leg, and then scrambled to get at him. One hand grasped the man's wrist, the other his throat. With all the power that was in him, Mike shut down on both hands.

Fernandez fought like an injured wildcat, but Mike's strength was too great. Gripping the throat with his left hand, Mike slammed the Mexican's head against the floor again and again, his throttling grip freezing tighter and tighter.

The outlaw's face went dark with blood, and his struggles grew weaker. Mike let go of his throat hold suddenly and slugged him three times on the chin with his fist.

Jerking the knife from the unconscious man's hand, Mike slashed at the thongs that bound his ankles. He got to his feet shakily. Glancing down at the sprawled-out Fernandez, he hesitated. The man was not wearing a gun, but must have had one. It could be outside the door. Easing to the door, Mike opened it a crack.

The street was deserted as far as he could see. His hands felt awkward from their long constraint, and he worked his fingers to loosen them up. There was no gun in sight, so he pushed the door wider. Fernandez's gun belts hung over the chair on the end of the porch.

He had taken two steps toward them when a man stepped out of the bunkhouse. The fellow had a toothpick lifted to his lips, but when he saw Mike Bastian, he let out a yelp of surprise and went for his gun.

It was scarcely fifteen paces and Mike threw the knife underhanded, pitching it point first off the palm of his hand. It flashed in the sun as the fellow's gun came up. Then Mike could see the haft protruding from the man's middle section.

The fellow screamed and, dropping the gun, clutched at the knife hilt in an agony of fear. His breath came in horrid gasps that Mike could hear as he grabbed Fernandez's guns and belted them on. Then he lunged for the mess hall, where his own guns had been taken from him. Shoving open the door, he sprang inside, gun in hand.

Then he froze. Doc Sawyer was standing there smiling, and Doc had a shotgun on four of Perrin's men. He looked up with relief.

"I was hoping you would escape," he said. "I didn't want to kill these men and didn't know how to go about tying them up by myself."

Mike caught up his own guns, removed Fernandez's gun belts, and strapped on his own. Then he shoved the outlaw's guns inside the waistband of his pants.

"Down on the floor," he ordered. "I'll tie them, and fast."

It was the work of only a few minutes to have

the four outlaws bound hand and foot. He gathered up their guns. "Where's Roundy?" he asked.

"I haven't seen him since he left here," Doc said. "I've been wondering."

"Let's go up to the house. We'll get Ben Curry, and then we'll have things under control in a hurry."

Together, they went out the back door and walked swiftly down the line of buildings. Mike took off his hat and sailed it into the brush, knowing he could be seen from the stone house and hoping that Ben Curry would recognize him. Sawyer was excited, but trying to appear calm. He had been a gambler and, while handy with guns, was not a man accustomed to violence. Always before, he had been a bystander rather than an active participant.

Side-by-side, gambling against a shot from someone below, they went up the stone stairs.

There was no sound from within the house. They walked into the wide living room and glanced around. There was no sign of anyone. Then Mike saw a broken box of rifle shells.

"He's been around here," he said. Then he looked up and shouted: "Dad!"

A muffled cry reached them, and Mike was out of the room and up another staircase. He entered the room at the top, and then froze in his tracks. Sawyer was behind him now.

This was the fortress room, a heavy-walled

stone room that had water trickling from a spring in the wall of the cliff and running down a stone trough and out through a pipe. There was food stored here, and plenty of ammunition.

The door was heavy and could be locked and barred from within. The walls of this room were all of four feet thick, and nothing short of dynamite could have blasted a way in.

This was Ben Curry's last resort, and he was here now. But he was sprawled on the floor, his face contorted with pain.

"Broke my leg," he panted. "Too heavy. Tried to move too . . . fast. Slipped on the steps, dragged myself up here." He looked up at Mike. "Good for you, Son! I was afraid they had killed you. You got away by yourself?"

"Yes, Dad."

Sawyer had dropped to his knees, and now he looked up.

"This is a bad break, Mike," he said. "He won't be able to move."

"Get me on a bed where I can see out of that window." Ben Curry's strength seemed to flow back with his son's presence. "I'll stand them off. You and me, Mike, we can do it!"

"Dad," Mike said. "I can't stay. I've got to go."

Ben Curry's face went gray with shock, then slowly the blood flowed back into it. Bastian dropped down beside him.

"Dad, I know where Perrin's going. He's gone to

make a raid on the Ragan Ranch. He wants the cattle and the women."

The old man lunged so mightily that Sawyer cried out and tried to push him back. Before he could speak, Mike said: "Dad, you must tell me about the secret crossing of the Colorado that you know. I must beat them to the ranch."

Ben Curry's expression changed to one of vast relief and then quick calculation. He nodded.

"You could do it, but it'll take tall riding." Quickly he outlined the route, and then added: "Now, listen! At the river there's an old Navajo. He keeps some horses for me, and he has six of the finest animals ever bred. You cross that river and get a horse from him. He knows about you."

Mike got up. "Make him comfortable, Doc. Do all you can."

Sawyer stared at Mike. "What about Dave Lenaker? He'll kill us all!"

"I'll take care of Lenaker!" Curry flared. "I'm not dead by a danged sight. I'll show that renegade where he heads in. The moment he comes up that street, I'm going to kill him." He looked at Mike again. "Son, maybe I've done wrong to raise you like I have, but if you kill Kerb Perrin or Lenaker, you would be doing the West a favor. If I don't get Dave Lenaker, you may have to. So remember this, *watch his left hand!*"

Mike ran down the steps and stopped in his room to grab his .44 Winchester. It was the work

71

of a minute to throw a saddle on a horse, and then he hit the trail. Ben Curry and Doc Sawyer could, if necessary, last for days in the fortress-like room—unless, somehow, dynamite was pitched into the window. He would have to get to the Ragan Ranch and then get back here as soon as possible.

Mike Bastian left the stable and wheeled the gray he was riding into the long, winding trail through the stands of ponderosa and fir. The horse was in fine fettle and ready for the trail, and he let it out. His mind was leaping over the trail, turning each bend, trying to see how it must lay.

This was all new country to him, for he was heading southwest now into the wild, unknown region toward the great cañons of the Colorado, a region he had never traversed and, except for old Ben Curry, was perhaps never crossed by any except Indians.

How hard the trail would be on the horse, Mike could not guess, but he knew he must ride fast and keep going. His route was the shorter, but Kerb Perrin had a lead on him and would be hurrying to make his strike and return.

Patches of snow still hid themselves around the roots of the brush and in the hollows under the end of some giant deadfall. The air was crisp and chill, but growing warmer, and by afternoon it would be hot in the sunlight. The wind of riding whipped his black hair. He ran the horse down a long path bedded deep with pine needles, and then turned at a blazed tree and went out across the arid top of a plateau.

This was the strange land he loved, the fiery, heat-blasted land of the sun. Riding along the crest of a long ridge, he looked out over a long valley dotted with mesquite and sagebrush. Black dots of cattle grazing offered the only life beyond the lonely, lazy swing of a high-soaring buzzard.

He saw the white rock he had been told to look for and turned the free-running horse into a cleft that led downward. They moved slowly here, for it was a steep slide down the side of the mesa and out on the long roll of the hill above the valley.

Time and time again Mike's hand patted his guns, as if to reassure himself they were there. His thoughts leaped ahead, trying to foresee what would happen. Would he arrive only to find the buildings burned and the girls gone?

He knew only that he must get there first, that he must face them, and that at all costs he must kill Kerb Perrin and Ducrow. Without them, the others might run, might not choose to fight it out. Mike had an idea that without Perrin, they would scatter to the four winds.

Swinging along the hillside, he took a trail that led again to a plateau top and ran off through the sage, heading for the smoky-blue distance of the cañon.

VII

Mike's mind lost track of time and distance, leaping ahead to the river and the crossing, and beyond it to Ragan's V Bar Ranch. Down steep trails through the great, broken cliffs heaped high with the piled-up stone of ages, and down through the wild, weird jumble of boulders, and across the flat top lands that smelled of sage and piñon, he kept the horse moving.

Then he was once more in the forests of the Kaibab. The dark pines closed around him, and he rode on in the vast stillness of virgin timber, the miles falling behind, the trail growing dim before him.

Then suddenly the forest split aside and he was on the rim of the cañon—an awful blue immensity yawning before him that made him draw the gray to a halt in gasping wonder. Far out over that vast, misty blue rose islands of red sandstone, islands that were laced and crossed by bands of purple and yellow. The sunset was gleaming on the vast plateaus and buttes and peaks with a ruddy glow, fading into opaqueness in the deeper cañon.

The gray was beaten and weary now. Mike turned the horse toward a break in the plateau and rode down it, giving the animal its head. They came out upon a narrow trail that hung above a vast gorge, its bottom lost in the darkness of gathering dusk. The gray stumbled on, seeming to know its day was almost done.

Dozing in the saddle, almost two hours later Mike Bastian felt the horse come to a halt. He jerked his head up and opened his eyes. He could feel the dampness of a deep cañon and could hear the thundering roar of the mighty river as it charged through the rock-walled slit. In front of him was a square of light.

"Halloo, the house!" he called.

He swung down as the door opened.

"Who's there?" a voice cried out.

"Mike Bastian!" he said, moving toward the house with long, swinging strides. "For Ben Curry!"

The man backed into the house. He was an ancient Navajo, but his eyes were keen and sharp.

"I want a horse," Mike said.

"You can't cross the river tonight." The Navajo spoke English well. "It is impossible."

"There'll be a moon later," Mike answered. "When it comes up, I'm going across."

The Indian looked at him, and then shrugged.

"Eat," he said. "You'll need it."

"There are horses?"

"Horses?" The Navajo chuckled. "The best a man ever saw. Do you suppose Ben Curry would have horses here that were not the best? But they are on the other side of the stream, and safe enough. My brother is with them."

Mike fell into a seat. "Take care of my horse, will you? I've most killed him."

When the Indian was gone, Mike slumped over on the table, burying his head in his arms. In a moment he was asleep, dreaming wild dreams of a mad race over a strange misty-blue land with great crimson islands, riding a splendid black horse and carrying a girl in his arms. He awakened with a start. The old Indian was sitting by the fireplace, and he looked up.

"You'd better eat," he said. "The moon is rising."

They went out together, walking down the path to the water's edge. As the moon shone down into the cañon, Mike stared at the tumbling stream in consternation. Nothing living could swim in that water! It would be impossible.

"How do you cross?" he demanded. "No horse could swim that. And a boat wouldn't get fifty feet before it would be dashed to pieces."

The Indian chuckled. "That isn't the way we cross it. You are right in saying no boat could cross here, for there is no landing over there, and the cañon is so narrow that the water piles up back of the narrows and comes down with a great rush."

Mike looked at him again. "You talk like an educated man," he said. "I don't understand."

The Navajo shrugged. "I was for ten years with a missionary, and after I traveled with him as an interpreter he took me back to the States, where I stayed with him for two years. Then I lived in Sante Fé."

He was leading the way up a steep path that skirted the cliff but was wide enough to walk comfortably. Opposite them, the rock wall of the cañon lifted and the waters of the tumbling river roared down through the narrow chasm.

"Ben Curry does things well, as you shall see," the guide said. "It took him two years of effort to get this bridge built."

Mike stared. "Across there?"

"Yes. A bridge for a man with courage. It is a rope bridge, made fast to iron rings sunk in the rock."

Mike Bastian walked on the rocky ledge at the edge of the trail and looked out across the gorge. In the pale moonlight he could see two slim threads trailing across the cañon high above the tumbling water. Just two ropes, and one of them four feet above the other.

"You mean," he said, "that Ben Curry crossed on *that?*"

"He did. I have seen him cross that bridge a dozen times, at least."

"Have you crossed it?"

The Navajo shrugged. "Why should I? The other side is the same as this, is it not? There is nothing over there that I want."

Mike looked at the slender strands, and then he

took hold of the upper rope and tentatively put a foot on the lower one. Slowly, carefully he eased out above the raging waters.

One slip and he would be gone, for no man could hope to live in those angry flood waters. He slid his foot along, then the other, advancing his handholds as he moved. Little by little, he worked his way across the cañon.

He was trembling when he got his feet in the rocky cavern on the opposite side and so relieved to be safely across that he scarcely was aware of the old Indian who sat there awaiting him.

The Navajo got up and without a word started down the trail. He quickly led Mike to a cabin built in the opening of a dry, branch cañon, and tethered before the door of the cabin was a huge bay stallion.

Waving at the Indian, Mike swung into the saddle, and the bay turned, taking to the trail as if eager to be off.

Would Perrin travel at night? Mike doubted it, but it was possible, so he kept moving himself. The trail led steadily upward, winding finally out of the cañon to the plateau.

The bay stallion seemed to know the trail; it was probable that Curry had used this horse himself. It was a splendid animal, big and very fast. Letting the horse have his head, Mike felt the animal gather his legs under him. Then he broke into a long, swinging lope that literally ate up the ground. How long the horse could hold that speed he did not know, but it was a good start.

It was at least a ten-hour ride to the Ragan V Bar Ranch.

The country was rugged and wild. Several times, startled deer broke and ran before him, and there were many rabbits. Dawn was breaking faintly in the east now, and shortly after daybreak he stopped near a pool of melted snow water and made coffee. Then he remounted the rested stallion and raced on.

Drusilla Ragan brushed her hair thoughtfully, and then pinned it up. Outside, she could hear her mother moving about and the Mexican girls who helped around the house whenever they were visiting. Julie was up, she knew, and had been up for hours. She was outside, talking to that blond cowhand from New Mexico, the one Voyle Ragan had hired to break horses.

Suddenly she heard Julie's footsteps, and then the door opened.

"Aren't you ready yet?" Julie asked. "I'm famished!"

"I'll be along in a minute." Then as Julie turned to go: "What did you think of him, Julie . . . that cowboy who got the buckboard for us? Wasn't he the handsomest thing?"

"Oh, you mean that Mike Bastian?" Julie said. "I was wondering why you were mooning around in here. Usually you're the first one up. Yes, I expect he is good-looking. But did you see the way he looked when you mentioned Uncle Voyle? He acted so strange."

"I wonder if Uncle Voyle knows anything about him? Let's ask!"

"You ask," Julie replied, laughing. "He's *your* problem!"

Voyle Ragan was a tall man, but lean and without Ben Curry's weight. He was already seated at the table when they came in, and Dru was no sooner in her seat than she put her question. Voyle's face became a mask.

"Mike Bastian?" he said thoughtfully. "I don't know. Where'd you meet him?"

The girls explained, and he nodded.

"In Weaver?" Voyle Ragan knew about the gold train, and his eyes narrowed. "I think I know who he is, but I never saw him that I heard of. You probably won't see him again, because most of those riders from up in the strip stay there most of the time. They are a wild bunch."

"On the way down here," Julie said, "the man who drove was telling us that outlaws live up there."

"Could be. It's wild enough." Voyle Ragan lifted his head, listening. For a moment he had believed he heard horses. But it was too soon for Ben to be coming. If anyone else came, he would have to get rid of them, and quickly.

He heard the sound again, and then he saw the cavalcade of horsemen riding into the yard. Voyle came to his feet abruptly.

"Stay here!" he snapped.

His immediate thought was of a posse, and then he saw Kerb Perrin. He had seen Perrin many times, although Perrin had never met him. Slowly he moved up to the door, uncertain of his course. These were Ben's men, but Ben had always told him that none of them was aware that he owned this ranch or that Voyle was his brother.

"Howdy!" Voyle said. "What can I do for you?"

Kerb Perrin swung down from his horse. Behind him Monson, Ducrow, and Kiefer were getting down.

"You can make as little trouble as you know how," Perrin said, his eyes gleaming. "All you got to do is stay out of the way. Where's the girls? We want them, and we want your cattle."

"What is this?" Voyle demanded. He wasn't wearing a gun; it was hanging from a clothestree in the next room. "You men can't get away with anything here!"

Perrin's face was ugly as he strode toward the door. "That's what *you* think," he sneered.

The tall old man blocked his way, and Perrin shoved him aside. Perrin had seen the startled faces of the girls inside and knew the men behind him were spreading out.

Ragan swung suddenly, and his fist struck Perrin

in the mouth. The gunman staggered, and his face went white with fury.

A Mexican started from the corral toward the house, and Ducrow wheeled, firing from the hip. The man cried out and sprawled over on the hard-packed earth, moaning out his agony.

Perrin had drawn back slowly, his face ugly with rage, a slow trickling of blood from his lips. "For that, I'll kill you!" he snarled at Ragan.

"Not yet, Perrin!"

The voice had a cold ring of challenge, and Kerb Perrin went numb with shock. He turned slowly, to see Mike Bastian standing at the corner of the corral.

VIII

Kerb Perrin was profoundly shocked. He had left Bastian a prisoner at Toadstool Cañon. Since he was free now, it could mean that Ben Curry was back in the saddle. It could mean a lot of things. An idea came with startling clarity to him. He had to kill Mike Bastian, and kill him now!

"You men have made fools of yourselves!" Bastian's voice was harsh. He stood there in his gray buckskins, his feet a little apart, his black hair rippled by the wind. "Ben Curry's not through! And this place is under his protection. He sent me to stop you, and stop you I shall! Now, any of you who don't want to fight Ben Curry, get out while the getting is good!"

"Stay where you are!" Perrin snapped. "I'll settle with you, Bastian . . . right now!"

His hand darted down in the sweeping, lightning-fast draw for which he was noted. His lips curled in sneering contempt. Yet, as his gun lifted, he saw flame blossom from a gun in Bastian's hand, and a hard object slugged him. Perplexed and disturbed, he took a step backward. Whatever had hit him had knocked his gun out of line. He turned it toward Bastian again. The gun in Mike's hand blasted a second time, and a third.

Perrin could not seem to get his own gun leveled. His mind wouldn't function right, and he felt a strangeness in his stomach, his legs— suddenly he was on his knees. He tried to get up and saw a dark pool forming near his knees. He must have slipped, he must have—that was blood.

It was his blood!

From far off he heard shouts, then a scream, then the pound of horses' hoofs. Then the thunder of those hoofs seemed to sweep through his brain and he was lying facedown in the dirt. And then he knew. Mike Bastian had beaten him to the draw. Mike Bastian had shot him three times. Mike Bastian had killed him!

He started to scream a protest—and then he just

lay there on his face, his cheek against the bloody ground, his mouth half open.

Kerb Perrin was dead.

In the instant that Perrin had reached for his gun, Ducrow had suddenly cut and run toward the corner of the house. Kiefer, seeing his leader gunned down, then made a wild grab for his own weapon. The old man in the doorway killed him with a hastily caught up rifle.

The others broke for their horses. Mike rushed after them and got off one more shot as they raced out of the yard. It was then he heard the scream, and whirled.

Ducrow had acted with suddenness. He had come to the ranch for women, and women he intended to have. Even as Bastian was killing Perrin, he had rushed for the house. Darting around the corner where two saddle horses were waiting, he was just in time to see Juliana, horrified at the killing, run back into her bedroom. The bedroom window opened beside Ducrow, and the outlaw reached through and grabbed her.

Julie went numb with horror. Ducrow threw her across Perrin's saddle, and with a pigging string, which he always carried from his days as a cowhand, he jerked her ankles together under the horse's belly.

Instantly he was astride the other horse. Julie screamed then. Wheeling, he struck her across the mouth with a backhand blow. He caught up the

84

bridle of her horse and drove in spurs to his own mount, and they went out of the ranch yard at a dead run.

Mike hesitated only an instant when he heard Julie scream, and then ran for the corner of the house. By the time he rounded the corner, gun in hand, the two horses were streaking into the piñons. In the dust, he could only catch a glimpse of the riders. He turned and walked back.

That had been a woman's scream, but Dru was in the doorway and he had seen her. Only then did he recall Julie. He sprinted for the doorway.

"Where's Julie?" he shouted to Drusilla. "Look through the house!"

He glanced around quickly. Kerb Perrin, mouth agape, lay dead on the hard earth of the ranch yard. Kiefer lay near the body of the Mexican Ducrow had killed. The whole raid had been a matter of no more than two or three minutes.

Voyle Ragan dashed from the house. "Julie's gone!" he yelled hoarsely. "I'll get a horse!"

Bastian caught his arm. His own dark face was tense and his eyes wide.

"You'll stay here!" he said harshly. "Take care of the women and the ranch. I'll go after Julie."

Dru ran from the house. "She's gone, Mike, she's gone! They have her!"

Mike walked rapidly to his horse, thumbing shells into his gun. Dru Ragan started to mount another horse. "You go back to the house," he ordered.

Dru's chin came up. In that moment she reminded him of Ben Curry.

"She's my sister!" Dru cried. "When we find her, she may need a woman's care!"

"All right," Mike said, "but you'll have to do some riding."

He wheeled the big bay around. The horse Dru had mounted was one of Ben Curry's beautiful horses, bred not only for speed but for staying power.

Mike's mind leaped ahead. Would Ducrow get back with the rest of them? Would he join Monson and Clatt? If he did, it was going to be a problem. Ducrow was a handy man with a six-gun, and tackling the three of them, or more if they were all together, would be nothing less than suicide.

He held the bay horse's pace down. He had taken a swift glance at the hoof marks of the horses he was trailing and knew them both.

Would Ducrow head back for Toadstool Cañon? Bastian considered that as he rode, and decided he would not. Ducrow did not know that Julie was Ben Curry's daughter. But from what Mike had said, Ducrow had cause to believe that Ben was back in the saddle again. And men who went off on rebel raids were not lightly handled by Curry. Besides, he would want, if possible, to keep the girl for himself.

Mike had been taught by Roundy that there was more to trailing a man than following his tracks, for you trailed him down the devious paths of the mind as well. He tried to put himself in Ducrow's place.

The man could not have much food, yet on his many outlaw forays he must have learned the country and would know where there was water. Also, there were many ranch hang-outs of the outlaws that Ducrow would know. He would probably go to one of them. Remembering the maps that Ben Curry had shown him and made him study, Mike knew the locations of all those places.

The trail turned suddenly off through the chaparral, and Mike turned to follow. Drusilla had said nothing since they started. Once he glanced at her. Even now, with her face dusty and tear-streaked, she was lovely. Her eyes were fastened on the trail, and he noted with a little thrill of satisfaction that she had brought her rifle along.

Dru certainly was her father's daughter, and a fit companion for any man.

Bastian turned his attention back to the trail. Despite the small lead he had, Ducrow had vanished. That taught Mike something of the nature of the man he was tracing; his years of outlawry had taught him how to disappear when need be. The method was simple. Turning off into the thicker desert growth, he had ridden down into a sandy wash.

Here, because of the deep sand and the tracks of

horses and cattle, tracking was a problem and it took Mike several minutes to decide whether Ducrow had gone up or down the wash. Then he caught a hoof print and they were off, winding up the sandy wash. Yet Mike knew they would not be in that sand for long. Ducrow would wish to save his horses' strength.

True enough, the trail soon turned out. From then on, it was a nightmare. Ducrow ran off in a straight-away, and then turned at right angles, weaving about in the sandy desert. Several times he had stopped to brush out portions of his trail, but Roundy had not spent years training Mike Bastian in vain. He hung to the trail like a bloodhound.

Dru, riding behind him, saw him get off and walk, saw him pick up sign where she could see nothing.

Hours passed, and the day slowly drew toward an end. Dru, her face pale, realized night would come before they found her sister. She was about to speak, when Mike looked at her.

"You wanted to come," he said, "so you'll have to take the consequences. I'm not stopping because of darkness."

"How can you trail them?"

"I can't." He shrugged. "But I think I know where they are going. We'll take a chance."

Darkness closed around them. Mike's shirt stuck to his body with sweat, and a chill wind off the higher plateaus blew down through the trees. He rode on, his face grim and his body weary with long hours in the saddle. The big bay kept on, seemingly unhurt by the long hours of riding. Time and again he patted the big horse, and Dru could hear him talking to it in a low voice. Suddenly at the edge of a clearing, he reined in.

"Dru," he said, "there's a ranch ahead. It's an outlaw hang-out. There may be one or more men there. Ducrow may be there. I am going up to find out."

"I'll come, too," the girl said impulsively.

"You'll stay here." His voice was flat. "When I whistle, then you come. Bring my horse along."

He swung down and, slipping off his boots, pulled on his moccasins. Then he went forward into the darkness. Alone, she watched him vanish toward the dark bulk of the buildings. Suddenly a light came on—too soon for him to have arrived.

Mike weaved his way through sage and mesquite to the corral and worked his way along the bars. Horses were there, but it was too dark to make them out. One of them stood near, and he put his hand through the bars, touching the horse's flank. It was damp with sweat.

His face tightened.

The horse stepped away, snorting. As if waiting for just that sound, a light went on in the house; a lamp had been lighted. By that time Mike was at the side of the house, flattened against the wall, peering in.

He saw a heavy, square-faced man with a pistol in his hand. The man put the gun under a towel on the table, and then began pacing around the room, waiting. Mike smiled grimly, walked around the house, and stepped up on the porch. In his moccasins, he made no sound. He opened the door suddenly and stepped into the room.

IX

Obviously the man had been waiting for the sound of boots or horses, or the *jingle* of spurs. Even a knock. Mike Bastian's sudden appearance startled him, and he straightened up from the table, his hand near the towel that covered the gun.

Bastian closed the door behind him. The man stared at the black-haired young man who faced him, stared with puckered brow. This man didn't look like a sheriff to him. Not those tied-down guns or that gray buckskin stained with travel, and no hat.

"You're Walt Sutton," Mike snapped. "Get your hands off that table before I blow you wide open. Get 'em off!"

He drew his gun and jammed the muzzle into Sutton's stomach with such force that it doubled the man up.

Then he swept the towel from the gun on the table.

"You fool!" he said sharply. "If you'd tried that, I'd have killed you!"

Sutton staggered back, his face gray. He had never even seen Mike's hand move.

"Who are you?" he gasped, struggling to get his wind back.

"I'm Mike Bastian, Ben Curry's foster son. He owns this ranch. He set you up here and gave you stock to get started with. Now you double-cross him! Where's Ducrow?"

Sutton swallowed. "I ain't seen him!" he protested.

"You're a liar, Sutton. His horses are out in that corral. I could pistol-whip you, but I'm not going to. You're going to tell me where he is, and now . . . or I'm going to start shooting!"

Walt Sutton was unhappy. He knew Ducrow as one of Ben Curry's men who had come here before for fresh horses. He had never seen this man who called himself Mike Bastian, yet, so far as he knew, no one but Curry himself had ever known the true facts about his ranch. If this man was lying, how could he know?

"Listen, mister," he protested, "I don't want no trouble . . . least of all with old Ben. He did set me up here. Sure, I seen Ducrow, but he told me the law was after him."

"Do I look like the law?" Mike snapped. "He's kidnapped the daughter of a friend of Curry's, niece of Voyle Ragan. I've got to find him."

"Kidnapped Voyle's niece? Gosh, mister, I wondered why he wanted two saddle horses."

Mike whistled sharply. "Where'd he go?" he demanded then.

"Damned if I know," Sutton answered. "He come in here maybe an hour ago, wanted two saddle horses and a pack horse loaded with grub. He took two canteens then and lit out."

Drusilla appeared now in the doorway, and Walt Sutton's eyes went to her.

"I know you," he said. "You're one of Voyle Ragan's nieces."

"She is," Mike said. "Ducrow kidnapped the other one. I'm going to find him. Get us some grub, but fast!"

Mike paced restlessly while Sutton filled a pack and strapped it behind the saddle of one of the fresh horses he furnished them. The horses were some of those left at the ranch by Ben Curry's orders and were good.

"No pack horses," Mike had said. "We're traveling fast." Now, he turned to Sutton again. "You got any idea where Ducrow might be going?"

"Well"—Sutton licked his lips—"he'd kill me if he knowed I said anything, but he did say something about Peach Meadow Cañon."

"Peach Meadow?" Bastian stared at Sutton. The cañon was almost a legend in the Coconino country. "What did he ask you?"

"If I knowed the trail in there, an' if it was passable."

"What did you say?"

Sutton shrugged. "Well, I've heard tell of that there cañon ever since I been in this country, an' ain't seen no part of it. I've looked, all right. Who wouldn't look, if all they say is true?"

When they were about to mount their horses, Mike turned to the girl and put his hand on her arm.

"Dru," he said, "it's going to be rough, so if you want to go back, say so."

"I wouldn't think of it," she said firmly.

"Well, I won't say I'm sorry, because I'm not. I'll sure like having you beside me. In fact"—he hesitated, and then went on—"it will be nice having you."

That was not what he had started to say, and Dru knew it. She looked at Mike for a moment, her eyes soft. He was tired now, and she could see how drawn his face was. She knew only a little of the ride he had made to reach them before Perrin's outlaws came.

When they were in the saddle, Mike explained a little of what he had in mind. "I doubt Ducrow will stop for anything now," he said. "There isn't a good hiding place within miles, so he'll head right for the cañon country. He may actually know something about Peach Meadow Cañon. If he does, he knows a perfect hideaway. Outlaws often stumble across places in their getaways that a man couldn't find if he looked for it for years."

"What is Peach Meadow Cañon?" Dru asked.

"It's supposed to be over near the river in one of the deep cañons that branch off from the Colorado. According to the story, a fellow found the place years ago, but the Spanish had been there before him, and the Indians before them. There are said to be old Indian ruins in the place, but no way to get into it from the plateau. The Indians found a way through some caves in the Coconino sandstone, and the Spanish are supposed to have reached it by boat.

"Anyway," he continued, "this prospector who found it said the climate was tropical, or almost. That it was in a branch cañon, that there was fresh water and a nice meadow. Somebody had planted some fruit trees, and, when he went back, he took a lot of peach pits and was supposed to have planted an orchard.

"Nobody ever saw him or it again," Mike went on, "so the place exists only on his say-so. The Indians alive now swear they never heard of it. Ducrow might be trying to throw us off, or he might honestly know something."

For several miles the trail was a simple thing. They were riding down the floor of a high-walled cañon from which there was no escape. Nevertheless, from time to time Bastian stopped and examined the sandy floor with matches. Always the tracks were there and going straight down the cañon.

This was new country to Mike. He knew the altitude was gradually lessening and believed they would soon emerge on the desert plateau that ran toward the cañon and finally lost itself on the edge of the pine forest.

When they had traveled about seven miles, the cañon ended abruptly and they emerged in a long valley. Mike reined in and swung down.

"Like it or not," he said, "here's where we stop. We can't have a fire, because from here it could be seen for miles. We don't want Ducrow to believe we stopped."

Mike spread his poncho on the sand and handed Dru a blanket. She was feeling the chill and gathered it closely around her.

"Aren't you cold?" she said suddenly. "If we sat close together, we could share the blanket."

He hesitated, and then sat down alongside her and pulled the blanket across his shoulders, grateful for the warmth. Leaning back against the rock, warmed by their proximity and the blanket, they dozed a little.

Mike had loosened the girths and ground-hitched the horses. He wasn't worried about them straying off.

When the sky was just faintly gray, he opened his eyes. Dru's head was on his shoulder and she was sleeping. He could feel the rise and fall of her breathing against his body. He glanced down at her face, amazed that this could happen to him—that he, Mike Bastian, foster son of an outlaw, could be sitting alone in the desert, with this girl sleeping on his shoulder.

Some movement of his must have awakened her, for her breath caught, and then she looked up. He could see the sleepy smile in her eyes and on her mouth.

"I was tired." She whispered the words and made no effort to move her head from his shoulder. "You've nice shoulders," she said. "If we were riding anywhere else, I'd not want to move at all."

"Nor I." He glanced at the stars. "We'd better get up. I think we can chance a very small fire and a quick cup of coffee."

While he was breaking dried mesquite and greasewood, Dru got the pack open and dug out the coffee and some bread. There was no time for anything else.

The fire made but little light, shielded by the rocks and kept very small, and there was less glow now because of the grayness of the sky. They ate quickly.

When they were in the saddle again, he turned down the trail left by the two saddle horses and the pack horse he was following. Sign was dim, but could be followed without dismounting. Dawn broke, and the sky turned red and gold, then blue.

The sun lifted and began to take some of the chill from their muscles.

The trail crossed the valley, skirting an alkali lake, and then dipped into the rocky wilderness that preceded the pine forest. He could find no signs of a camp. Julie, who lacked the fire and also the strength of Dru, must be almost dead with weariness, for Ducrow was not stopping. Certainly the man had more than a possible destination before him. In fact, the farther they rode, the more confident Mike was that the out-law knew exactly where he was headed.

The pines closed around them, and the trail became more difficult to follow. It was slow going, and much of it Mike Bastian walked. Suddenly he stopped, scowling.

The trail, faint as it had been, had vanished into thin air!

"Stay where you are," he told Dru. "I've got to look around a bit."

Mike studied the ground carefully. Then he walked back to the last tracks he had seen. Their own tracks did not cover them, as he had avoided riding over them in case he needed to examine the hoof prints once more.

Slowly Mike paced back and forth over the pine needles. Then he stopped and studied the surrounding timber very carefully. It seemed to be absolutely uniform in appearance. Avoiding the trail ahead, he left the girl and circled into the woods, describing a slow circle around the horses.

There were no tracks.

He stopped, his brow furrowed. It was impossible to lose them after following so far—yet they were gone, and they had left no trail. He walked back to the horses again, and Dru stared at him, her eyes wide.

"Wait a minute," he said as she began to speak. "I want to think."

He studied, inch by inch, the woods on his left, the trail ahead, and then the trail on his right. Nothing offered a clue. The tracks of three horses had simply vanished as though the animals and their riders had been swallowed into space.

On the left the pines stood thick, and back inside the woods the brush was so dense as to allow no means of passing through it. That was out, then. He had studied that brush and had walked through those woods, and, if a horseman did turn that way there would be no place to go.

The trail ahead was trackless, so it had to be on the right. Mike turned and walked again to the woods on his right. He inched over the ground, yet there was nothing, no track, no indication that anything heavier than a rabbit had passed that way. It was impossible, yet it had happened.

"Could they have backtracked?" Dru asked suddenly. "Over their same trail?"

Mike shook his head. "There were no tracks,"

he said, "but those going ahead, I think . . ." He stopped dead still, and then swore. "I'm a fool! A darned fool!" He grinned at her. "Lend me your hat."

Puzzled, she removed her sombrero and handed it to him. He turned and, using the hat for a fan, began to wave it over the ground to let the wind disturb the surface needles. Patiently he worked over the area around the last tracks seen, and then to the woods on both sides of the trail. Suddenly he stopped.

"Got it," he said. "Here they are."

Dru ran to him. He pointed to a track, then several more.

"Ducrow was smart," Mike explained. "He turned at right angles and rode across the open space, and then turned back down the way he had come, riding over on the far side. Then he dismounted and, coming back, gathered pine needles from somewhere back in the brush and came along here, pressing the earth down and scattering the needles to make it seem there had been no tracks at all."

Mounting again, they started back, and from time to time he dismounted to examine the trail. Suddenly the tracks turned off into thick woods. Leading their horses, they followed.

"Move as quietly as you can," Mike said softly. "We may be close now. Or he may wait and try to ambush us."

"You think he knows we're following him?" Dru asked.

"Sure. And he knows I'm a tracker. He'll use every trick in the book now."

For a while, the trail was not difficult to follow, and they rode again. Mike Bastian could not take his mind from the girl who rode with him. What would she think when she discovered her father was an outlaw—that he was the mysterious leader of the outlaws?

X

Pine trees thinned out, and before them was the vast blue and misty distance of the cañon. Mike slid to the ground and walked slowly forward on moccasined feet. There were a few scattered pines and the cracked and splintered rim of the cañon, breaking sharply off to fall away into the vast depths. Carefully he scouted the edge of the cañon, and, when he saw the trail, he stopped, flat-footed, and stared, his heart in his mouth.

Had they gone down *there?* He knelt on the rock. Yes, there was the scar of a horse's hoof. He walked out a little farther, looking down.

The cliff fell away for hundreds of feet without even a hump in the wall. Then, just a little farther along, he saw the trail. It was a rocky ledge scarcely three feet wide that ran steeply down the side of the rock from the cañon's rim. On the left the wall, on the right the vast, astonishing emptiness of the cañon.

Thoughtfully he walked back and explained.

"All right, Mike." Dru nodded. "If you're ready, I am."

He hesitated to bring the horses, but decided it would be the best thing. He drew his rifle from the saddle scabbard and jacked a shell into the chamber.

Dru looked at him, steady-eyed. "Mike, maybe he'll be waiting for us," she said. "We may get shot. Especially you."

Bastian nodded. "That could be," he agreed.

She came toward him. "Mike, who are you? What are you? Uncle Voyle seemed to know you, or about you, and that outlaw, Perrin. He knew you. Then I heard you say Ben Curry had sent you to stop them from raiding the ranch. Are you an outlaw, Mike?"

For as long as a man might have counted a slow ten, Mike stared out over the cañon, trying to make up his mind. Now, at this stage, there was only one thing he could say.

"No, Dru, not exactly, but I was raised by an outlaw," he explained. "Ben Curry brought me up like his own son, with the idea that I would take over the gang when he stepped out."

"You lived with them in their hide-out?"

"When I wasn't out in the woods." He nodded.

"Ben Curry had me taught everything . . . how to shoot, to track, to ride, even to open safes and locks."

"What's he like, this Ben Curry?" Dru asked.

"He's quite a man," Mike Bastian said, smiling. "When he started outlawing, everybody was rustling a few cows, and he just went a step further and robbed banks and stages, or planned the robberies and directed them. I don't expect he really figured himself bad. He might have done a lot of other things, for he has brains. But he killed a man . . . and then, in getting away, he killed another. The first one was justified. The second one . . . well, he was in a hurry."

"Are you apologizing for him?" Dru said quickly. "After all, he was an outlaw and a killer."

He glanced at her. "He was, yes. And I am not making any apologies for him, nor would he want them. He's a man who always stood on his own two feet. Maybe he was wrong but there were the circumstances. And he was mighty good to me. I didn't have a home, no place to go, and he took me in and treated me right."

"Was he a big man, Mike? A big old man?"

He did not look her way. She knew, then?

"In many ways," he said, "he is one of the biggest men I know. We'd better get started."

It was like stepping off into space, yet the horses took it calmly enough. They were mountain bred and would go anywhere as long as they could get a foothold on something.

The red maw of the cañon gaped to receive them, and they went down, following the narrow, switchback trail that seemed to be leading them into the very center of the earth.

It was late afternoon before they started down, and now the shadows began to creep up the cañon walls, reaching with ghostly fingers for the vanished sunlight. Overhead the red blazed with the setting sun's reflection and seemed to be hurling arrows of flame back into the sky. The depths of the cañon seemed chill after the sun on the plateau, and Mike walked warily, always a little ahead of the horse he was leading.

Dru was riding, and, when he glanced back once, she smiled brightly at him, keeping her eyes averted from the awful depths below.

Mike had no flair for making love, for his knowledge of women was slight. He wished now that he knew more of their ways, knew the things to say that would appeal to a girl.

A long time later they reached the bottom, and far away on their right they could hear the river rushing through the cañon. Mike knelt, and, striking a match, he studied the trail. The tracks turned back into a long cañon that led back from the river.

He got into the saddle then, his rifle across his saddle, and rode forward.

At the end, it was simple. The long chase had led to a quiet meadow, and he could smell the grass before he reached it, could hear the babble of a small stream. The cañon walls flared wide, and he saw, not far away, the faint sparkle of a fire.

Dru came alongside him. "Is . . . that them?" she asked, low-voiced.

"It couldn't be anyone else." Her hand was on his arm and he put his own hand over it. "I've got to go up there alone, Dru. I'll have to kill him, you know."

"Yes," she said simply, "but don't *you* be killed." He started to ride forward, and she caught his arm. "Mike, why have you done all this?" she asked. "She isn't your sister."

"No." He looked very serious in the vague light. "She's yours."

He turned his head and spoke to the horse. The animal started forward.

When, shortly, he stopped the mount, he heard a sound nearby. Dru Ragan was close behind him.

"Dru," he whispered, "you've *got* to stay back. Hold my horse. I'm going up on foot."

He left her like that and walked steadily forward. Even before he got to the fire, he could see them. The girl, her head slumped over on her arms, half dead with weariness, and Ducrow, bending over the fire. From time to time Ducrow glanced at the girl. Finally he reached over and cuffed her on the head.

"Come on, get some of this coffee into you," he growled. "This is where we stay . . . in Peach Meadow Cañon. Might as well give up seein' that sister of yours, because you're my woman now." He sneered. "Monson and them, they ran like scared foxes. No bottom to them. I come for a woman, and I got one."

"Why don't you let me go?" Juliana protested. "My father will pay you well. He has lots of money."

"Your pa?" Ducrow stared at her. "I thought Voyle Ragan was your uncle?"

"He is. I mean Ben Ragan. He ranches up north of the cañon."

"North of the cañon?" Ducrow laughed. "Not unless he's a Mormon, he don't. What's he look like, this pa of yours?"

"He's a great big man, with iron-gray hair, a heavy jaw . . ." She stopped, staring at Ducrow. "What's the matter with you?"

Ducrow got slowly to his feet. "Your pa . . . Ben Ragan? A big man with gray hair, an' maybe a scar on his jaw . . . that him?"

"Oh, yes. Take me to him. He'll pay you well."

Suddenly Ducrow let out a guffaw of laughter. He slapped his leg and bellowed. "Man, oh, man! Is that a good one! You're Ben Curry's daughter! Why, that old . . ." He sobered. "What did you call him? Ragan? Why, honey, that old man of yours is the biggest outlaw in the world. Or was until today. Well, of all the . . ."

"You've laughed enough, Ducrow!"

As Mike Bastian spoke, he stepped to the edge of the firelight.

"You leave a tough trail, but I followed it."

Ducrow turned, half crouching, his cruel eyes glaring at Bastian.

"Roundy was right," he snarled. "You could track a snake across a flat rock! Well, now that you're here, what are you goin' to do?"

"That depends on you, Ducrow. You can drop your guns, and I'll take you in for a trial. Or you can shoot it out."

"Drop my guns?" Ducrow chuckled. "You'd actually take me in, too! You're too soft, Bastian. You'd never make the boss man old Ben Curry was. He would never even've said yes or no. He would have seen me and gone to blastin'! You got a sight to learn, youngster. Too bad you ain't goin' to live long enough to learn it."

Ducrow lifted one hand carelessly and wiped it across the tobacco-stained stubble of his beard. His right hand swept down for his gun even as his left touched his face. His gun came up, spouting flame.

Mike Bastian palmed his gun and momentarily held it rigid. Then he fired.

Ducrow winced like he had been slugged in

the chest, and then he lifted on his tiptoes. His gun came level again. "You're . . . fast," he gasped. "Devilish fast."

He fired, and then Mike triggered his gun once more. The second shot spun Ducrow around and he fell, facedown, at the edge of the fire.

Dru came running, her rifle in her hand, but when she saw Mike still standing, she dropped the rifle and ran to him. "Oh, Mike!" she sobbed. "I was so frightened! I thought you were killed!"

Julie started to rise, and then fell headlong in a faint. Dru rushed to her side.

Mike Bastian absently thumbed shells into his gun and stared down at the fallen man. He had killed a third man. Suddenly, and profoundly, he wished with all his heart he would never have to kill another.

He holstered his weapon and, gathering up the dead man, carried him away from the fire. He would bury him here, in Peach Meadow Cañon.

XI

Sunlight lay upon the empty street of the settlement in Toadstool Cañon when Mike Bastian, his rifle crosswise on his saddle, rode slowly into the lower end of the town.

Beside him, sitting straight in her saddle, rode Dru Ragan. Julie had stayed at the ranch, but Dru had flatly refused. Ben Curry was her father, and she was going to him, outlaw camp or not.

If Dave Lenaker had arrived, Mike thought, he was quiet enough, for there was no sound. No horses stood at the hitch rails, and the doors of the saloon were wide open.

Something fluttered on the ground, and Mike looked at it quickly. It was a torn bit of cloth on a man's body. The man was a stranger. Dru noticed it and her face paled.

His rifle at the ready, Mike rode on, eyes shifting from side to side. A man's wrist lay in sight across a windowsill, his pistol on the porch outside. There was blood on the stoop of another house.

"There's been a fight," Mike said, "and a bad one. You'd better get set for the worst."

Dru said nothing, but her mouth held firm. At the last building, the mess hall, a man lay dead in a doorway. They rode on, and then drew up at the foot of the stone steps, and dismounted. Mike shoved his rifle back in the saddle scabbard and loosened his six-guns.

"Let's go," he said.

The wide verandah was empty and still, but when he stepped into the huge living room, he stopped in amazement. Five men sat about a table playing cards.

Ben Curry's head came up and he waved at them. "Come on in, Mike!" he called. "Who's that with you? Dru, by all that's holy!"

Doc Sawyer, Roundy, Garlin, and Colley were there. Garlin's head was bandaged, and Colley had one foot stretched out, stiff and straight, as did Ben Curry. But all were smiling.

Dru ran to her father and fell on her knees beside him.

"Oh, Dad!" she cried. "We were so scared!"

"What happened here?" Mike demanded. "Don't sit there grinning! Did Dave Lenaker come?"

"He sure did, and what do you think?" Doc said. "It was Rigger Molina got him! Rigger got to Weaver and found out Perrin had double-crossed him before he ever pulled the job. He discovered that Perrin had lied about the guards, so he rushed back. When he found out that Ben was crippled and that Kerb Perrin had run out, he waited for Lenaker himself.

"He was wonderful, Mike," Doc continued. "I never saw anything like it! He paced the verandah out there like a bear in a cage, swearing and waiting for Lenaker. Muttered . . . 'Leave you in the lurch, will they? I'll show 'em! Lenaker thinks he can gun you down because you're gettin' old, does he? Well, killer I may be, but I can kill him!' And he did, Mike. They shot it out in the street down there. Dave Lenaker, as slim and tall as you, and that great bear of a Molina.

"Lenaker beat him to the draw," Doc went on. "He got two bullets into the Rigger, but Molina wouldn't go down. He stood there, spraddle-legged, in the street and shot until both guns were empty. Lenaker kept shooting and must have hit Molina five times, but when he went down, Rigger walked over to him and spat in his face. 'That's for double-crossers!' he said. He was magnificent!"

"They fooled me, Mike," Roundy said. "I seen trouble a-comin' an' figured I'd better get to old Ben. I never figured they'd slip in behind you like they done. Then the news of Lenaker comin' got me. I knowed him an' was afraid of him, so I figured in order to save Ben Curry I'd get down the road and dry-gulch him. Never killed a gunslinger like him in my life, Mike, but I was sure aimin' to. But he got by me on another trail. After Molina killed Lenaker, his boys and some of them from here started after the gold they'd figured was in this house."

"Doc here," Garlin said, "is some fighter. I didn't know he had it in him."

"Roundy, Doc, Garlin, an' me," Colley said, "we sided Ben Curry. It was a swell scrap while it lasted. Garlin got one through his scalp, and I got two bullets in the leg. Aside from that, we came out all right."

Briefly, then, Mike explained all that had transpired, how he had killed Perrin, and then had trailed Ducrow to Peach Meadow Cañon and the fight there.

"Where's the gang?" he demanded now. "All gone?"

"All the live ones." Ben Curry nodded grimly. "There's a few won't go anywhere. Funny, the only man who ever fooled me was Rigger Molina. I never knew the man was that loyal, yet he stood by me when I was in no shape to fight Lenaker. Took that fight right off my hands. He soaked up lead like a sponge soaks water."

Ben Curry looked quickly at Dru. "So you know you're the daughter of an outlaw? Well, I'm sorry, Dru. I never aimed for you to know. I was gettin' shet of this business and planned to settle down on a ranch with your mother and live out the rest of my days plumb peaceful."

"Why don't you?" Dru demanded.

He looked at her, his admiring eyes taking in her slim, well-rounded figure. "You reckon she'll have me?" he asked. "She looked a sight like you when she was younger, Dru."

"Of course, she'll have you. She doesn't know . . . or didn't know until Julie told her. But I think she guessed. *I* knew. I saw you talking with some men once, and later heard they were outlaws, and then I began hearing about Ben Curry."

Curry looked thoughtfully from Dru to Mike.

"Is there something between you two? Or am I an old fool?"

Mike flushed and kept his eyes away from Dru.

111

"He's a fine man, Dru," Doc Sawyer said. "And well educated, if I do say so . . . who taught him all he knows."

"All he knows!" Roundy stared at Doc with contempt. "Book larnin'! Where would that gal be but for what I told him? How to read sign, how to foller a trail? Where would she be?"

Mike took Dru out to the verandah then.

"I can read sign, all right," he said, "but I'm no hand at reading the trail to a woman's heart. You would have to help me, Dru."

She laughed softly, and her eyes were bright as she slipped her arm through his. "Why, Mike, you've been blazing a trail over and back and up again, ever since I met you in the street at Weaver." Suddenly she sobered. "Mike, let's get some cattle and go back to Peach Meadow Cañon. You said you could make a better trail in, and it would be a wonderful place. Just you and I and . . ."

"Sure," he said. "In Peach Meadow Cañon."

Roundy craned his head toward the door, and then he chuckled.

"That youngster," he said. "He may not know all the trails, but he sure gets where he's goin'. He sure does!"

The Trail to
Crazy Man

I

In the dark, odorous forecastle a big man with wide shoulders sat at a scarred mess table, his feet spread to brace himself against the roll of the ship. A brass hurricane lantern, its light turned low, swung from a beam overhead, and in the vague light the big man studied a worn and sweat-stained chart. There was no sound in the forecastle but the distant rustle of the bow wash about the hull, the lazy creak of the square rigger's timbers, a few snores from sleeping men, and the hoarse, rasping breath of a man who was dying in the lower bunk.

The big man who bent over the chart wore a slipover jersey with alternate red and white stripes, a broad leather belt with a brass buckle, and coarse jeans. On his feet were woven leather sandals of soft, much-oiled leather. His hair was shaggy and uncut, but he was clean-shaven except for a mustache and burnsides. The chart he studied showed the coast of northern California. He marked a point on it with the tip of his knife, then checked the time with a heavy gold watch. After a swift calculation, he folded the chart and replaced it in an oilskin packet with other papers, and tucked the packet under his jersey above his belt.

Rising, he stood for an instant, canting to the roll of the ship, staring down at the white-haired man in the lower bunk. There was that about the big man to make him stand out in any crowd. He was a man born to command, not only because of his splendid physique and the strength of his character, but because of his personality. He knelt beside the bunk and touched the dying man's wrist. The pulse was feeble. Rafe Caradec crouched there, waiting, watching, thinking.

In a few hours at most, possibly even in a few minutes, this man would die. In the long year at sea his health had broken down under forced labor and constant beatings, and this last one had broken him up internally. When Charles Rodney was dead he, Rafe Caradec, would do what he must.

The ship rolled slightly, and the older man sighed and his lids opened suddenly. For a moment he stared upward into the ill-smelling darkness, then his head turned. He saw the big man crouched beside him. He smiled. His hand fumbled for Rafe's.

"Yuh . . . yuh've got the papers? Yuh won't forget?"

"I won't forget."

"Yuh must be careful."

"I know."

"See my wife, Carol. Explain to her that I didn't run away, that I wasn't afraid. Tell her I had the money, was comin' back. I'm worried about the mortgage I paid. I don't trust Barkow." Then the man lay silently, breathing deeply, hoarsely. For the first time in three days he was conscious and aware. "Take care of 'em, Rafe," he continued, rising up slightly. "I've got to trust yuh! Yuh're the only chance I have! Dyin' ain't bad, except for them. And to think . . . a whole year has gone by. Anything may have happened."

"You'd better rest," Rafe said gently.

"It's late for that. He's done me in this time. Why did this happen to me, Rafe? To us?"

Caradec shrugged his powerful shoulders. "I don't know. No reason, I guess. We were just there at the wrong time. We took a drink we shouldn't have taken."

The old man's voice lowered. "Yuh're goin' to try . . . tonight?"

Rafe smiled then. "Try? Tonight we're goin' ashore, Rodney. This is our only chance. I'm goin' to see the captain first."

Rodney smiled, and lay back, his face a shade whiter, his breathing more gentle.

A year they had been together, a brutal, ugly, awful year of labor, blood, and bitterness. It had begun, that year, one night in San Francisco in Hongkong Bohl's place on the Barbary Coast. Rafe Caradec was just back from Central America with a pocketful of money, his latest revolution cleaned up, and the proceeds in his pocket, and some of it in the bank. The months just past had been jungle months, dripping jungle, fever-ridden and stifling with heat and humidity. It had been a period of raids and battles, but finally it was over, and Rafe had taken his payment in cash and moved on. He had been on the town, making up for lost time—Rafe Caradec, gambler, soldier of fortune, wanderer of the far places.

Somewhere along the route that night he had met Charles Rodney, a sun-browned cattleman who had come to San Francisco to raise money for his ranch in Wyoming. They had had a couple of drinks and dropped in at Hongkong Bohl's dive. They'd had a drink there, too, and, when they awakened, it had been to the slow, long roll of the sea and the brutal voice of Bully Borger, skipper of the *Mary S*. Rafe had cursed himself for a tenderfoot and a fool. To have been shanghaied like any drunken farmer! He had shrugged it off, knowing the uselessness of resistance. After all, it was not his first trip to sea. Rodney had been wild. He had rushed to the captain and demanded to be put ashore, and Bully Borger had knocked him down and booted him senseless while the mate stood by with a pistol. That had happened twice more until Rodney returned to work almost a cripple, and frantic with worry over his wife and daughter.

As always, the crew had split into cliques. One of these consisted of Rafe, Rodney, Roy Penn,

Rock Mullaney, and Tex Brisco. Penn had been a law student and occasional prospector. Mullaney was an able-bodied seaman, hardrock miner, and cowhand. They had been shanghaied in San Francisco in the same lot with Rafe and Rodney. Tex Brisco was a Texas cowhand who had been shanghaied from a waterfront dive in Galveston where he had gone to look at the sea.

Finding a friend in Rafe, Rodney had told him the whole story of his coming to Wyoming with his wife and daughter, of what drought and Indians had done to his herd, and how finally he had mortgaged his ranch to a man named Barkow. Rustlers had invaded the country, and he had lost cattle. Finally reaching the end of his rope, he had gone to San Francisco to get a loan from an old friend. In San Francisco, surprisingly, he had met Barkow and some others, and paid off the mortgage. A few hours later, wandering into Hongkong Bohl's place, which had been recommended to him by Barkow's friends, he had been doped, robbed, and shanghaied.

When the ship returned to San Francisco after a year, Rodney had demanded to be put ashore, and Borger had laughed at him. Then Charles Rodney had tackled the big man again, and that time the beating had been final. With Rodney dying, the *Mary S.* had finished her loading and slipped out of port so he could be conveniently "lost at sea."

The cattleman's breathing had grown gentler,

and Rafe leaned his head on the edge of the bunk, dozing. Rodney had given him the deed to the ranch, a deed that gave him half a share, the other half belonging to Rodney's wife and daughter. Caradec had promised to save the ranch if he possibly could. Rodney had also given him Barkow's signed receipt for the money.

Rafe's head came up with a jerk. How long he had slept he did not know. He stiffened as he glanced at Charles Rodney. The hoarse, rasping breath was gone; the even, gentle breath was no more. Rodney was dead.

For an instant, Rafe held the old man's wrist, then drew the blanket over Rodney's face. Abruptly then, he got up. A quick glance at his watch told him they had only a few minutes until they would sight Cape Mendocino. Grabbing a small bag of things off the upper bunk, he turned quickly to the companionway.

Two big feet and two hairy ankles were visible on the top step. They moved, and step by step a man came down the ladder. He was a big man, bigger than Rafe, and his small, cruel eyes stared at him, then at Rodney's bunk.

"Dead?"

"Yes."

The big man rubbed a fist along his unshaven jowl. He grinned at Rafe. "I heerd him speak aboot the ranch. It could be a nice thing, that. I heerd aboot them ranches. Money in 'em." His eyes brightened with cupidity and cunning. "We share an' share alike, eh?"

"No." Caradec's voice was flat. "The deed is made out to his daughter and me. His wife is to share, also. I aim to keep nothin' for myself."

The big man chuckled hoarsely. "I can see that," he said. "Josh Briggs is no fool, Caradec! You're intendin' to get it *all* for yourself. I want mine." He leaned on the handrail of the ladder. "We can have a nice thing, Caradec. They said there was trouble over there, huh? I guess we can handle any trouble, an' make some ourselves."

"The Rodneys get it all," Rafe said. "Stand aside. I'm in a hurry."

Briggs's face was ugly. "Don't get high an' mighty with me!" he said roughly. "Unless you split even with me, you don't get away. I know aboot the boat you've got ready. I can stop you there, or here."

Rafe Caradec knew the futility of words. There are some natures to whom only violence is an argument. His left hand shot up suddenly, his stiffened fingers and thumb making a V that caught Briggs where his jawbone joined his throat. The blow was short, vicious, unexpected. Briggs's head jerked back, and Rafe hooked short and hard with his right, then followed through with a smashing elbow that flattened Briggs's nose and showered him with blood.

Rafe dropped his bag, then struck, left and right to the body, then left and right to the chin. The last two blows cracked like pistol shots. Josh Briggs hit the foot of the ladder in a heap, rolled over, and lay still, his head partly under the table. Rafe picked up his bag and went up the ladder without so much as a backward glance.

II

On the dark deck Rafe Caradec moved aft along the starboard side. A shadow moved out from the mainmast.

"You ready?"

"Ready, Rock."

Two more men got up from the darkness near the foot of the mast, and all four hauled the boat from its place and got it to the side.

"This the right place?" Penn asked.

"Almost." Caradec straightened. "Get her ready. I'm going to call on the Old Man."

In the darkness he could feel their eyes on him. "You think that's wise?"

"No, but he killed Rodney. I've got to see him."

"You goin' to kill Borger?"

It was like them that they did not doubt he could if he wished. Somehow he had always impressed men so that what he wanted to accomplish, he would accomplish."No, just a good beatin'. He's had it comin' for a long time."

Mullaney spat. He was a stocky, muscular man. "Yuh cusséd right he has! I'd like to help."

"No, there'll be no help for either of us. Stand by and watch for the mate."

Penn chuckled. "He's tied up aft, by the wheel."

Rafe Caradec turned and walked forward. His soft leather sandals made no noise on the hardwood deck, or on the companionway as he descended. He moved like a shadow along the bulkhead, and saw the door of the captain's cabin standing open. He was inside and had taken two steps before the captain looked up.

Bully Borger was big, almost a giant. He had a red beard around his jawbone under his chin. He squinted from cold, gray eyes at Rafe. "What's wrong?" he demanded. "Trouble on deck?"

"No, Captain," Rafe said shortly, "there's trouble here. I've come to beat you within an inch of your life, Captain. Charles Rodney is dead. You ruined his life, Captain, and then you killed him."

Borger was on his feet, cat-like. Somehow he had always known this moment would come. A dozen times he had told himself he should kill Caradec, but the man was a seaman, and in the lot of shanghaied crews there were few. So he had delayed.

He lunged at the drawer for his brass knuckles. Rafe had been waiting for that, poised on the balls of his feet. His left hand dropped to the captain's wrist in a grip like steel, and his right hand sank to the wrist in the captain's middle. It stopped Borger, that punch did, stopped him flat-footed for only an instant, but that instant was enough. Rafe's head darted forward, butting the bigger man in the face, as Rafe felt the bones crunch under his hard skull.

Yet the agony gave Borger a burst of strength, and he tore the hand with the knuckles loose and got his fingers through their holes. He lunged, swinging a roundhouse blow that would have dropped a bull elephant. Rafe went under the swing, his movements timed perfectly, his actions almost negligent. He smashed left and right to the wind, and the punches drove hard at Borger's stomach, and he doubled up, gasping. Rafe dropped a palm to the back of the man's head and shoved him down, hard. At the same instant, his knee came up, smashing Borger's face into a gory pulp.

Bully Borger, the dirtiest fighter on many a waterfront, staggered back, moaning with pain. His face expressionless, Rafe Caradec stepped in and threw punches with both hands, driving, wicked punches that had the power of those broad shoulders behind them, and timed with the rolling of the ship. Left, right, left, right, blows that cut and chopped like meat cleavers. Borger tottered and fell back across the settee.

Rafe wheeled to see Penn's blond head in the doorway. Roy Penn stared at the bloody hulk, then at Rafe. "Better come on. The cape's showing off the starb'rd bow."

When they had the boat in the water, they slid down the rope one after the other, then Rafe slashed it with his belt knife, and the boat dropped back. The black hulk of the ship swept by them. Her stern lifted, then sank, and Rafe, at the tiller, turned the bow of the boat toward the monstrous blackness of the cape.

Mullaney and Penn got the sail up, when the mast was stepped, then Penn looked around at Rafe.

"That was mutiny, you know."

"It was," Rafe said calmly. "I didn't ask to go aboard, and knockout drops in a Barbary Coast dive ain't my way of askin' for a year's job!"

"A year?" Penn swore. "Two years and more for me. For Tex, too."

"Yuh know this coast?" Mullaney asked.

Rafe nodded. "Not well, but there's a place just north of the cape where we can run in. To the south the sunken ledges and rocks might tear our bottom out, but I think we can make this other place. Can you all swim?"

The mountainous headland loomed black against the gray-turning sky of the hours before daybreak. The seaward face of the cape was rocky and water-worn along the shoreline. Rafe, studying the currents and the rocks, brought the boat neatly in among them and headed for a boulder-strewn gray beach where water curled and left a white ruffle of surf. They scrambled out of the boat and threw their gear on the narrow beach.

"How about the boat?" Texas demanded. "Do we leave it?"

"Shove her off, cut a hole in the bottom, and let her sink," Rafe said.

When the hole had been cut, they let the sea take the boat offshore a little, watching it fill and sink. Then they picked up their gear, and Rafe Caradec led them inland, working along the shoulder of the mountain. The northern slope was covered with brush and trees and afforded some concealment. Fog was rolling in from the sea, and soon the gray, cottony shroud of it settled over the countryside.

When they had several miles behind them, Rafe drew to a halt. Penn opened the sack he was carrying and got out some bread, figs, coffee, and a pot.

"Stole 'em out of the captain's stores," he said. "Figured we might as well eat."

"Got anything to drink?" Mullaney rubbed the dark stubble on his wide jaws.

"Uhn-huh. Two bottles of rum. Good stuff from Jamaica."

"Yuh'll do to ride the river with," Tex said,

squatting on his heels. He glanced up at Rafe. "What comes now?"

"Wyomin', for me." Rafe broke some sticks and put them into the fire Rock was kindling. "I made my promise to Rodney, and I'll keep it."

"He trusted yuh." Tex studied him thoughtfully.

"Yes. I'm not goin' to let him down. Anyway," he added, smiling, "Wyomin's a long way from here, and we should be as far away as we can. They may try to find us. Mutiny's a hangin' offense."

"Ever run any cattle?" Tex wanted to know.

"Not since I was a kid. I was born in New Orleans, grew up near San Antonio. Rodney tried to tell me all he could."

"I been over the trail to Dodge twice," Tex said, "and to Wyomin' once. I'll be needin' a job."

"You're hired," Rafe said, "if we ever get the money to pay you."

"I'll chance it," Tex Brisco agreed. "I like the way yuh do things."

"Me for the gold fields in Nevady," Rock said.

"That's good for me," Penn said. "If me and Rock don't strike it rich, we may come huntin' a feed."

There was no trail through the tall grass but the one the mind could make, or the instinct of the cattle moving toward water, yet as the long-legged zebra dun moved along the flank of the little herd, Rafe Caradec thought he was coming home. This was a land for a man to love, a long, beautiful land of rolling grass and trees, of towering mountains pushing their dark peaks against the sky and the straight, slim beauty of lodgepole pines.

He sat easy in the saddle, more at home than in many months, for almost half his life had been lived astride a horse, and he liked the dun, which had an easy, space-eating stride. He had won the horse in a poker game in Ogden, and won the saddle and bridle in the same game. The new Winchester '73, newest and finest gun on the market, he had bought in San Francisco.

A breeze whispered in the grass, turning it to green and shifting silver as the wind stirred along the bottomland. Rafe heard the gallop of a horse behind him and reined in, turning. Tex Brisco rode up alongside.

"We should be about there, Rafe," he said, digging in his pocket for the makings. "Tell me about that business again, will yuh?"

Rafe nodded. "Rodney's brand was one he bought from an *hombre* named Shafter Mason. It was the Bar M. He had two thousand acres in Long Valley that he bought from Red Cloud, paid him good for it, and he was runnin' cattle on that, and some four thousand acres outside the valley. His cabin was built in the entrance to Crazy Man Cañon. He borrowed money, and mortgaged the land to a man named Bruce Barkow. Barkow's a big cattleman there, tied in with three or four others. He has several gunmen workin' for him, but he was the only man around who could loan him the money he needed."

"What's yore plan?" Brisco asked, his eyes following the cattle.

"Tex, I haven't got one. I couldn't plan until I saw the lay of the land. The first thing will be to find Missus Rodney and her daughter and, from them, learn what the situation is. Then we can go to work. In the meantime, I aim to sell these cattle and hunt up Red Cloud."

"That'll be tough," Tex suggested. "There's been some Injun trouble, and he's a Sioux. Mostly, they're on the prod right now."

"I can't help it, Tex," Rafe said. "I've got to see him, tell him I have the deed, and explain so's he'll understand. He might turn out to be a good friend, and he would certainly make a bad enemy."

"There may be some question about these cattle," Tex suggested dryly.

"What of it?" Rafe shrugged. "They are all strays, and we culled them out of cañons where no white man has been in years, and slapped our own brand on 'em. We've driven them two hundred miles, so nobody here has any claim on them. Whoever started cattle where we found these left the country a long time ago. You remember what that old trapper told us?"

"Yeah," Tex agreed, "our claim's good enough." He glanced again at the brand, then looked curiously at Rafe. "Man, why didn't yuh tell me yore old man owned the C Bar? My uncle rode for 'em a while! I heard a lot about 'em! When yuh said to put the C Bar on these cattle, yuh could have knocked me over with a axe! Why, Uncle Joe used to tell me all about the C Bar outfit. The old man had a son who was a ring-tailed terror as a kid. Slick with a gun . . . say!" Tex Brisco stared at Rafe. "You wouldn't be the same one, would yuh?"

"I'm afraid I am," Rafe said. "For a kid I was too slick with a gun. Had a run-in with some old enemies of Dad's, and, when it was over, I hightailed for Mexico."

"Heard about it."

Tex turned his sorrel out in a tight circle to cut a steer back into the herd, and they moved on. Rafe Caradec rode warily, with an eye on the country. This was all Indian country, and the Sioux and Cheyennes had been hunting trouble ever since Custer had ridden into the Black Hills, which was the heart of the Indian country and almost sacred to the plains tribes. This was the near end of Long Valley where Rodney's range had begun, and it could be no more than a few miles to Crazy Man Cañon and his cabin.

Rafe touched a spur to the dun and cantered toward the head of the drive. There were three hundred head of cattle in this bunch, and, when the old trapper had told him about them, curiosity had impelled him to have a look. In the green bottom of several adjoining cañons these cattle, remnants of a herd brought into the country several years before, had looked fat and fine. It had been brutal, bitter work, but he and Tex had rounded up and branded the cattle, then hired two drifting cowhands to help them with the drive.

He passed the man riding point and headed for the strip of trees where Crazy Man Creek curved out of the cañon and turned in a long, sweeping semicircle out to the middle of the valley, then down its center, irrigating some of the finest grassland he had ever seen. Much of it, he noted, was sub-irrigated from the mountains that lifted on both sides of the valley. The air was fresh and cool after the long, hot drive over the mountains and desert. The heavy fragrance of the pines and the smell of the long grass shimmering with dew lifted to his nostrils. He moved the dun down to the stream, and sat his saddle while the horse dipped its muzzle into the clear, cold water of the Crazy Man. When the gelding lifted its head, Rafe waded him across the stream and climbed the opposite bank, then turned upstream toward the cañon.

III

The bench beside the stream, backed by its stand of lodgepole pines, looked just as Rodney had described it. Yet, as the cabin came into sight, Rafe's lips tightened with apprehension, for there was no sign of life. The dun, feeling his anxiety, broke into a canter. One glance sufficed. The cabin was empty, and evidently had been so for a long time.

Rafe was standing in the door when Tex rode up. Brisco glanced around, then at Rafe. "Well," he said, "looks like we've had a long ride for nothin'."

The other two hands rode up—Johnny Gill and Bo Marsh, both Texans. With restless saddles, they had finished a drive in the Wyoming country, then headed west and had ridden clear to Salt Lake. On their return they had run into Rafe and Tex, and hired on to work the herd east to Long Valley.

Gill, a short, leather-faced man of thirty, stared around. "I know this place," he said. "Used to be the Rodney Ranch. Feller name of Dan Shute took over. Rancher."

"Shute, eh?" Tex glanced at Caradec. "Not Barkow?"

Gill shook his head. "Barkow made out to be

helpin' Rodney's women folks, but he didn't do much good. Personal, I never figgered he cut no great swath a-tryin'. Anyway, this here Dan Shute is a bad *hombre*."

"Well," Rafe said casually, "mebbe we'll find out how bad. I aim to settle right here."

Gill looked at him thoughtfully. "Yuh're buyin' yoreself a piece of trouble, mister," he said. "But I never cottoned to Dan Shute myself. Yuh got any rightful claim to this range? This is where yuh was headed, ain't it?"

"That's right," Rafe said, "and I have a claim."

"Well, Bo," Gill said, hooking a leg over the saddle horn, "want to drift on, or do we stay and see how this gent stacks up with Dan Shute?"

Marsh grinned. He had a reckless, infectious grin. "Shore, Johnny," he said. "I'm for stayin' on. Shute's got him a big, red-headed hand ridin' for him that I never liked, no ways."

"Thanks, boys," Rafe said. "Looks like I've got an outfit. Keep the cattle in pretty close the next few days. I'm ridin' in to Painted Rock."

"That town belongs to Barkow," Gill advised. "Might pay yuh to kind of check up on Barkow and Shute. Some of the boys talkin' around the chuck wagon sort of figgered there was more to that than met the eye. That Bruce Barkow is a right important gent around here, but when yuh read his sign, it don't always add up."

"Mebbe," Rafe suggested thoughtfully, "you'd

better come along. Let Tex and Marsh worry with the cattle."

Rafe Caradec turned the dun toward Painted Rock. Despite himself, he was worried. His liking for the little cattleman, Rodney, had been very real, and he had come to know and respect the man while aboard the *Mary S.* In the weeks that had followed the flight from the ship, he had been considering the problem of Rodney's ranch so much that it had become much his own problem. Now, Rodney's worst fears seemed to have been realized. The family had evidently been run off their ranch, and Dan Shute had taken possession. Whether there was any connection between Shute and Barkow remained to be seen, but Caradec knew that chuck wagon gossip can often come close to the truth, and that cowhands could many times see men more clearly than people who saw them only on their good behavior or when in town.

As he rode through the country toward Painted Rock, he studied it curiously and listened to Johnny Gill's comments. The little Texan had punched cattle in here two seasons, and knew the area better than most.

Painted Rock was the usual cowtown. A double row of weather-beaten, false-fronted buildings, most of which had never been painted, and a few scattered dwellings, some of logs, most of stone. There was a two-story hotel, and a stone building, squat and solid, whose sign identified it as the PAINTED ROCK BANK.

Two buckboards and a spring wagon stood on the street, and a dozen saddle horses stood three-hoofed at hitching rails. A sign ahead of them and cater-cornered across from the stage station told them that here was the NATIONAL BAR.

Gill swung his horse in toward the hitching rail and dropped to the ground. He glanced across his saddle at Caradec. "The big *hombre* lookin' us over is the redhead Bo didn't like," he said in a low voice.

Rafe did not look around until he had tied his own horse with a slipknot. Then he hitched his guns into place on his hips. He was wearing two walnut-stocked pistols, purchased in San Francisco. He wore jeans, star boots, and a buckskin jacket. Stepping up on the boardwalk, Rafe glanced at the burly redhead. The man was studying them with frank curiosity.

"Howdy, Gill!" he said. "Long time no see."

"Is that bad?" Gill said, and shoved through the doors into the dim, cool interior of the National.

At the bar, Rafe glanced around. Two men stood nearby, drinking. Several others were scattered around at tables.

"Red-eye," Gill said, then in a lower tone: "Bruce Barkow is the big man with the black mustache, wearin' black and playin' poker. The Mexican-lookin' *hombre* across from him is

Dan Shute's gun-slingin' *segundo*, Gee Bonaro."

Rafe nodded, and lifted his glass. Suddenly he grinned. "To Charles Rodney!" he said clearly.

Barkow jerked sharply and looked up, his face a shade paler. Bonaro turned his head slowly, like a lizard watching a fly. Gill and Rafe both tossed off their drinks and ignored the stares.

"Man," Gill said, grinning, his eyes dancing, "yuh don't waste no time, do yuh?"

Rafe Caradec turned. "By the way, Barkow," he said, "where can I find Missus Rodney and her daughter?"

Bruce Barkow put down his cards. "If yuh've got any business," he said smoothly, "I'll handle it for 'em."

"Thanks," Rafe said. "My business is personal, and with them."

"Then," Barkow said, his eyes hardening, "yuh'll have trouble. Missus Rodney is dead. Died three months ago."

Rafe's lips tightened. "And her daughter?"

"Ann Rodney," Barkow said carefully, "is here in town. She is to be my wife soon. If yuh've got any business . . ."

"I'll transact it with her!" Rafe said sharply.

Turning abruptly, he walked out the door, Gill following. The little cowhand grinned, his leathery face folding into wrinkles that belied his thirty-odd years. "Like I say, boss," he chuckled, "yuh shore throw the hooks into 'em." He nodded toward a building across the street. "Let's try the Emporium. Rodney used to trade there, and Gene Baker who runs it was a friend of his."

The Emporium smelled of leather, dry goods, and all the varied and exciting smells of the general store. Rafe rounded a bale of jeans and walked back to the long counter, backed by shelves holding everything from pepper to rifle shells.

"Where am I to find Ann Rodney?" he asked.

The white-haired proprietor gave him a quick glance, then nodded to his right. Rafe turned and found himself looking into the large, soft dark eyes of a slender, yet beautifully shaped, girl in a print dress. Her lips were delicately lovely; her dark hair was gathered in a loose knot at the nape of her neck. She was so lovely that it left him a little breathless.

She smiled, and her eyes were questioning. "I'm Ann Rodney," she said. "What is it you want?"

"My name is Rafe Caradec," he said gently. "Your father sent me."

Her face went white to the lips, and she stepped back suddenly, dropping one hand to the counter as though for support. "You come . . . from my *father?* Why, I . . ."

Bruce Barkow, who had apparently followed them from the saloon, stepped in front of Rafe, his face flushed with anger. "Yuh've scared her to death," he snapped. "What do yuh mean, comin' in here with such a story? Charles Rodney has been dead for almost a year."

Rafe's eyes measured Barkow, his thoughts racing. "He has? How did he die?"

"He was killed," Barkow said, "for the money he was carryin', it looked like." Barkow's eyes suddenly turned triumphant. "Did you kill him?"

Rafe was suddenly aware that Johnny Gill was staring at him, his brows drawn together, puzzled and wondering. Gill, he realized, knew him but slightly and might easily become suspicious of his motives. Gene Baker, also, was studying him coldly, his eyes alive with suspicion. Ann Rodney stared at him, as if stunned by what he had said, and somehow uncertain.

"No," Rafe said coolly, "I didn't kill him, but I'd be plumb interested to know who made yuh believe he was dead."

"Believe he was dead?" Barkow laughed harshly. "I was with him when he died. We found him beside the trail, shot through the body by bandits. I brought back his belongings to Miss Rodney."

"Miss Rodney," Rafe began, "if I could talk to you a few minutes. . . ."

"No," she whispered. "I don't want to talk to you. What can you be thinking of? Coming to me with such a story? What is it you want from me?"

"Somehow," Rafe said quietly, "you've got hold of some false information. Your father has been dead for no more than two months."

"Get out of here!" Barkow ordered, his hand on his gun. "Yuh're torturin' that poor young lady! Get out, I say! I don't know what scheme yuh've cooked up, but it won't work! If yuh know what's good for yuh, yuh'll leave this town while the goin' is good!"

Ann Rodney turned sharply around and ran from the store, heading for the storekeeper's living quarters.

"Yuh'd better get out, mister," Gene Baker said harshly. "We know how Rodney died. Yuh can't work no underhanded schemes on that young lady. Her pa died, and he talked before he died. Three men heard him."

Rafe Caradec turned and walked outside, standing on the boardwalk, frowning at the skyline. He was aware that Gill had moved up beside him.

"Boss," Gill said, "I ain't no lily, but neither am I takin' part in no deal to skin a young lady out of what is hers by rights. Yuh'd better throw a leg over yore saddle and get."

"Don't jump to conclusions, Johnny," Rafe advised, "and before you make any change in your plans, suppose you talk to Tex about this? He was with me, an' he knows all about Rodney's death as well as I do. If they brought any belongin's of his back here, there's somethin' more to this than we believed."

Gill kicked his boot toe against a loose board. "Tex was with yuh? Damn it, man! What of that yarn of theirs? It don't make sense."

"That's right," Caradec replied, "it don't, and before it will, we've got to do some diggin'." He added: "Suppose I told you that Barkow back there held a mortgage on the Rodney Ranch, and Rodney went to Frisco, got the money, and paid it in Frisco . . . then never got home?"

Gill stared at Rafe, his mouth tightening. "Then nobody here would know he ever paid that mortgage but Barkow? The man he paid it to?"

"That's right."

"Then I'd say this Barkow was a sneakin' polecat," Gill said harshly. "Let's brace him!"

"Not yet, Johnny. Not yet!"

A horrible thought had occurred to him. He had anticipated no such trouble, yet if he explained the circumstances of Rodney's death and was compelled to prove them, he would be arrested for mutiny on the high seas—a hanging offense! Not only his own life depended on silence, but the lives of Brisco, Penn, and Mullaney. There must be a way out. There had to be.

IV

As Rafe Caradec stood there in the bright sunlight, he began to understand a lot of things and wonder about them. If some of the possessions of Charles Rodney had been returned to Painted Rock, it implied that those who returned them knew something of the shanghaiing of Rodney. How else could they have come by his belongings? Bully Borger had shanghaied his own crew with the connivance of Hongkong Bohl. Had he taken Rodney by suggestion? Had the man been marked for him? Certainly it would not be the first time somebody had got rid of a man in such a manner. If that was the true story, it would account for some of Borger's animosity when he had beaten Rodney.

No doubt they had all been part of a plan to make sure that Charles Rodney never returned to San Francisco alive, or to Painted Rock. Yet believing such a thing and proving it were two vastly different things. Also, it presented a problem of motive. Land was not scarce in the West, and much of it could be had for the taking. Why, then, people would ask, would Barkow go to such efforts to get one piece of land? Rafe had Barkow's signature on the receipt, but that could be claimed to be a forgery. First, a motive beyond the mere value of two thousand acres of land and the money paid on the debt must be established. That might be all, and certainly men had been killed for less, but Bruce Barkow was no fool, nor was he a man who played for small stakes.

Rafe lit a cigarette and stared down the street. He must face another fact. Barkow was warned. Whatever he was gambling for, including the girl, was in danger now and would remain in peril as long as Rafe Caradec remained alive or in the country. That fact stood out cold and clear. Barkow knew by now that he must kill Rafe Caradec.

Rafe understood the situation perfectly. His life had been lived among men who played ruthlessly for the highest stakes. It was no shock to him that men would stoop to killing, or a dozen killings, if they could gain a desired end. From now on he must ride with cat eyes, always aware, and always ready.

Sending Gill to find and buy two pack horses, Rafe turned on his heel and went into the store. Barkow was gone, and Ann Rodney was still out of sight.

Baker looked up and his eyes held no welcome. "If yuh've got any business here," he said, "state it and get out. Charles Rodney was a friend of mine."

"He needed some smarter friends," Rafe replied shortly. "I came here to buy supplies, but if you want to, start askin' yourself some questions. Who profits by Rodney's death? What evidence have you got besides a few of his belongings, that might have been stolen, that he was killed a year ago? How reliable were the three men who were with him? If he went to San Francisco for the money, what were Barkow and the others doin' on the trail?"

"That's neither here nor there," Baker said roughly. "What do yuh want? I'll refuse no man food."

Coolly Caradec ordered what he wanted, aware that Baker was studying him. The man seemed puzzled.

"Where yuh livin'?" Baker asked suddenly. Some of the animosity seemed to have gone from his voice.

"At the Rodney cabin on the Crazy Man," Caradec said. "I'm stayin', too, till I get the straight of this. If Ann Rodney is wise, she won't get married or get rid of any rights to her property till this is cleared up."

"Shute won't let yuh stay there."

"I'll stay." Rafe gathered up the boxes of shells and stowed them in his pockets. "I'll be right there. While you're askin' yourself questions, ask why Barkow, who holds a mortgage that he claims is unpaid on the Rodney place, lets Dan Shute take over?"

"He didn't want trouble because of Ann," Baker

143

said defensively. "He was right nice about it. He wouldn't foreclose. Givin' her a chance to pay up."

"As long as he's goin' to marry her, why should he foreclose?" Rafe turned away from the counter. "If Ann Rodney wants to see me, I'll tell her all about it, any time. I promised her father I'd take care of her, and I will, whether she likes it or not! Also," he added, "any man who says he talked to Rodney as he was dyin' *lies!*"

The door closed at the front of the store, and Rafe Caradec turned to see the dark, Mexican-looking gunman Gill had indicated in the National Saloon, the man known as Gee Bonaro. The gunman came toward him, smiling and showing even white teeth under a thread of mustache.

"Would you repeat that to me, *señor*?" he asked pleasantly, a thumb hooked in his belt.

"Why not?" Rafe said sharply. He let his eyes, their contempt unveiled, go over the man slowly from head to foot, then back. "If you was one of 'em that said that, you're a liar. And if you touch that gun, I'll kill you."

Gee Bonaro's spread fingers hovered over the gun butt, and he stood flat-footed, an uncomfortable realization breaking over him. This big stranger was not frightened. In the green eyes was a coldness that turned Bonaro a little sick inside. He was uncomfortably aware that he stood, perilously, on the brink of death.

"Were you one of 'em?" Rafe demanded.

"*Sí, señor.*" Bonaro's tongue touched his lips.

"Where was this supposed to be?"

"Where he died, near Pilot Peak, on the trail."

"You're a white-livered liar, Bonaro. Rodney never got back to Pilot Peak. You're bein' trapped for somebody else's gain, and, if I were you, I'd back up and look the trail over again." Rafe's eyes held the man. "You say you saw him. How was he dressed?"

"Dressed?" Bonaro was startled and confused. Nobody had asked such a thing. He had no idea what to say. Suppose the same question was answered in a different way by one of the others? He wavered and was lost. "I . . . I don't know. I . . ."

He looked from Baker to Caradec and took a step back, his tongue at his lips, his eyes like those of a trapped animal. He was confused. The big man facing him somehow robbed him of his sureness, his poise, and he had come here to kill him.

"Rodney talked to me only a few weeks ago, Bonaro," Rafe said coldly. "Think! How many others did he talk to? You're bein' mixed up in a cold-blooded killin', Bonaro! Now turn around and get out! And get out fast!"

Bonaro backed up, and Rafe took a forward step. Wheeling, the man scrambled for the door.

Rafe turned and glanced at Baker. "Think that over," he said coolly. "You'll take the word of a coyote like that about an honest man! Some-body's tryin' to rob Miss Rodney, and because you're believin' that cock-and-bull story, you're helpin' it along."

Gene Baker stood stockstill, his hands flat on the counter. What he had seen he would not have believed. Gee Bonaro had slain two men since coming to Painted Rock, and here a stranger had backed him down without lifting a hand or moving toward a gun. Baker rubbed his ear thoughtfully.

Johnny Gill met Rafe in front of the store with two pack horses. A glance told Caradec that the little cowhand had bought well.

Gill glanced questioningly at Rafe. "Did I miss somethin'? I seen that gun hand *segundo* of Shute's come out of that store like he was chased by the devil. You and him have a run-in?"

"I called him, and he backed down," Rafe told Gill. "He said he was one of the three who heard Rodney's last words. I told him he was a liar."

Johnny drew the rope tighter. He glanced out of the corner of his eye at Rafe. This man had come into town and put himself on record for what he was and what he planned faster than anybody he had ever seen. *Shucks,* Johnny thought, grinning at the horse, *why go back to Texas? There'll be ruckus enough here, ridin' for that* hombre.

The town of Painted Rock numbered exactly eighty-nine inhabitants, and by sundown the arrival of Rafe Caradec and his challenge to Gee Bonaro was the talk of all of them. It was a behind-the-hand talking, but the story was going the rounds. Also, that Charles Rodney was alive—or had been alive until recently.

By nightfall Dan Shute heard that Caradec had moved into the Rodney house on Crazy Man, and an hour later he had stormed furiously into his bunkhouse and given Bonaro a tongue-lashing that turned the gunman livid with anger. Bruce Barkow was worried, and he made no pretense about it in his conference with Shute. The only hopeful note was that Caradec had said that Rodney was dead.

Gene Baker, sitting in his easy chair in his living quarters behind the store, was uneasy. He was aware that his silence was worrying his wife. He was also aware that Ann was silent herself, an unusual thing, for the girl was usually gay and full of fun and laughter. The idea that there could have been anything wrong about the story told by Barkow, Weber, and Bonaro had never entered the storekeeper's head. He had accepted the story as others had, for many men had been killed along the trails or had died in fights with Indians. It was another tragedy of the westward march, and he had done what he could—he and his wife had taken Ann Rodney into their home and loved her as their own child.

Now this stranger had come with his questions.

Despite Baker's irritation that the matter had come up at all, and despite his outward denials of truth in what Caradec had said, he was aware of an inner doubt that gnawed at the walls of his confidence in Bruce Barkow. Whatever else he might be, Gene Baker was a fair man. He was forced to admit that Bonaro was not a man in whom reliance could be placed. He was a known gunman, and a suspected outlaw. That Shute hired him was bad enough in itself, yet when he thought of Shute, Baker was again uneasy. The twin ranches of Barkow and Shute surrounded the town on three sides. Their purchases represented no less than fifty percent of the storekeeper's business, and that did not include what the hands bought on their own. The drinking of the hands from the ranches supported the National Saloon, too, and Gene Baker, who for all his willingness to live and let live was a good citizen, or believed himself to be, found himself examining a situation he did not like. It was not a new situation in Painted Rock, and he had been unconsciously aware of it for some time, yet, while aware of it, he had tacitly accepted it. Now there seemed to be someone in the woodpile, or several of them.

As Baker smoked his pipe, he found himself realizing with some discomfort and growing doubt that Painted Rock was completely subservient to Barkow and Shute. Pod Gomer, who was town marshal, had been nominated for the job by Barkow at the council meeting. Joe Benson of the National had seconded the motion, and Dan Shute had calmly suggested that the nomination be closed, and Gomer was voted in. Gene Baker had never liked Gomer, but the man was a good gun hand and certainly unafraid. Baker had voted with the others, as had Pat Higley, another responsible citizen of the town. In the same manner, Benson had been elected mayor of the town, and Roy Gargan had been made judge.

Remembering that the town was actually in the hands of Barkow and Shute, Baker also recalled that at first the tactics of the two big ranchers had caused grumbling among the smaller holders of land. Nothing had ever been done, largely because one of them, Stu Martin, who talked the loudest, had been killed in a fall from a cliff. A few weeks later another small rancher, Al Chase, had mistakenly tried to draw against Bonaro, and had died. Looked at in that light, the situation made Baker uneasy. Little things began to occur to him that had remained unconsidered, and he began to wonder just what could be done about it, even if he knew for sure that Rodney had been killed. Not only was he dependent on Shute and Barkow for business, but Benson, their partner and friend, owned the freight line that brought in his supplies.

Law was still largely a local matter. The Army maintained a fort not too far away, but the soldiers were busy keeping an eye on the Sioux and their allies who were becoming increasingly restive, what with the blooming gold camps at Bannock and Alder Gulch, Custer's invasion of the Black Hills, and the steady roll of wagon trains over the Bozeman and Laramie Trails. If there were trouble here, Baker realized with a sudden, sickening fear, it would be settled locally, and that meant it would be settled by Dan Shute and Bruce Barkow. Yet, even as he thought of that, Baker recalled the tall man in the black, flat-crowned hat and buckskin jacket. There was something about Rafe Caradec that was convincing, something that made a man doubt he would be controlled by anybody or anything, at any time, or anywhere.

V

Rafe Caradec rode silently alongside Johnny Gill when they moved out of Painted Rock, trailing the two pack horses. The trail turned west by south and crossed the north fork of Clear Creek. They turned then along a narrow path that skirted the huge boulders fringing the mountains.

Gill turned his head slightly. "Might not be a bad idea to take to the hills, boss," he said carelessly. "There's a trail up that-a-way . . . ain't much used, either."

Caradec glanced quickly at the little 'puncher,

then nodded. "All right," he said, "lead off, if you want."

Johnny was riding with his rifle across his saddle, and his eyes were alert. That, Rafe decided, was not a bad idea. He jerked his head back toward Painted Rock. "What you think Barkow will do?"

Gill shrugged. "No tellin', but Dan Shute will know what to do. He'll be gunnin' for yuh, if yuh've shore enough got the straight of this. What yuh figger happened?"

Rafe hesitated, then he said carefully: "What happened to Charles Rodney wasn't any accident. It was planned and carried out mighty smooth." He waited while the horse took a half dozen steps, then looked up suddenly. "Gill, you size up like a man to ride the river with. Here's the story, and if you ever tell it, you'll hang four good men."

Briefly and concisely, he outlined the shanghaiing of Rodney and himself, the events aboard ship, the escape.

"See?" he added. "It must have looked foolproof to them. Rodney goes away to sea and never comes back. Nobody but Barkow knows that mortgage was paid, and what did happen was somethin' they couldn't plan for, and probably didn't even think about."

Gill nodded. "Rodney must have been tougher'n anybody figgered," he said admiringly. "He never quit tryin', yuh say?"

"Right. He had only one idea, it looked like, and that was to live to get home to his wife and daughter. If," Rafe added, "the wife was anything like the daughter, I don't blame him."

The cowhand chuckled. "Yeah, I know what yuh mean. She's purty as a papoose in a red hat."

"You know, Gill," Rafe said speculatively, "there's one thing that bothers me. Why do they want that ranch so bad?"

"That's got me wonderin', too," Gill agreed. "It's a good ranch, mostly, except for that land at the mouth of the valley. Rises there to a sort of a dome, and the Crazy Man swings around it. Nothin' much grows there. The rest of it's a good ranch."

"Say anything about Tex or Bo?" Caradec asked.

"No," Gill said. "It figgers like war, now. No use lettin' the enemy know what you're holdin'."

The trail they followed left the grasslands of the creek bottom and turned back up into the hills to a long plateau. They rode on among the tall pines, scattered here and there with birch or aspen along the slopes. A cool breeze stirred among the pines, and the horses walked along slowly, taking their time, their hoof beats soundless on the cushion of pine needles. Once the trail wound down the steep side of a shadowy cañon, weaving back and forth, finally to reach bottom in a brawling, swift-running stream. Willows skirted the banks, and, while the horses were drinking, Rafe saw a trout leap in a pool above the rapids. A brown thrasher swept like a darting red-brown arrow past his head, and he could hear yellow warblers gossiping among the willows.

He himself was drinking when he saw the sand crumble from a spot on the bank and fall with a tiny splash into the creek. Carefully he got to his feet. His rifle was in his saddle boot, but his pistols were good enough for anything he could see in this narrow place. He glanced casually at Gill, and the cowhand was tightening his cinch, all unawares.

Caradec drew a long breath and hitched up his trousers, then hooked his thumbs in his belt near the gun butts. He had no idea who was there, but that sand did not fall without a reason. In his own mind he was sure that someone was standing in the willow thicket across and downstream, above where the sand had fallen. Someone was watching them.

"Ready?" Johnny suggested, looking at him curiously.

"Almost," Rafe drawled casually. "Sort of like this little place. It's cool and pleasant. Sort of place a man might like to rest a while, and where a body could watch his back trail, too." He was talking at random, hoping Gill would catch on. The 'puncher was looking at him intently now. "At least," Rafe added, "it would be nice here if a man *was* alone. He could think better."

It was then that his eye caught the color in the willows. It was a tiny corner of red, a bright, flaming crimson, and it lay where no such color should be. That was not likely to be a cowhand unless he was a Mexican or a dude, and they were scarce in this country. It could be an Indian. If whoever it was had planned to fire, a good chance had been missed while he and Gill drank. Two well-placed shots would have done for them both. Therefore, it was logical to discount the person in the willows as an enemy, or, if so, a patient enemy. To all appearances whoever lay in the willows preferred to remain unseen. It had all the earmarks of being someone or something trying to avoid trouble.

Gill was quiet and puzzled. Cat-like, he watched Rafe for some sign to indicate what the trouble was. A quick scanning of the brush had revealed nothing, but Caradec was not the man to be spooked by a shadow.

"You speak Sioux?" Rafe asked casually.

Gill's mouth tightened. "A mite. Not so good, mebbe."

"Speak loud and say we are friends."

Johnny Gill's eyes were wary as he spoke. There was no sound, no reply.

"Try it again," Rafe suggested. "Tell him we want to talk. Tell him we want to talk to Red Cloud, the great chief."

Gill complied, and there was still no sound.

Rafe looked up at him. "I'm goin' to go over into those willows," he said softly. "Something's wrong."

"You watch yoreself!" Gill warned. "The Sioux are plenty smart."

Moving slowly, so as to excite no hostility, Rafe Caradec walked his horse across the stream, then swung down. There was neither sound nor movement from the willows. He walked back among the slender trees, glancing around, yet even then, close as he was, he might not have seen her had it not been for the red stripes. Her clothing blended perfectly with the willows and flowers along the stream bank.

She was a young squaw, slender and dark, with large, intelligent eyes. One look told Rafe that she was frightened speechless, and, knowing what had happened to squaws found by some of the white men, he could understand. Her legs were outstretched, and from the marks on the grass and the bank of the stream he could see she had been dragging herself. The reason was plain to see. One leg was broken just below the knee.

"Johnny," he said, not too loudly, "here's a young squaw. She's got a busted leg."

"Better get away quick!" Gill advised. "The Sioux are pretty mean where squaws are concerned."

"Not till I set that leg," Rafe said.

"Boss," Gill advised worriedly, "don't do it.

155

She's liable to yell like blazes if yuh lay a hand on her. Our lives won't be worth a nickel. We've got troubles enough, without askin' for more."

Rafe walked a step nearer, and smiled at the girl. "I want to fix your leg," he said gently, motioning to it. "Don't be afraid."

She said nothing, staring at him, yet he walked up and knelt down. She drew back from his touch, and he saw then she had a knife. He smiled and touched the break with gentle fingers.

"Better cut some splints, Gill," he said. "She's got a bad break. Just a little jolt and it might pop right through the skin."

Working carefully, he set the leg. There was no sound from the girl, no sign of pain. Gill shook his head wonderingly.

"Nervy, ain't she?" Rafe suggested.

Taking the splints Gill had cut, he bound them on her leg.

"Better take the pack off that paint and split it between the two of us and the other hoss," he said. "We'll put her up on the hoss."

When they had her on the paint's back, Gill asked her, in Sioux: "How far to Indian camp?"

She looked at him, then at Rafe. Then she spoke quickly to him.

Gill grinned. "She says she talks to the chief. That means you. Her camp is about an hour south and west, in the hills."

"Tell her we'll take her most of the way."

Rafe swung into saddle, and they turned their horses back into the trail. Rafe rode ahead, the squaw and the pack horse following, and Johnny Gill, rifle still across the saddle bows, bringing up the rear.

They had gone no more than a mile when they heard voices, then three riders swung around a bend in the trail, reining in sharply. Tough-looking, bearded men, they stared from Rafe to the Indian girl. She gasped suddenly, and Rafe's eyes narrowed a little.

"See yuh got our pigeon!" A red-bearded man rode toward them, grinning. "We been a-chasin' her for a couple of hours. Purty thing, ain't she?"

"Yeah." A slim, wiry man with a hatchet face and a cigarette dangling from his lips was speaking. "Glad yuh found her. We'll take her off yore hands now."

"That's all right," Rafe said quietly. "We're taking her back to her village. She's got a broken leg."

"Takin' her back to the village?" the red-bearded man exclaimed. "Why, we cut that squaw out for ourselves, and we're slappin' our own brand on her. You get yore own squaws." He nodded toward the hatchet-faced man. "Get that lead rope, Boyne."

"Keep your hands off that rope!" Rafe's voice was cold. "You blasted fools will get us all killed. This girl's tribe would be down on your ears before night."

"We'll take care of that," Red persisted. "Get her, Boyne!"

Rafe smiled suddenly. "If you boys are lookin' for trouble, I reckon you've found it. I don't know how many of you want to die for this squaw, but any time you figger to take her away from us, some of you'd better start sizing up grave space."

Boyne's eyes narrowed wickedly. "Why, he's askin' for a ruckus, Red! Which eye shall I shoot him through?"

Rafe Caradec sat his horse calmly, smiling a little. "I reckon," he said, "you boys ain't any too battle wise. You're bunched too much. Now, from where I sit, all three of you are dead in range and grouped nice for even one gun shootin', and I'm figurin' to use two." He spoke to Gill. "Johnny," he said quietly, "suppose these *hombres* start smokin' it, you take that fat one. Leave the redhead and this Boyne for me."

The fat cowhand shifted in his saddle uncomfortably. He was unpleasantly aware that he had turned his horse so he was sideward to Gill and, while presenting a fair target himself, would have to turn half around in the saddle to fire.

Boyne's eyes were hard and reckless. Rafe knew he was the one to watch. He wore his gun slung low, and that he fancied himself as a gun hand was obvious. Suddenly Rafe knew the man was going to draw.

"Hold it!" The voice cut sharply across the air

like the crack of a whip. "Boyne, keep yore hand shoulder high! You, too, Red! Now turn yore horses with yore knees and start down the trail. If one of yuh even looks like yuh wanted to use a gun, I'll open up with this Henry and cut yuh into little pieces."

Boyne cursed wickedly. "Yuh're gettin' out of it easy this time!" he said viciously. "I'll see yuh again!"

Rafe smiled. "Why, shore, Boyne! Only next time you'd better take the rawhide lashin' off the butt of your Colt. Mighty handy when ridin' over rough country, but mighty unhandy when you need your gun in a hurry."

With a startled gasp, Boyne glanced down. The rawhide thong was tied over his gun to hold it in place. His face two shades whiter than a snake's belly, he turned his horse with his knees and started the trek down trail.

Bo Marsh stepped out of the brush with his rifle in his hands. He was grinning.

"Hey, boss! If I'd known that six-gun was tied down, I'd 'a' let yuh mow him down! That skunk needs it. That's Lem Boyne. He's a gunslinger for Dan Shute."

Gill laughed. "Man! Will our ears burn tonight! Rafe's run two of Shute's boys into the ground today!"

Marsh grinned. "Figgered yuh'd be headed home soon, and I was out after deer." He glanced at the squaw with the broken leg. "Got more trouble?"

"No," Rafe said. "Those *hombres* had been runnin' this girl down. She busted her leg gettin' away, so we fixed it up. Let's ride."

VI

The trail was smoother now and drifted casually from one cañon to another. Obviously it had been a game trail that had been found and used by Indians, trappers, and wandering buffalo hunters before the coming of the cowhands and trail drivers.

When they were still several miles from the cabin on the Crazy Man, the squaw spoke up suddenly. Gill looked over at Rafe.

"Her camp's just over that rise in a draw," he said.

Caradec nodded. Then he turned to the girl. She was looking at him, expecting him to speak.

"Tell her," he said, "that we share the land Rodney bought from Red Cloud. That we share it with the daughter of Rodney. Get her to tell Red Cloud we will live on the Crazy Man, and we are friends to the Sioux, that their women are safe with us, their horses will not be stolen, that we are friends to the warriors of Red Cloud and the great chiefs of the Sioux people."

Gill spoke slowly, emphatically, and the girl nodded. Then she turned her horse and rode up through the trees.

"Boss," Johnny said, "she's got our best hoss. That's the one I give the most money for!"

Rafe grinned. "Forget it. The girl was scared silly but wouldn't show it for anything. It's a cheap price to pay to get her home safe. Like I said, the Sioux make better friends than enemies."

When the three men rode up, Tex Brisco was carrying two buckets of water to the house. He grinned at them. "That grub looks good," he told them. "I've eaten so much antelope meat, the next thing you know I'll be boundin' along over the prairie myself."

While Marsh got busy with the grub, Johnny told Tex about the events of the trip.

"Nobody been around here," Brisco said. "I seen three Injuns, but they was off a couple of miles and didn't come this way. There hasn't been nobody else around."

During the three days that followed the trip to Painted Rock, Rafe Caradec scouted the range. There were a lot of Bar M cattle around, and most of them were in fairly good shape. His own cattle were mingling freely with them. The range would support many more head than it carried, and the upper end of Long Valley was almost untouched.

There was much good grass in the mountain meadows, also, and in several cañons south of the Crazy Man.

Johnny Gill and Bo Marsh explained the lay of the land as they knew it.

"North of here," Gill said, "back of Painted Rock, and mostly west of there, the mountains rise up nigh onto nine thousand feet. Good huntin' country, some of the best I ever seen. South, toward the end of the valley, the mountains thin out. There's a pass through to the head of Otter Creek, and that country west of the mountains is good grazin' land, and nobody much in there yet. Injuns got a big powwow grounds over there. Still farther south there's a long road wall, runnin' purty much north and south. Only one entrance in thirty-five miles. Regular hole in the wall. A few men could get into that hole and stand off an army, and, if they wanted to hightail it, they could lose themselves in that back country."

Rafe scouted the crossing toward the head of Otter Creek, and rode down the creek to the grasslands below. This would be good grazing land, and mentally he made a note to make some plans for it.

He rode back to the ranch that night, and, when he was sitting on the stoop after the sun was down, he looked around at Tex Brisco. "You been over the trail from Texas?" he asked.

"Uhn-huh."

"Once aboard ship you were tellin' me about a stampede you had. Only got back about sixteen hundred head of a two-thousand-head herd. That sort of thing happen often?"

Tex laughed. "Shucks, yes! Stampedes are regular things along the trail. Yuh lose some cattle, yuh mebbe get more back, but there's plenty of maverick stock runnin' on the plains south of the Platte . . . all the way to the Canadian, as far as that goes."

"Reckon a few men could slip over there and round up some of that stock?"

Brisco sat up and glanced at Rafe. "Shore could. Wild stuff, though, and it would be a man-sized job."

"Mebbe," Caradec suggested, "we'll try and do it. It would be one way of gettin' a herd pretty fast, or turnin' some quick money."

There followed days of hard, driving labor. Always one man stayed at the cabin keeping a sharp look-out for any of the Shute or Barkow riders. Caradec knew they would come and, when they did, they would be riding with only one idea in mind—to get rid of him.

In the visit to Painted Rock he had laid his cards on the table, and they had no idea how much he knew, or what his story of Charles Rodney could be. Rafe Caradec knew Barkow was worried, and that pleased him. Yet while the delayed attack was a concern, it was also a help.

There was some grumbling from the hands, but he kept them busy, cutting hay in the meadows and stacking it. Winter in this country was going to be bad—he needed no weather prophet to tell him that—and he had no intention of losing a lot of stock.

In a cañon that branched off from the head of Crazy Man, he had found a warm spring. There was small chance of it freezing, yet the water was not too hot to drink. In severe cold it would freeze, but otherwise it would offer an excellent watering place for his stock. They made no effort to bring hay back to the ranch, but arranged it in huge stacks back in the cañons and meadows.

There had been no sign of Indians, and Rafe avoided their camp, yet once, when he did pass nearby, there was no sign of them. It seemed as if they had moved out and left the country.

Then one night he heard a noise at the corral, and the snorting of a horse. Instantly he was out of bed and had his boots on when he heard Brisco swearing in the next room. They got outside in a hurry, fearing someone was rustling their stock. In the corral they could see the horses, and there was no one nearby.

Bo Marsh had walked over to the corral, and suddenly he called out.

"Boss! Look it here!"

They all trooped over, then stopped. Instead of five horses in the corral there were ten! One of them was the paint they had loaned the young squaw, but the others were strange horses, and every one was a picked animal.

"Well, I'll be damned!" Gill exploded. "Brung our own hoss and an extra for each of us. Reckon that big black is for you, boss."

By daylight, when they could examine the horses, Tex Brisco walked around them admiringly.

"Man," he said, "that was the best horse trade I ever heard of! There's four of the purtiest horses I ever laid an eye on! I always did say the Sioux knowed hossflesh, and this proves it. Reckon yore bread cast on the water shore come back to yuh, boss!"

Rafe studied the valley thoughtfully. They would have another month of good haying weather if there was no rain. Four men could not work much harder than they were, but the beaver were building their houses bigger and in deeper water, and from that and all other indications the winter was going to be hard.

He made his decision suddenly, and mentioned it that night at the supper table. "I'm ridin' to Painted Rock. Want to go along, Tex?"

"Yeah." The Texan looked at him calculatingly. "Yeah, I'd like that."

"How about me?" Bo asked, grinning. "Johnny went last time. I could shore use a belt of that red-eye the National peddles, and mebbe a look around town."

"Take him along, boss," Johnny said. "I can hold this end. If he stays, he'll be ridin' me all the time, anyway."

"All right. Saddle up first thing in the mornin'."

"Boss . . ." Johnny threw one leg over the other, and lit his smoke. "One thing I better tell yuh. I hadn't said a word before, but two, three days ago, when I was down to the bend of the Crazy Man, I run into a couple fellers. One of 'em was Red Blazer, that big galoot who was with Boyne. Remember?"

Rafe turned around and looked down at the little, leather-faced cowhand. "Well," he said, "what about him?"

Gill took a long drag on his cigarette. "He told me he was carryin' a message from Trigger Boyne, and that Trigger was goin' to shoot on sight, next time yuh showed up in Painted Rock."

Rafe reached over on the table and picked up a piece of cold cornbread. "Then I reckon that's what he'll do," he said. "If he gets into action fast enough."

"Boss," Marsh pleaded, "if that red-headed Tom Blazer, brother to the one yuh had the run-in with . . . if he's there, I want him."

"That the one we saw on the National stoop?" Rafe asked Gill.

"Uhn-huh. There's five of them brothers. All gun-toters."

Gill got up and stretched. "Well, I'll have it

purty lazy while you *hombres* are down there dustin' lead." He added: "It would be a good idea to sort of keep an eye out. Gee Bonaro's probably in town and could be feelin' mighty mad."

Rafe walked outside, strolling toward the corral. Behind him, Marsh turned to Gill. "Reckon he can sling a gun?"

Tex chuckled. "Mister, that *hombre* killed one of the fastest, slickest gun throwers that ever came out of Texas, and done it when he was no more'n sixteen, down on the C Bar. Also, while I've never seen him shoot, if he can shoot like he can fistfight, Mister Trigger Boyne had better grab hisself an armful of hossflesh and start makin' tracks for the blackest part of the Black Hills . . . *fast!*"

VII

Nothing about the town of Painted Rock suggested drama or excitement. It lay sprawled comfortably in the morning sunlight in an elbow of Rock Creek. A normally roaring and plunging stream, the creek had decided here to loiter a while, enjoying the warm sun and the graceful willows that lined the banks. Behind and among the willows the white, slender trunks of the birch trees marched in neat ranks, each tree so like its neighbor that it was almost impossible to

167

distinguish between them. Clumps of mountain alder, yellow rose, puffed clematis, and antelope bush were scattered along the far bank of the stream and advanced up the hill beyond in skirmishing formation. In a few weeks now the aspen leaves would be changing, and Painted Rock would take on a background of flaming color—a bank of trees, rising toward the darker growth of spruce and fir along the higher mountain side.

Painted Rock's one street was the only thing about the town that was ordered. It lay between two neat rows of buildings that stared at each other down across a long lane of dust and, during the rainy periods, of mud. At any time of day or night a dozen saddle horses would be standing three-legged at the hitching rails, usually in front of Joe Benson's National Saloon. A buckboard or a spring wagon would also be present, usually driven by some small rancher in for his supplies. The two big outfits sent two wagons together, drawn by mules.

Bruce Barkow sat in front of the sheriff's office this morning, deep in conversation with Pod Gomer. It was a conversation that had begun over an hour before. Gomer was a short, thick-set man, almost as deep from chest to spine as from shoulder to shoulder. He was not fat and was considered a tough man to tangle with. He was also a man who liked to play on the winning side,

168

and long ago he had decided there was only one side to consider in this light—the side of Dan Shute and Bruce Barkow. Yet he was a man who was sensitive to the way the wind blew, and he frequently found himself puzzled when he considered his two bosses. There was no good feeling between them. They met on business or pleasure, saw things through much the same eyes, but each wanted to be kingpin. Sooner or later, Gomer knew, he must make a choice between them.

Barkow was shrewd, cunning. He was a planner and a conniver. He was a man who would use any method to win, but in most cases he kept himself in the background of anything smacking of crime or wrongdoing. Otherwise, he was much in the foreground. Dan Shute was another type of man. He was tall and broad of shoulder. Normally he was sullen, hard-eyed, and surly. He had little to say to anyone and was more inclined to settle matters with a blow or a gun than with words. He was utterly cold-blooded, felt slightly about anything, and would kill a man as quickly and with as little excitement as he would brand a calf.

Barkow might carve a notch on his gun butt. Shute wouldn't even understand such a thing. Shute was a man who seemed to be without vanity, and such men are dangerous. For the vanity is there, only submerged, and the slow-burning, deep fires of hatred for the vain smolder within them until suddenly they burst into flame and end in sudden, dramatic climax and ugly violence.

Pod Gomer understood little of Dan Shute. He understood the man's complex character just enough to know that he was dangerous, that as long as Shute rode along, Barkow would be top dog, but that if ever Barkow incurred Shute's resentment, the deep-seated fury of the gunman would brush his partner aside as he would swat a fly. In a sense, both men were using each other, but of the two Dan Shute was the man to be reckoned with. Yet Gomer had seen Barkow at work. He had seen how deviously the big rancher planned, how carefully he made friends. At the fort, they knew and liked him, and what little law there was outside the town of Painted Rock was in the hands of the commanding officer at the fort. Knowing this, Bruce Barkow had made it a point to know the personnel there, and to plan accordingly.

The big black that Rafe was riding was a powerful horse, and he let the animal have its head. Behind him in single file trailed Tex Brisco and Bo Marsh. Rafe Caradec was thinking as he rode. He had seen too much of violence and struggle to fail to understand men who lived lives along the frontier. He had correctly gauged the kind of courage Gee Bonaro possessed, yet he knew the man was dangerous and, if the opportunity offered, would shoot and shoot instantly.

Trigger Boyne was another proposition. Boyne was reckless, wickedly fast with a gun, and the type of man who would fight at the drop of a hat, and had his own ready to drop on the slightest pretext. Boyne liked the name of being a gunman, and he liked being top dog. If Boyne had sent a warning to Caradec, it would be only because he intended to back up that warning.

Rafe took the black along the mountain trail, riding swiftly. The big horse was the finest he had ever had between his knees. When a Sioux gave gifts, he apparently went all the way. A gift had been sent to each of the men on the Crazy Man, which was evidence that the Sioux had looked them over at the cabin. The black had a long, space-eating stride that seemed to put no strain on his endurance. The horses given to the others were almost as good. There were not four men in the mountains mounted as well, Rafe knew.

He rounded the big horse into the dusty street of Painted Rock and rode down toward the hitching rail at a spanking trot. He pulled up and swung down, and the other men swung down alongside him.

"Just keep your eyes open," Rafe said guardedly. "I don't want trouble. But if Boyne starts anything, he's my meat."

Marsh nodded, and walked up on the boardwalk alongside of Brisco, who was sweeping the street with quick, observant eyes.

"Have a drink?" Rafe suggested, and led the way inside the National.

Joe Benson was behind the bar. He looked up warily as the three men entered. He spoke to Bo, then glanced at Tex Brisco. He placed Tex as a stranger, and his mind leaped ahead. It took no long study to see that Tex was a hard character and a fighting man.

Joe was cautious and shrewd. Unless he was mistaken, Barkow and Shute had their work cut out for them. These men didn't look like the sort to back water for anything or anyone. The town's saloonkeeper-mayor had an uncomfortable feeling that a change was in the offing, yet he pushed the feeling aside with irritation. That must not happen. His own failure and his own interests were too closely allied to those of Barkow and Shute. Of course, when Barkow married the Rodney girl that would give them complete title to the ranch. That would leave them in the clear, and these men, if alive, could be run off the ranch with every claim to legal process.

Caradec tossed off his whisky and looked up sharply. His glance pinned Joe Benson to the spot. "Trigger Boyne sent word he was looking for me," he said abruptly. "Tell him I'm in town . . . ready."

"How should I know Trigger better'n any other man who comes into this bar?" Benson demanded.

"You know him. Tell him."

Rafe hitched his guns into a comfortable position and strode through the swinging doors. There were a dozen men in sight, but none of them resembled Boyne or either of the Blazers he had seen.

He started for the Emporium. Behind him, Tex stopped by one of the posts that supported the wooden awning over the walk, and leaned a negligent shoulder against it, a cigarette drooping from the corner of his mouth.

Bo Marsh sat back in a chair against the wall, his interested eyes sweeping the street. Several men who passed spoke to him and glanced at Tex Brisco's tall, lean figure.

Rafe opened the door of the Emporium and strode inside. Gene Baker looked up, frowning when he saw him. He was not glad to see Rafe, for the man's words on his previous visit had been responsible for some doubts and speculations.

"Is Ann Rodney in?"

Baker hesitated. "Yes," he said finally. "She's back there."

Rafe went around the counter toward the door, hat in his left hand.

"I don't think she wants to see yuh," Baker advised.

"All right," Rafe said, "we'll see."

He pushed past the screen, and stepped into the living room beyond.

Ann Rodney was sewing, and, when the quick

step sounded, she glanced up. Her eyes changed. Something inside her seemed to turn over slowly. This big man who had brought such disturbing news affected her as no man ever had. Considering her engagement to Bruce Barkow, she didn't like to feel that way about any man. Since he had last been here, she had worried a good deal about what he had said and her reaction to it. Why would he come with such a tale? Shouldn't she have heard him out?

Bruce said no, that the man was an imposter and someone who hoped to get money from her. Yet she knew something of Johnny Gill, and she had danced with Bo Marsh, and knew that these men were honest and had been so as long as she had known of them. They were liked and respected in Painted Rock.

"Oh," she said, rising. "It's you?"

Rafe stopped in the center of the room, a tall, picturesque figure in his buckskin coat and with his waving black hair. He was, she thought, a handsome man. He wore his guns low and tied down, and she knew what that meant.

"I was goin' to wait," he said abruptly, "and let you come to me and ask questions, if you eve did, but when I thought it over, rememberin' what I'd promised your father, I decided I must come back now, lay all my cards on the table, and tell you what happened."

She started to speak, and he lifted his hand.

"Wait. I'm goin' to talk quick, because in a few minutes I have an appointment outside that I must keep. Your father did not die on the trail back from California. He was shanghaied in San Francisco, taken aboard a ship while unconscious, and forced to work as a seaman. I was shanghaied at the same time and place. Your father and I in the months that followed were together a lot. He asked me to come here, to take care of you and his wife, and to protect you. He died of beatin's he got aboard ship, just before the rest of us got away from the ship. I was with him when he died, settin' beside his bed. Almost his last words were about you."

Ann Rodney stood very still, staring at him. There was a ring of truth in the rapidly spoken words, yet how could she believe this? Three men had told her they saw her father die, and one of them was the man she was to marry, the man who had befriended her, who had refused to fore-close on the mortgage he held and take from her the last thing she possessed in the world.

"What was my father like?" she asked.

"Like?" Rafe's brow furrowed. "How can any-body say what any man is like? I'd say he was about five feet eight or nine. When he died, his hair was almost white, but when I first saw him, he had only a few gray hairs. His face was a heap like yours. So were his eyes, except they weren't so large nor so beautiful. He was a kind man who wasn't used to violence, I think, and he

175

didn't like it. He planned well, and thought well, but the West was not the country for him, yet. Ten years from now, when it has settled more, he'd have been a leadin' citizen. He was a good man, and a sincere man."

"It sounds like him," Ann said hesitantly, "but there is nothing you could not have learned here, or from someone who knew him."

"No," he said frankly. "That's so. But there's somethin' else you should know. The mortgage your father had against his place was paid."

"What?" Ann stiffened. "Paid? How can you say that?"

"He borrowed the money in Frisco and paid Barkow with it. He got a receipt for it."

"Oh, I can't believe that! Why, Bruce would have . . ."

"Would he?" Rafe asked gently. "You shore?"

She looked at him. "What was the other thing?"

"I have a deed," he said, "to the ranch made out to you and to me."

Her eyes widened, then hardened with suspicion. "So? Now things become clearer. A deed to my father's ranch made out to you and to me! In other words, you are laying claim to half of my ranch?"

"Please . . . ," Rafe said. "I . . ."

She smiled. "You needn't say anything more, Mister Caradec. I admit I was almost coming to believe there was something in your story. At least, I was wondering about it, for I couldn't understand how you hoped to profit from any such tale. Now it becomes clear. You are trying to get half my ranch. You have even moved into my house without asking permission." She stepped to one side of the door and pulled back the curtain. "I'm sorry, but I must ask you to leave. I must also ask you to vacate the house on Crazy Man at once. I must ask you to refrain from calling on me again, or from approaching me."

"Please," Rafe said, "you're jumping to conclusions. I never aimed to claim any part of the ranch. I came here only because your father asked me to."

"Good day, Mister Caradec!" Ann still held the curtain.

He looked at her, and for an instant their eyes held. She was first to look away. He turned abruptly and stepped through the curtain, and, as he did, the door opened and he saw Bo Marsh.

Marsh's eyes were excited and anxious. "Rafe," he said, "that Boyne *hombre*'s in front of the National. He wants yuh!"

"Why, shore," Rafe said quietly. "I'm ready."

He walked to the front door, hitching his guns into place. Behind him, he heard Ann Rodney asking Baker: "What did he mean? That Boyne was waiting for him?"

Baker's reply came to Rafe as he stepped out into the morning light. "Trigger Boyne's goin' to kill him, Ann. Yuh'd better go back inside."

Rafe smiled slightly. Kill him? Would that be it? No man knew better than he the tricks that Destiny plays on a man, or how often the right man dies at the wrong time and place. A man never wore a gun without inviting trouble; he never stepped into a street and began the gunman's walk without the full knowledge that he might be a shade too slow, that some small thing might disturb him just long enough.

VIII

Morning sun was bright, and the street lay empty of horses or vehicles. A few idlers loafed in front of the stage station, but all of them were on their feet.

Rafe Caradec saw his black horse switch his tail at a fly, and he stepped down into the street. Trigger Boyne stepped off the boardwalk to face him, some distance off. Rafe did not walk slowly; he made no measured, quiet approach. He started to walk toward Boyne, going fast.

Trigger walked down the street easily, casually. He was smiling. Inside, his heart was throbbing, and there was a wild reckless eagerness within him. This one he would finish off fast. This would be simple, easy. He squared in the street, and suddenly the smile was wiped from his face. Caradec was coming toward him, shortening the

178

distance at a fast walk. That rapid approach did something to the calm on Boyne's face and in his mind. It was wrong. Caradec should have come slowly; he should have come poised and ready to draw. Knowing his own deadly marksmanship, Boyne felt sure he could kill this man at any distance. But as soon as he saw that walk, he knew that Caradec was going to be so close in a few more steps that he himself would be killed. It is one thing to know you are to kill another man, quite a different thing to know you are to die yourself. Why, if Caradec walked that way, he would be so close he couldn't miss!

Boyne's legs spread and the wolf sprang into his eyes, but there was panic there, too. He had to stop his man, get him now. His hand swept down for his gun. Yet something was wrong. For all his speed he seemed incredibly slow, becausethat other man, that tall, moving figure in the buckskin coat and black hat, was already shooting.

Trigger's own hand moved first, his own hand gripped the gun butt first, and then he was staring into a smashing, blossoming rose of flame that seemed to bloom beyond the muzzle of that big black gun in the hand of Rafe Caradec. Something stabbed at his stomach, and he went numb to his toes. Stupidly he swung his gun up, staring over it. The gun seemed awfully heavy. He must get a smaller one. That gun opposite him blossomed with rose again, and something struck him again in the stomach. He started to speak, half turning toward the men in front of the stage station, his mouth opening and closing.

Something was wrong with him, he tried to say. Why, everyone knew he was the fastest man in Wyoming, unless it was Shute! Everyone knew that! The heavy gun in his hand bucked, and he saw the flame stab at the ground. He dropped the gun, swayed, then fell flat on his face.

He would have to get up. He was going to kill that stranger, that Rafe Caradec. He would have to get up. The numbness from his stomach climbed higher, and he suddenly felt himself in the saddle of a bucking horse, a monstrous and awful horse that leaped and plunged, and it was going up! Up! Up! Then it came down hard, and he felt himself leave the saddle, all sprawled out. The horse had thrown him. Bucked off into the dust. He closed his hands spasmodically.

Rafe Caradec stood tall in the middle of the gunman's walk, the black, walnut-stocked pistol in his right hand. He glanced once at the still figure sprawled in the street, then his eyes lifted, sweeping the walks in swift, accurate, appraisal. Only then, some instinct prodded his unconscious and warned him. The merest flicker of a curtain, and in the space between the curtain and the edge of the window the black muzzle of a rifle! His .44 lifted, and the heavy gun bucked in his hand just as flame leaped from the rifle barrel, and he felt quick, urgent fingers pluck at his sleeve. The .44 jolted again, and a rifle rattled on the shingled porch roof. The curtain made a tearing sound, and the head and shoulders of a man fell through, toppling over the sill. Overbalanced, the heels came up, and the man's body rolled over slowly, seemed to hesitate, then rolled over again, poised an instant on the edge of the roof, and dropped suddenly into the street. Dust lifted from around the body, settled back. Gee Bonaro thrust hard with one leg, and his face twisted a little. In the quiet street there was no sound, no movement.

For the space of a full half-minute the watchers held themselves, shocked by the sudden climax, stunned with disbelief. Trigger Boyne had been beaten to the draw and killed; Gee Bonaro had made his try, and died.

Rafe Caradec turned slowly and walked back to his horse. Without a word he swung into saddle. He turned the horse and, sitting tall in the saddle, swept the street with a cold, hard eye that seemed to stare at each man there. Then, as if by his own wish, the black horse turned. Walking slowly, his head held proudly, he carried his rider down the street and out of town.

Behind him, coolly and without smiles, Bo Marsh and Tex Brisco followed. Like him, they rode slowly; like him they rode proudly. Something in their bearing seemed to say: *We were challenged. We came. You see the result.*

In the window of the National, Joe Benson chewed his mustache. He stared at the figure of Trigger Boyne with vague disquiet, then irritation. "Cuss it!" he muttered under his breath. "You was supposed to be a gunman? What in thunder was wrong with yuh?"

A bullet from Boyne's gun, or from Bonaro's, for that matter, could have ended it all. A bullet now could settle the whole thing, quiet the gossip, remove the doubts, and leave Barkow free to marry Ann, and the whole business could go forward. Instead, they had failed. It would be a long time now, Benson knew, before it was all over. A long time. Barkow was slipping. The man had better think fast and get something done. Rafe Caradec must die.

The Fort Laramie Treaty of 1868 had forbidden white men to enter the Powder River country, yet gold discoveries had brought prospectors north in increasing numbers. Small villages and mining camps had come into existence. Following them, cattlemen discovered the rich grasses of northern Wyoming, and a few herds came over what later was to be known as the Texas Trail.

Indian attacks and general hostility caused many of these pioneers to retreat to more stable localities, but a few of the more courageous had stayed on. Prospectors had entered the Black Hills, following the Custer expedition in 1874, and the Sioux, always resentful of any incursion upon their hunting grounds or any flaunting of their rights, were preparing to do something more than talk.

The names of such chiefs as Red Cloud, Dull Knife, Crazy Horse, and the medicine man, Sitting Bull, came more and more into frontier gossip. A steamboat was reported to be *en route* up the turbulent Yellowstone, and river traffic on the upper Mississippi was an accepted fact. There were increasing reports of gatherings of Indians in the hills, and white men rode warily, never without arms.

Cut off from contact with the few scattered ranchers, Rafe Caradec and his riders heard little of the gossip except what they gleaned from an occasional prospector or wandering hunter. Yet no gossip was needed to tell them how the land lay.

Twice they heard sounds of rifle fire, and once the Sioux ran off a number of cattle from Shute's ranch, taking them from a herd kept not far from Long Valley. Two of Shute's riders were killed. None of Caradec's men was molested. He was left strictly alone. Indians avoided his place, no matter what their mission.

Twice, riders from the ranch went to Painted Rock. Each time they returned, they brought stories of an impending Indian outbreak. A few of the less courageous ranchers sold out and left the country. In all this time, Rafe Caradec lived in the saddle, riding often from dawn until dusk, avoiding the tangled brakes, but studying the lay of the land with care. There was, he knew, some particular reason for Bruce Barkow's interest in the ranch that belonged to Ann Rodney. What that reason was, he must know. Without it, he knew he could offer no real reason why Barkow would go to the lengths he had gone to get a ranch that was on the face of things of no more value than any piece of land in the country, most of which could be had for the taking. . . .

Ann spent much of her time alone. Business at the store was thriving, and Gene Baker and his wife, and often Ann as well, were busy. In her spare time the thought kept returning to her that Rafe Caradec might be honest. Yet she dismissed the thought as unworthy. If she admitted even for an instant that he was honest, she must also admit that Bruce Barkow was dishonest, a thief, and possibly a killer. Yet somehow the picture of her father kept returning to her mind. It was present there on one of the occasions when Bruce Barkow came to call.

A handsome man, Barkow understood how to appeal to a woman. He carried himself well, and his clothes were always the best in Painted Rock. He called this evening, looking even better than he had on the last occasion, his black suit neatly pressed, his mustache carefully trimmed.

They had been talking for some time when Ann mentioned Rafe Caradec. "His story sounded so sincere!" she said, after a minute. "He said he had been shanghaied in San Francisco with Father, and that they had become acquainted on the ship."

"He's a careful man," Barkow commented, "and a dangerous one. He showed that when he killed Trigger Boyne and Bonaro. He met Boyne on the range, and they had some trouble over an Indian girl."

"An Indian girl?" Ann looked at him questioningly.

"Yes." Barkow frowned as if the subject was distasteful to him. "You know how some of the cowhands are . . . always running after some squaw. They have stolen squaws, kept them for a while, then turned them loose or killed them. Caradec had a young squaw, and Boyne tried to argue with him to let her go. They had words, and there'd have been a shooting then if one of Caradec's other men hadn't come up with a rifle, and Shute's boys went away."

Ann was shocked. She had heard of such things happening and was well aware of how much trouble they caused. That Rafe Caradec would be a man like that was hard to believe. Yet, what did she know of the man? He disturbed her more than she allowed herself to believe. Despite the fact that he seemed to be trying to work some scheme to get all or part of her ranch, and despite all she had heard of him at one time or another from Bruce, she couldn't make herself believe that all she heard was true.

That he appealed to her, she refused to admit. Yet when with him, she felt drawn to him. She liked his rugged masculinity, his looks, his voice, and was impressed with his sincerity. Yet the killing of Boyne and Bonaro was the talk of the town. The Bonaro phase of the incident she could understand from the previous episode in the store. But no one had any idea of why Boyne should be looking for Caradec. The solution now offered by Barkow was the only one. A fight over a squaw! Without understanding why, Ann felt vaguely resentful.

For days a dozen of Shute's riders had hung around town. There had been talk of lynching Caradec, but nothing came of it. Ann had heard the talk, and asked Baker about it.

The old storekeeper looked up, nodding.

"There's talk, but it'll come to nothin'. None of these boys aim to ride out there to Crazy Man and tackle that crowd. You know what Gill and Marsh are like. They'll fight, and they can. Well, Caradec's showed what he could do with a gun when he killed those two in the street. I don't know whether yuh saw that other feller with Caradec or not. The one from Texas. Well, if he ain't tougher than either Marsh or Gill, I'll pay off! Notice how he wore his guns? Nope, nobody'll go looking for them. If they got their hands on Caradec, that would be somethin' else."

Baker rubbed his jaw thoughtfully. "Unless they are powerful lucky, they won't last long, anyway. That's Injun country, and Red Cloud or Man-Afraid-Of-His-Hoss won't take kindly to white men livin' there. They liked yore pa, and he was friendly to 'em."

As a result of his conversations with Barkow, Sheriff Pod Gomer had sent messages south by stage to Cheyenne and the telegraph. Rafe Caradec had come from San Francisco, and Bruce Barkow wanted to know who and what he was. More than that, he wanted to find out how he had been allowed to escape the *Mary S*. With that in mind he wrote to Bully Borger.

Barkow had known nothing about Caradec when the deal was made, but Borger had agreed to take Charles Rodney to sea and let him die there, silencing the truth forever. Allowing Rafe Caradec to come ashore with his story was not keeping the terms of the bargain. If Caradec had actually been aboard the ship and left it, there might be something in that to make him liable to the law. Barkow intended to leave no stone unturned, and in the meanwhile he spread his stories around about Caradec's reason for killing Boyne.

IX

Caradec went on with his haying. The nights were already growing chillier. At odd times, when not haying or handling cattle, he and the boys built another room onto the cabin, and banked the house against the wind. Fortunately its position was sheltered. Wind would not bother them greatly where they were, but there would be snow and lots of it.

Rafe rode out each day, and several times brought back deer or elk. The meat was jerked and stored away. Gill got the old wagon Rodney had brought from Missouri and made some repairs. It would be the easiest way to get supplies out from Painted Rock. He worked over it and soon had it in excellent shape.

On the last morning of the month, Rafe walked out to where Gill was hitching a team to the wagon.

"Looks good," he agreed. "You've done a job on it, Johnny."

Gill looked pleased. He nodded at the hubs of the wheels. "Notice 'em? No squeak!"

"Well, I'll be hanged." Rafe looked at the grease on the hubs. "Where'd you get the grease?"

"Sort of a spring back over in the hills. I brung back a bucket of it."

Rafe Caradec looked up sharply. "Johnny, where'd you find that spring?"

"Why,"—Gil looked puzzled—"it's just a sort of hole, back over next to that mound. You know, in that bad range. Ain't much account down there, but I was down there once and found this here spring. This stuff works as well as the grease yuh buy."

"It should," Rafe said dryly. "It's the same stuff!"

He caught up the black and threw a saddle on it. Within an hour he was riding down toward the barren knoll Gill had mentioned. What he found was not a spring, but a hole among some sparse rushes, dead and sick-looking. It was an oil seepage.

Oil! Swiftly his mind leaped ahead. This, then, could be the reason why Barkow and Shute were so anxious to acquire title to this piece of land, so anxious that they would have a man shanghaied and killed. Caradec recalled that Bonneville had reported oil seepages on his trip through the state some forty years or so before, and there had been a well drilled in the previous decade. One of the largest markets for oil was the patent medicine business, for it was the main ingredient in so-called "British Oil."

The hole in which the oil was seeping in a thick stream might be shallow, but sounding with a six-foot stick found no bottom. Rafe doubted if it was much deeper. Still, there would be several barrels here, and he seemed to recall some talk of selling oil for twenty dollars a barrel.

Swinging into the saddle, he turned the big black down the draw and rode rapidly toward the hills. This could be the reason, for certainly it was reason enough. The medicine business was only one possible market, for machinery of all kinds needed lubricants. There was every chance that the oil industry might really mean something in time. If the hole was emptied, how fast would it refill? How constant was the supply? On one point he could soon find out.

He swung the horse up out of the draw, forded the Crazy Man, and cantered up the hill to the cabin. As he reined in and swung down at the door, he noticed two strange horses.

Tex Brisco stepped to the door, his face hard. "Watch it, boss!" he said sharply.

Pod Gomer's thick-set body thrust into the doorway. "Caradec," he said calmly, "yuh're under arrest."

Rafe swung down, facing him. Two horses. Who had ridden the other one?

"For what?" he demanded.

His mind was racing. *The mutiny? Have they found out about that?*

"For killin'. Shootin' Bonaro."

"Bonaro?" Rafe laughed. "You mean for defendin' myself? Bonaro had a rifle in that window. He was all set to shoot me."

Gomer nodded coolly. "That was most folks' opinion, but it seems nobody *saw* him aim any gun at yuh. We've only got yore say-so. When we got to askin' around, it begun to look sort of funny-like. It appears to a lot of folks that yuh just took that chance to shoot him and get away with it. Anyway, yuh'd be better off to stand trial."

"Don't go, boss," Brisco said. "They don't ever aim to have a trial."

"Yuh'd better not resist," Gomer replied calmly. "I've got twenty Shute riders down in the valley. I made 'em stay back. The minute any shootin' starts, they'll come a-runnin', and yuh all know what that would mean."

Rafe knew. It would mean the death of all four of them and the end to any opposition to Barkow's plans. Probably that was what the rancher hoped would happen.

"Why, shore, Gomer," Caradec said calmly, "I'll go."

Tex started to protest, and Rafe saw Gill hurl his hat into the dust.

"Give me yore guns, then," Gomer said, "and mount up."

"No." Rafe's voice was flat. "I keep my guns till I get to town. If that bunch of Shute's starts anything, the first one I'll kill will be you, Gomer."

Pod Gomer's face turned sullen. "Yuh ain't goin' to be bothered. I'm the law here. Let's go!"

"Gomer," Tex Brisco said viciously, "if anything happens to him, I'll kill you and Barkow both!"

"That goes for me, too!" Gill said harshly.

"And me," Marsh put in. "I'll get you if I have to dry-gulch yuh, Gomer."

"Well, all right!" Gomer said angrily. "It's just a trial. I told 'em I didn't think much of it, but the judge issued this warrant."

He was scowling blackly. It was all right for them to issue warrants, but if they thought he was going to get killed for them, they were bloody well wrong. Pod Gomer jammed his hat down on his head. This was a far cry from the coal mines of Lancashire, but sometimes he wished he was back in England. There was a look in Brisco's eyes he didn't like. *No,* he told himself, *he'll be turned loose before I take a chance. Let Barkow kill his own pigeons. I don't want these Bar M hands gunnin' for me!*

The man who had ridden the other horse stepped out of the cabin, followed closely by Bo Marsh. There was no smile on the young cowhand's face. The man was Bruce Barkow. For an instant, his eyes met Caradec's. "This is just a formality," Barkow said smoothly. "There's been some talk around Painted Rock, and a trial will clear the air a lot, and, of course, if yuh're innocent, Caradec, yuh'll be freed."

"You shore of that?" Rafe's eyes smiled cynically. "Barkow, you hate me and you know it.

If I ever leave that jail alive, it won't be your fault."

Barkow shrugged. "Think what you want," he said indifferently. "I believe in law and order. We've got a nice little community at Painted Rock, and we want to keep it that way. Boyne had challenged yuh, and that was different. Bonaro had no part in the fight."

"No use arguin' that here," Gomer protested. "Court's the place for that. Let's go."

Tex Brisco lounged down the steps, his thumbs hooked in his belt. He stared at Gomer. "I don't like you," he said coolly. "I don't like you a bit. I think yuh're yeller as a coyote. I think yuh bob ever' time this here Barkow says bob."

Gomer's face whitened, and his eyes shifted. "Yuh've got no call to start trouble," he said. "I'm doin' my duty."

"Let it ride," Caradec told Tex. "There's plenty of time."

"Yeah," Tex drawled, his hard eyes on Gomer, "but just for luck I'm goin' to mount and trail yuh into town, keepin' to the hills. If that bunch of Shute riders gets fancy, I'm goin' to get myself a sheriff, and"—his eyes shifted—"mebbe another *hombre.*"

"Is that a threat?" Barkow asked contemptuously. "Talk is cheap."

"Want to see how cheap?" Tex prodded. His eyes were ugly, and he was itching for a fight. It showed in every line of him. "Want to make it expensive?"

Bruce Barkow was no fool. He had not seen Tex Brisco in action, yet there was something chill and deadly about the tall Texan. Barkow shrugged. "We came here to enforce the law. Is this resistance, Caradec?"

"No," Rafe said. "Let's go."

The three men turned their horses and walked them down the trail toward Long Valley. Tex Brisco threw a saddle on his horse, then mounted. Glancing back, Pod Gomer saw the Texan turn his horse up a trail into the trees. He swore viciously.

Caradec sat his horse easily. The trouble would not come now. He was quite sure the plan had been to get him away, then claim the Shute riders had taken him from the law. Yet he was sure it would not come to that now. Pod Gomer would know that Brisco's Winchester was within range. Also, Rafe was still wearing his guns.

Rafe rode warily, lagging a trifle behind the sheriff. He glanced at Barkow, but the rancher's face was expressionless. Ahead of them, in a tight bunch, waited the Shute riders. The first he recognized were the Blazers. There was another man, known as Joe Gorman, whom he also recognized.

Red Blazer started forward abruptly. "He come, did he?" he shouted. "Now we'll show him!"

"Get back!" Gomer ordered sharply.

"Huh?" Red glared at Gomer. "Who says I'll get back! I'm stringin' this *hombre* to the first tree we get to."

"You stay back!" Gomer ordered. "We're takin' this man in for trial!"

Red Blazer laughed. "Come on, boys!" he yelled. "Let's hang the skunk!"

"I wouldn't, Red," Rafe Caradec said calmly. "You've overlooked somethin'. I'm wearin' my guns. Are you faster than Trigger Boyne?"

Blazer jerked his horse's head around, his face pale but furious. "Hey!" he yelled. "What the devil is this? I thought . . ."

"That you'd have an easy time of it?" Rafe shoved the black horse between Gomer and Barkow, pushing ahead of them. He rode right up to Blazer and let the big black shove into the other horse. "Well, get this, Blazer, any time you kill me, you'll do it with a gun in your hand, savvy? You're nothin' but a lot of lynch-crazy coyotes! Try it, damn it! Try it now, and I'll blow you out of that saddle so full of lead you'll sink a foot into the ground!" Rafe's eyes swept the crowd. "Think this is a joke? That goes for any of you. As for Gomer, he knows that if you *hombres* want any trouble, he gets it, too. There's a man up in the hills with a Winchester, and, if you don't think he can empty saddles, start somethin'. That Winchester carries sixteen shots, and I've seen him empty it and get that many rabbits! I'm packing two guns. I'm askin' you now so, if you want any of what I've got, start the ball rollin'. Mebbe you'd get me, but I'm tellin' you there'll be more dead men around here than you can shake a stick at."

Joe Gorman spoke quickly. "Watch it, boys! There is an *hombre* up on the mountain with a rifle. I seen him."

"What the hell is this?" Red Blazer repeated.

"The fun's over," Rafe replied shortly. "You might as well head for home and tell Dan Shute to kill his own wolves. I'm wearin' my guns, and I'm goin' to keep 'em. I'll stand trial, but you know and I know that Bonaro got what he was askin' for." Caradec turned his eyes on Blazer. "As for you, stay out of my sight. You're too blasted willin' to throw your hemp over a man you think is helpless. I don't like skunks and never did."

"Yuh can't call me a skunk!" Blazer bellowed.

Rafe stared at him. "I just did," he said calmly.

X

For a full minute their eyes held. Rafe's hand was on his thigh within inches of his gun. If it came to gun play now, he would be killed, but Blazer and Barkow would go down, too, and there would be others. He had not exaggerated when he spoke of Tex Brisco's shooting. The man was a wizard with the rifle.

Red Blazer was trapped. White to the lips, he stared at Rafe and could see cold, certain death looking back at him. He could stand it no longer. "Why don't some of yuh do somethin'?" he bellowed.

Joe Gorman spat: "You done the talkin', Red."

"Tarnation with it!"

Blazer swung his horse around, touched spurs to the animal, and raced off at top speed.

Bruce Barkow's hand hovered close to his gun. A quick draw, a shot, and the man would be dead. Just like that. His lips tightened, and his elbow crooked.

Gomer grabbed his wrist. "Don't, Bruce! Don't! That *hombre* up there . . . look!"

Barkow's head swung. Brisco was in plain sight, his rifle resting over the limb of a tree. At that distance, he could not miss. Yet he was beyond pistol range, and, while some of the riders had rifles, they were out in the open without a bit of cover.

Barkow jerked his arm away and turned his horse toward town. Rafe turned the black and rode beside him. He said nothing, but Barkow was seething at the big man's obvious contempt. Rafe Caradec had outfaced the lot of them. He had made them look fools. Yet Barkow remembered as well as each of the riders remembered that Rafe had fired but three shots in the street battle, that all the shots had scored, and two men had died.

When the cavalcade reached the National, Rafe turned to Pod Gomer. "Get your court goin'," he said calmly. "We'll have this trial now."

"Listen here!" Gomer burst out, infuriated. "Yuh can do things like that too often! We'll have our court when we get blamed good and ready!"

"No," Rafe said, "you'll hold court this afternoon . . . now. You haven't got any calendar to interfere. I have business to attend to that can't wait, and I won't. You'll have yore trial today, or I'll leave, and you can come and get me."

"Who you tellin' what to do?" Gomer said angrily. "I'll have you know . . ."

"Then you tell him, Barkow . . . or does he take his orders from Shute? Call that judge of yours and let's get this over."

Bruce Barkow's lips tightened. He could see that Gene Baker and Ann Rodney were standing in the doorway of the store, listening.

"All right," Barkow said savagely. "Call him down here."

Not much later Judge Roy Gargan walked into the stage station and looked around. He was a tall, slightly stooped man with a lean, hangdog face and round eyes. He walked up to the table and sat down in the chair behind it. Bruce Barkow took a chair to one side where he could see the judge.

Noting the move, Rafe Caradec sat down where both men were visible. Barkow, nettled, shifted his chair irritably. He glanced up and saw Ann Rodney come in, accompanied by Baker and Pat Higley. He scowled again. *Why couldn't they stay out of this?*

Slowly the hangers-on around town filed in. Joe Benson came in and sat down close to Barkow. They exchanged looks. Benson's questioning glance made Barkow furious. If they wanted so much done, why didn't someone do something besides him?

"I'll watch from here," drawled a voice.

Barkow's head came up. Standing in the window behind and to the right of the judge was Tex Brisco. At the same instant Barkow noted him, the Texan lifted a hand.

"Hi, Johnny! Glad to see you."

Bruce Barkow's face went hard. Johnny Gill and, beside him, Bo Marsh. If anything rusty was pulled in this courtroom, the place would be a shambles. Maybe Dan Shute was right, after all. If they were going to be crooked, why not dry-gulch the fellow and get it over? All Barkow's carefully worked-out plans to get Caradec had failed.

There had been three good chances. Resistance, that would warrant killing in attempting an arrest; attempted escape, if he so much as made a wrong move; or lynching by the Shute riders. At every point they had been outguessed.

Judge Gargan slammed a six-shooter on the table.

"Order!" he proclaimed. "Court's in session! Reckon I'll appoint a jury. Six men will do. I'll have Joe Benson, Tom Blazer, Sam Mawson, Doe Otto, and . . ."

"Joe Benson's not eligible," Caradec interrupted.

Gargan frowned. "Who's runnin' this court?"

"Supposedly," Rafe said quietly, "the law, supposedly the interests of justice. Joe Benson was a witness to the shootin', so he'll be called on to give testimony."

"Who yuh tellin' how to run this court?" Gargan demanded belligerently.

"Doesn't the defendant even have a chance to defend himself?" Caradec asked gently. He glanced around at the crowd. "I think you'll all agree that a man on trial for his life should have a chance to defend himself, that he should be allowed to call and question witnesses, and that he should have an attorney. But since this court hasn't provided an attorney, and because I want to, I'll act for myself. Now,"—he looked around— "the judge picked out three members of the jury. I'd like to pick out three more. I'd like Pat Higley, Gene Baker, and Ann Rodney as members of the jury."

"What?" Gargan roared. "I'll have no woman settin' on the jury in my court! Why, of all the . . ."

Rafe said smoothly: "It kind of looks like Your Honor does not know the law in Wyomin'. By an act approved in December Eighteen Sixty-Nine, the first Territorial Legislature granted equal rights to women. Women served on juries in Laramie in Eighteen Seventy, and one was servin' as justice of the peace that year."

Gargan swallowed and looked uncomfortable. Barkow sat up, started to say something, but before he could open his mouth, Caradec was speaking again.

"As I understand, the attorney for the State and the defense attorney usually select a jury. As the Court has taken it upon himself to appoint a jury, I was just suggestin' the names of three responsible citizens I respect. I'm shore none of these three can be considered friends of mine, sorry as I am to say it. Of course," he added, "if the court objects to these three people . . . if there's somethin' about their characters I don't know, or if they are not good citizens . . . then I take back my suggestion." He turned to look at Bruce Barkow. "Or mebbe Mister Barkow objects to Ann Rodney servin' on the jury?"

Barkow sat up, flushing. Suddenly he was burning with rage. This whole thing had got out of hand. What had happened to bring this about? He was acutely conscious that Ann was staring at him, her eyes wide, a flush mounting in her cheeks at his hesitation. "No!" he said violently.

"No, of course, no. Let her sit, but let's get this business started."

Pod Gomer was slumped in his chair, watching cynically. His eyes shifted to Barkow with a faintly curious expression. The planner and schemer had missed out on this trial. It had been his idea to condemn the man in public, then see to it that he was hanged.

"Yuh're actin' as prosecutin' attorney?" Gargan asked Barkow.

The rancher got to his feet, cursing the thought that had given rise to this situation. That Rafe Caradec had won the first round he was unpleasantly aware. Somehow they had never contemplated any trouble on the score of the jury. In the few trials held thus far the judge had appointed the jury, and there had been no complaint. All the cases had gone off as planned.

"Yore Honor," he began, "and gentlemen of the jury. Yuh all know none of us here are lawyers. This court is bein' held only so's we can keep law and order in this community, and that's the way it will be till the county is organized. This prisoner was in a gunfight with Lemuel Boyne, known as Trigger. Boyne challenged him . . . some of yuh know the reason for that . . . and Caradec accepted. In the fight out in the street, Caradec shot Boyne and killed him. In almost the same instant, he lifted his gun and shot Gee Bonaro, who was innocently watchin' the battle from his window. If a thing like this isn't punished, any gunfighter is apt to shoot anybody he don't like at any time, and nothin' done about it. We've all heard that Caradec claims Bonaro had a rifle and was about to shoot at him, which was a plumb good excuse, but a right weak one. We know this Caradec had words with Bonaro at the Emporium, and almost got into a fight then and there. I say Caradec is guilty of murder in the first degree, and should be hung." Barkow turned his head and motioned to Red Blazer. "Red, you get up there and tell the jury what yuh know."

Red strode up to the chair that was doing duty for a witness stand and slouched down in the seat. He was unshaven, and his hair was uncombed. He sprawled his legs out and stuck his thumbs in his belt. He rolled his quid in his jaws, and spat. "I seen this here Caradec shoot Boyne," he said, "then he ups with his pistol and cut down on Bonaro, who was a-standin' in the window, just a-lookin'."

"Did Bonaro make any threatening moves toward Caradec?"

"Him?" Red's eyes opened wide. "Shucks, no. Gee was just a-standin' there. Caradec was afeerd of him, an' seen a chance to kill him and get plumb away."

Rafe looked thoughtfully at Barkow. "Is the fact that the witness was not sworn in the regular way in this court? Or is his conscience delicate on the subject of perjury?"

"Huh?" Blazer sat up. "What'd he say?"

Barkow flushed. "It hasn't usually been the way here, but . . ."

"Swear him in," Caradec said calmly, "and have him say under oath what he's just said."

He waited until this was done, and then, as Red started to get up, Rafe motioned him back. "I've got a few questions," he said.

"Huh?" Red demanded belligerently. "I don't have to answer no more questions."

"Yes, you do." Rafe's voice was quiet. "Get back on that witness stand."

"Do I have to?" Blazer demanded of Barkow, who nodded.

If there had been any easy way out, he would have taken it, but there was none. He was beginning to look at Rafe Caradec with new eyes.

Rafe got up and walked over to the jury. "Gentlemen," he said, "none of you know me well. None of us, as Barkow said, knows much about how court business should be handled. All we want to do is get at the truth. I know that all of you here are busy men. You're willin' and anxious to help along justice and the beginnin's of law hereabouts, and all of you are honest men. You want to do the right thing. Red Blazer has just testified that I shot a man who was makin' no threatenin' moves, that Bonaro was standing in a window, just watching."

Caradec turned around and looked at Blazer

thoughtfully. He walked over to him, squatted on his haunches, and peered into his eyes, shifting first to one side, then the other.

Red Blazer's face flamed. "What's the matter?" he blared. "Yuh gone crazy?"

"No," Caradec said, "just lookin' at your eyes. I was curious to see what kind of eyes a man had who could see through a shingle roof and a ceilin'."

"Huh?" Blazer glared.

The jury sat up, and Barkow's eyes narrowed. The courtroom crowd leaned forward.

"Why, Red, you must have forgot," Rafe said. "You were in the National when I killed Boyne. You were standin' behind Joe Benson. You were the first person I saw when I looked around. You could see me, and you could see Boyne . . . but you couldn't see the second-story window across the street."

Somebody whooped, and Pat Higley grinned.

"I reckon he's right," Pat said coolly. "I was standin' right alongside of Red."

"That's right!" somebody from back in the courtroom shouted. "Blazer tried to duck out without payin' for his drink, and Joe Benson stopped him!"

Everybody laughed, and Blazer turned fiery red, glaring back into the room to see who the speaker was, and not finding him.

Rafe turned to Barkow, and smiled. "Have you got another witness?"

XI

Despite herself, Ann Rodney found herself admiring Rafe Caradec's composure, his easy manner. Her curiosity was stirred. What manner of man was he? Where was he from? What background had he? Was he only a wanderer, or was he something different? His language, aside from his characteristic Texas drawl, and his manner spoke of refinement, yet she knew of his gun skill as exhibited in the Boyne fight.

"Tom Blazer's my next witness," Barkow said. "Swear him in."

Tom Blazer, a hulking redhead even bigger than Red, took the stand. Animosity glared from his eyes.

"Did you see the shootin'?" Barkow asked.

"Yuh're darned right I did!" Tom declared, staring at Rafe. "I seen it, and I wasn't inside no saloon! I was right out in the street!"

"Was Bonaro where yuh could see him?"

"He shore was!"

"Did he make any threatenin' moves?"

"Not any!"

"Did he lift a gun?"

"He shore didn't!"

"Did he make any move that would give an idea he was goin' to shoot?"

"Nope. Not any." As Tom Blazer answered each question, he glared triumphantly at Caradec.

Barkow turned to the jury. "Well, there yuh are. I think that's enough evidence. I think . . ."

"Let's hear Caradec ask his questions," Pat Higley said. "I want both sides of this yarn."

Rafe got up and walked over to Tom Blazer, then looked at the judge. "Your Honor, I'd like permission to ask one question of a man in the audience. He can be sworn or not, just as you say."

Gargan hesitated uncertainly. Always before things had gone smoothly. Trials had been railroaded through, objections swept aside, and the wordless little ranchers or other objectors to the rule of Barkow and Shute had been helpless. This time preparations should have been more complete. He didn't know what to do. "All right," he said, his misgiving showing in his expression and tone.

Caradec turned to look at a short, stocky man with a brown mustache streaked with gray. "Grant," he said, "what kind of a curtain have you got over that window above your harness and saddle shop?"

Grant looked up. "Why, it ain't rightly no curtain," he said frankly. "It's a blanket."

"You keep it down all the time? The window covered?"

"Uhn-huh. Shore do. Sun gets in there otherwise

and makes the floor hot and she heats up the store thataway. Keepin' that window covered keeps her cooler."

"It was covered the day of the shooting?"

"Shore was."

"Where did you find the blanket after the shootin'?"

"Well, she laid over the sill, partly inside, partly outside."

Rafe turned to the jury. "Miss Rodney and gentlemen, I believe the evidence is clear. The window was covered by a blanket. When Bonaro fell after I shot him, he tumbled across the sill, tearin' down the blanket. Do you agree?"

"Shore!" Gene Baker found his voice. The whole case was only too obviously a frame-up to get Caradec. It was like Bonaro to try a sneak killing, anyway. "If that blanket hadn't been over the window, then he couldn't have fallen against it and carried part out with him."

"That's right." Rafe turned on Tom Blazer. "Your eyes seem to be as amazin' as your brother's. You can see through a wool blanket!"

Blazer sat up with a jerk, his face dark with sullen rage. "Listen!" he said, "I'll tell yuh . . ."

"Wait a minute!" Rafe whirled on him and thrust a finger in his face. "You're not only a perjurer but a thief! What did you do with that Winchester Bonaro dropped out of the window?"

"It wa'n't no Winchester!" Blazer blared

furiously. "It was a Henry!" Then, seeing the expression on Barkow's face, and hearing the low murmur that swept the court, he realized what he had said. He started to get up, then sat back, angry and confused.

Rafe Caradec turned toward the jury. "The witness swore that Bonaro had no gun, yet he testified that the rifle Bonaro dropped was a Henry. Gentlemen and Miss Rodney, I'm goin' to ask that you recommend the case be dismissed, and also that Red and Tom Blazer be held in jail to answer charges of perjury."

"What?" Tom Blazer came out of the witness chair with a lunge. "Jail? Me? Why, you . . ."

He leaped, hurling a huge red-haired fist in a roundhouse swing. Rafe Caradec stepped in with a left that smashed Blazer's lips, then a solid right that sent him crashing to the floor.

He glanced at the judge. "And that, I think," he said quietly "is contempt of court."

Pat Higley got up abruptly. "Gargan, I reckon yuh better dismiss this case. Yuh haven't got any evidence or anything that sounds like evidence, and I guess ever'body here heard about Caradec facin' Bonaro down in the store. If he wanted to shoot him, there was his chance."

Gargan swallowed. "Case dismissed," he said.

He looked up at Bruce Barkow, but the rancher was walking toward Ann Rodney. She glanced at him, then her eyes lifted, and beyond him she saw Rafe Caradec. How fine his face was! It was a rugged, strong face. There was character in it, and sincerity. She came to with a start. Bruce was speaking to her.

"Gomer told me he had a case," Barkow said, "or I'd never have been a party to this. He's guilty as can be, but he's smooth."

Ann looked down at Bruce Barkow, and suddenly his eyed looked different to her than they ever had before. "He may be guilty of a lot of things," she said tartly, "but if ever there was a cooked-up, dishonest case, it was this one. And everyone in town knew it. If I were you, Bruce Barkow, I'd be ashamed of myself."

Abruptly she turned her back on him and started for the door, yet, as she went, she glanced up, and for a brief instant her eyes met those of Rafe Caradec's, and something within her leaped. Her throat seemed to catch. Head high, she hurried past him into the street. The store seemed a long distance away.

When Bruce Barkow walked into Pod Gomer's office, the sheriff was sitting in his swivel chair. In the big leather armchair across the room Dan Shute was waiting. He was a big man, with massive shoulders, powerfully muscled arms, and great hands. A shock of dusky blond hair covered the top of his head, and his eyebrows were the color of corn silk. He looked up as Barkow came in, and, when he spoke, his voice was rough. "You shore played hob!"

"The man's smart, that's all," Barkow said. "Next time we'll have a better case."

"Next time?" Dan Shute lounged back in the big chair, the contempt in his eyes unconcealed. "There ain't goin' to be a next time. Yuh're through, Barkow. From now on, this is my show, and we run it my way. Caradec needs killin', and we'll kill him. Also, yuh're goin' to foreclose that mortgage on the Rodney place." He held up a hand as Barkow started to speak. "No, you wait. Yuh was all for pullin' this slick stuff. Winnin' the girl, gettin' the property the easy way, the legal way. To blazes with that! This Caradec is makin' a monkey of yuh! Yuh're not slick! Yuh're just a country boy playin' with a real smooth lad! To blazes with that smooth stuff! You foreclose on that mortgage and do it plumb quick. I'll take care of Mister Rafe Caradec! With my own hands, or guns if necessary. We'll clean that country down there so slick of his hands and cattle they won't know what happened."

"That won't get it," Barkow protested. "You let me handle this. I'll take care of things."

Dan Shute looked up at Barkow, his eyes sardonic. "I'll run this show. You're takin' the back seat, Barkow, from now on. All yuh've done is make us out fumblin' fools. Also," he added calmly, "I'm takin' over that girl."

211

"What?" Barkow whirled, his face livid. In his wildest doubts of Shute, and he had had many of them, this was one thing that had never entered his mind.

"You heard me," Shute replied. "She's a neat little lady, and I can make a place for her out to my ranch. You messed up all around, so I'm takin' over."

Barkow laughed, but his laugh was hollow with something of fear in it. Always before Dan Shute had been big, silent, and surly, saying little, letting Barkow plan and plot and take the lead. Bruce Barkow had always thought of the man as a sort of strong-arm squad to use in a pinch. Suddenly he was shockingly aware that this big man was completely sure of himself, that he held him, Barkow, in contempt. He would ride roughshod over everything. "Dan," Barkow protested, trying to keep his thoughts ordered, "yuh can't play with a girl's affections. She's in love with me. Yuh can't do anything about that. Yuh think she'd fall out of love with one man, and . . . ?"

Dan Shute grinned. "Who said anything about love? You talk about that all yuh want. Talk it to yoreself. I want the girl, and I'm goin' to have her. It doesn't make any difference who says no, and that goes for Gene Baker, her, or you."

Bruce Barkow stood flat-footed and pale. Suddenly he felt sick and empty. Here it was, then. He was through. Dan Shute had told him off, and in front of Pod Gomer. Out of the tail of his eye he could see the calm, yet cynical, expression on Gomer's face. He looked up, and he felt small under the flat, ironic gaze of Shute's eyes. "All right, Dan, if that's the way yuh feel. I expect we'd better part company."

Shute chuckled, and his voice was rough when he spoke. "No," he said, "we don't part company. You sit tight. Yuh're holdin' that mortgage, and I want that land. Yuh had a good idea there, Barkow, but yuh're too weak-kneed to swing it. I'll swing it, and mebbe, if yuh're quiet and obey orders, I'll see yuh get some of it."

Bruce Barkow glared at Shute. For the first time he knew what hatred was. Here, in a few minutes, he had been destroyed. This story would go the rounds, and before nightfall everyone in town would know it. Dan Shute, big, slow-talking Dan Shute with his hard fists and his guns had crushed Barkow. He stared at Shute with hatred livid in his eyes. "Yuh'll go too far!" he said viciously.

Shute shrugged. "Yuh can live, an' come out of this with a few dollars," he said calmly, "or yuh can die. I'd just as soon kill yuh, Barkow, as look at yuh." He picked up his hat. "We had a nice thing. That shanghaiin' idea was yores. Why yuh didn't shoot him, I'll never know. If yuh had, this Caradec would never have run into him at all and would never have come in here, stirrin' things up. Yuh could have foreclosed that mortgage,

213

and we could be makin' a deal on that oil now."

"Caradec don't know anything about that," Barkow protested.

"Like sin he don't!" Dan Shute sneered. "Caradec's been watched by my men for days. He's been wise there was somethin' in the wind, and he's scouted all over that place. Well, he was down to the knob the other day, and he took a long look at that oil seepage. He's no fool, Barkow."

Bruce Barkow looked up. "No," he replied suddenly, "he's not, and he's a hand with a gun, too, Dan. He's a hand with a gun. He took Boyne."

Shute shrugged. "Boyne was nothin'. I could have spanked him with his own gun. I'll kill Caradec someday, but first I want to beat him, to beat him with my own hands."

He heaved himself out of the chair and stalked outside. For an instant, Barkow stared after him, then his gaze shifted to Pod Gomer.

The sheriff was absently whittling a small stick. "Well," he said, "he told yuh."

XII

Hard and grim, Barkow's mouth tightened. So Gomer was in it, too. He started to speak, then hesitated. Like Caradec, Gomer was no fool, and he, too, was a good hand with a gun. Barkow shrugged. "Dan sees things wrong," he said. "I've still got an ace in the hole." He looked at Gomer. "I'd like it better if you were on my side."

Pod Gomer shrugged. "I'm with the winner. My health is good. All I need is more money."

"Yuh think Shute's the winner?"

"Don't you?" Gomer asked. "He told yuh plenty, and yuh took it."

"Yes, I did, because I know I'm no match for him with a gun. Nor for you." He studied the sheriff thoughtfully. "This is goin' to be a nice thing, Pod. It would split well, two ways."

Gomer got up and snapped his knife shut. "You show me the color of some money," he said, "and how Dan Shute's out, and we might talk. Also," he added, "if yuh mention this to Dan, I'll call yuh a liar in the street or in the National. I'll make you use that gun."

"I won't talk," Barkow said. "Only I've been learnin' a few things. When we get answers to some of the messages yuh sent, and some I sent, we should know more. Borger wouldn't let Caradec off that ship willin'ly after he knew Rodney. I think he deserted. I think we can get something on him for mutiny, and that means hangin'."

"Mebbe yuh can," Gomer agreed. "You show me yuh're holdin' good cards, and I'll back yuh to the limit."

Bruce Barkow walked out on the street. Gomer, at least, he understood. He knew the man had no use for him, but if he could show evidence that he was to win, then Gomer would be a powerful ally. Judge Gargan would go as Gomer went, and would always adopt the less violent means. The cards were on the table now. Dan Shute was running things. What he could do, Barkow was not sure. He realized suddenly, with no little trepidation, that after all his association with Shute he knew little of what went on behind the hard brutality of the rancher's face. Yet he was not a man to lag or linger. What he did would be sudden, brutal, and thorough, but it would make a perfect shield under which he, Barkow, could operate and carry to fulfillment his own plans.

Dan Shute's abrupt statement of his purpose in regard to Ann Rodney had jolted Barkow. Somehow, he had taken Ann for granted. He had always planned a marriage. That he wanted her land was true. Perhaps better than Shute he knew what oil might mean in the future, and Barkow was a farsighted man. But Ann Rodney was lovely and interesting. She would be a good wife for him. There was one way he could defeat Dan Shute on that score. To marry Ann at once.

True, it might precipitate a killing, but already Bruce Barkow was getting ideas on that score. He was suddenly less disturbed about Rafe Caradec than Dan Shute. The rancher loomed large and formidable in his mind. He knew the brutality of the man, had seen him kill, and knew with what coldness he regarded people or animals. Bruce Barkow made up his mind. Come what may, he was going to marry Ann Rodney.

He could, he realized, marry her and get her clear away from here. His mind leaped ahead. Flight to the northwest to the gold camps would be foolhardy. To the Utah country would be as bad. In either case, Shute might and probably would overtake him. There remained another way out, and one that Shute probably would never suspect—he could strike for Fort Phil Kearney not far distant, and then, with or without a scouting party for escort, could head across country and reach the Yellowstone. Or he might even try the nearer Powder River. A steamer had ascended the Yellowstone earlier that year, and there was every chance that another would come. If not, with a canoe or barge they could head downstream until they encountered such a boat, and buy passage to St. Louis.

Ann and full title to her land would be in his hands then, and he could negotiate a sale or the leasing of the land from a safe distance. The more he thought of this, the more he was positive it remained the only solution for him.

Let Gomer think what he would. Let Dan Shute believe him content with a minor rôle. He would go ahead with his plans, then strike suddenly and swiftly and be well on his way before Shute realized what had happened. Once he made the fort, he would be in the clear. Knowing the officers as well as he did, he was sure he could get an escort to the river. He had never seen the Yellowstone, nor did he know much about either that river or Powder River. But they had been used by many men as a high road to the West, and he could use a river as an escape to the East.

Carefully he considered the plan. There were preparations to be made. Every angle must be considered. At his ranch were horses enough. He would borrow Baker's buckboard to take Ann for a ride, then at his ranch they would mount and be off. With luck they would be well on their way before anyone so much as guessed what had happened.

Stopping by the store, he bought ammunition from Baker. He glanced up to find the store-keeper's eyes studying him, and he didn't like the expression.

"Is Ann in?" he asked.

Baker nodded, and jerked a thumb toward the curtain. Turning, Barkow walked behind the curtain and looked at Ann, who arose as he entered. Quickly he sensed a coolness that had not been there before. This was no time to talk of marriage. First things first.

He shrugged shamefacedly. "I suppose yuh're thinkin' pretty bad of me," he suggested ruefully. "I know now I shouldn't have listened to Dan Shute or to Gomer. Pod swore he had a case, and

Shute claims Caradec is a crook and a rustler. If I had realized, I wouldn't have had any hand in it."

"It was pretty bad," Ann agreed as she sat down and began knitting. "What will happen now?"

"I don't know," he admitted, "but I wish I could spare you all this. Before it's over I'm afraid there'll be more killin's and trouble. Dan Shute is plenty roused up. He'll kill Caradec."

She looked at him. "You think that will be easy?"

Surprised, he nodded. "Yes. Dan's a dangerous man, and a cruel and brutal one. He's fast with a gun, too."

"I thought you were a friend to Dan Shute?" she asked, looking at him hard. "What's changed you, Bruce?"

He shrugged. "Oh, little things. He showed himself up today. He's brutal, unfeelin'. He'll stop at nothin' to gain his ends."

"I think he will," Ann said composedly. "I think he'll stop at Rafe Caradec."

Barkow stared at her. "He seems to have impressed yuh. What makes yuh think that?"

"I never really saw him until today, Bruce," she admitted. "Whatever his motives, he is shrewd and capable. I think he is a much more dangerous man than Dan Shute. There's something behind him, too. He has background. I could see it in his manner more than his words. I wish I knew more about him."

Nettled at her defense of the man, and her apparent respect for him, Bruce shrugged his shoulders. "Don't forget, he probably killed your father."

She looked up. "Did he, Bruce?"

Her question struck fear into him. Veiling his eyes, he shrugged again. "Yuh never know. I'm worried about you, Ann. This country's going to be flamin' within a few days or weeks. If it ain't the fight here, it'll be the Indians. I wish I could get yuh out of it."

"But this is my home," Ann protested. "It is all I have."

"Not quite all." Her eyes fell before his gaze. "Ann, how would yuh like to go to Saint Louis?"

She looked up, startled. "To Saint Louis? But how . . . ?"

"Not so loud." He glanced apprehensively at the door. There was no telling who might be listening. "I don't want anybody to know about it unless yuh decide, and nobody to know till after we're gone. But Ann, we *could* go. I've always wanted to marry yuh, and there's no time better than now."

She got up and walked to the window. St. Louis. It was another world. She hadn't seen a city in six years, and, after all, they had been engaged for several months now. "How would we get there?" she asked, turning to face him.

"That's a secret." He laughed. "Don't tell

anybody about it, but I've got a wonderful trip planned for yuh. I always wanted to do things for yuh, Ann. We could go away and be married within a few hours."

"Where?"

"By the chaplain, at the fort. One of the officers would stand up with me, and there are a couple of officers' wives there, too."

"I don't know, Bruce," she said hesitantly. "I'll have to think about it."

He smiled and kissed her lightly. "Then think fast, honey. I want to get yuh away from all this trouble, and quick."

When he got outside in the street, he paused, smiling with satisfaction. *I'll show that Dan Shute a thing or two,* he told himself grimly. *I'll leave him standin' here flat-footed, holdin' the bag. I'll have the girl and the ranch, and won't be within miles of this place.* Abruptly he turned toward the cabin where he lived.

Dan Shute stood on the boardwalk, staring into the dust, big hands on his hips above the heavy guns, his gray hat pulled low, a stubble of corn-white beard along his hard jaws. *I think,* he said to himself, looking up, *that I'll kill Bruce Barkow. And I'm goin' to like the doin' of it.*

XIII

Gene Baker was sweeping his store and the stoop in front of it when he saw a tight little cavalcade of horsemen trot around the corner into the street. It was the morning after the fiasco of the trial, and he had been worried and irritated while wondering what the reaction would be from Barkow and Shute. Then word had come to him of the break between the two at Gomer's office.

Dan Shute, riding a powerful gray, was in the van of the bunch of horsemen. He rode up to the stoop of Baker's store, and reined in. Behind him were Red and Tom Blazer, Joe Gorman, Fritz Handl, Fats McCabe, and others of the hard bunch that trailed with Shute.

"Gene," Shute said abruptly, resting his big hands on the pommel of the saddle, "don't sell any more supplies to Caradec or any of his crowd." He added harshly: "I'm not askin' yuh. I'm tellin' yuh. And if yuh do, I'll put you out of business and run you out of the country. You know I don't make threats. The chances are Caradec won't be alive by daybreak, anyway, but, just in case, yuh've been told."

Without giving Baker a chance to reply, Dan Shute touched spurs to his horse and led off down the south trail toward the Crazy Man. The door slammed behind Baker.

"Where are they going?" Ann wanted to know, her eyes wide. "What are they going to do?"

Gene stared after them bleakly. This was the end of something.

"They are goin' after Caradec and his crowd, Ann."

"What will they do to him?" Something inside her went sick and frightened. She had always been afraid of Dan Shute. The way he looked at her made her shrink. He was the only human being of whom she had ever been afraid. He seemed without feeling, without decency, without regard for anything but his own immediate desires.

"Kill him," Baker said. "They'll kill him. Shute's a hard man, and with him that's a mighty wicked lot of men."

"But can't someone warn him?" Ann protested.

Baker glanced at her. "So far as we know, that Caradec is a crook, and mebbe a killer, Ann. You ain't gettin' soft on him, are yuh?"

"No!" she exclaimed, startled. "Of course not! What an idea! Why, I've scarcely talked to him."

Yet there was a heavy, sinking feeling in her heart as she watched the riders disappear in the dust along the southward trail. If there were only something she could do! If she could warn them!

Suddenly she remembered the bay horse her father had given her. Because of the Indians, she had not been riding in a long time, but if she took the mountain trail . . . Hurrying through the door, she swiftly saddled the bay. There was no thought in her mind. She was acting strictly on impulse, prompted by some memory of the way the hair swept back from Rafe's brow, and the look in his eyes when he met her gaze. She told herself she wanted to see no man killed, that Bo Marsh and Johnny Gill were her friends. Yet even in her heart she knew the excuse would not do. She was thinking of Rafe, and only of Rafe.

The bay was in fine shape and impatient after his long restraint in the corral. He started for the trail, eagerly, and his ears pricked up at every sound. The leaves had turned to red and gold now, and in the air there was a hint of frost. Winter was coming. Soon the country would be blanketed, inches deep, under a thick covering of snow.

Hastily Ann's mind leaped ahead. The prairie trail, which the Shute riders had taken, swept wide into the valley, then crossed the Crazy Man, and turned to follow the stream up the cañon. By cutting across over the mountain trail, there was every chance she could beat them to the ranch. In any case, her lead would be slight due to the start the bunch had had.

The trail crossed the mountain side through a long grove of quaking aspens, their leaves shimmering in the cool wind, dark green above, a gray below. Now with oncoming autumn, most of the leaves had turned to bright yellow intermixed with crimson, and here and there among the forest of mounting color were the darker arrowheads of spruce and lodgepole pine.

Once, coming out in a small clearing, she got a view of the valley below. She had gained a little, but only a little. Frightened, she touched spurs to the bay, and the little horse leaped ahead and swept down through the woods at a rapid gallop. Ahead, there was a ledge. It was a good six miles off yet, but from there she would be able to see the cañon of the Crazy Man and the upper cañon. A rider had told her that Caradec had been putting up hay in the wind-sheltered upper cañon and was obviously planning on feeding his stock there near the warm spring.

She recalled it because she remembered it was something her father had spoken of doing. There was room in the upper valley for many cattle, and, if there was hay enough for them, the warm water would be a help, and with only that little help the cattle should survive even the coldest weather.

Fording the stream where Caradec had encountered the young squaw, she rode higher on the mountain, angling across the slope under a magnificent stand of lodgepole pine. It was a splendid avenue of trees, all seemingly of the same size and shape as though cast from a mold. Once she glimpsed a deer, and another time in the distance in a small, branching valley she saw a small bunch of elk. This was her country. No wonder her father had loved it, wanted it, worked to get and to keep it.

Had her father paid the mortgage? Wouldn't Bruce have told her if he had? She could not believe Bruce dishonest or deceitful, and certainly he had made no effort to foreclose, but had been most patient and thoughtful with her. What would he think of this ride? To warn a man he regarded as an enemy. But she could never forgive herself if Rafe Caradec were killed, and she had made no effort to avert it.

Too often she had listened to her father discourse on the necessity for peace and consideration of the problems of others. She believed in that policy whole-heartedly, and the fact that occasionally violence was necessary did not alter her convictions one whit. No system of philosophy or ethics, no growth of government, no improvement in living came without trial and struggle. Struggle, she had often heard her father say, quoting Hegel, was the law of growth.

Without giving too much thought to it, she understood that such men as Rafe Caradec, Tex Brisco, and others of their ilk were needed. For all their violence, their occasional heedlessness and the desire to go their own way, they were men building a new world in a rough and violent land where everything tended to extremes. Mountains were high, the prairies wide, the streams roaring, the buffalo by the thousand and tens of thousands. It was a land where nothing was small, nothing was simple. Everything, the lives of men and the stories they told, ran to extremes.

The bay pony trotted down the trail, then around a stand of lodgepole. Ann brought him up sharply on the lip of the ledge that had been her first goal. Below her, a vast and magnificent panorama, lay the ranch her father had pioneered. The silver curve of the Crazy Man lay below and east of her, and opposite the ledge was the mighty wall of the cañon. From below, a faint thread of smoke among the trees marked the cabin.

Turning her head, she looked west and south into the upper cañon. Far away, she seemed to see a horseman moving, and the black dot of a herd. Turning the bay, she started west, riding fast. If they were working the upper cañon, she still had a chance.

An hour later, the little bay showing signs of his rough traveling, she came down to the floor of the cañon. Not far away, she could see Rafe Caradec, moving a bunch of cattle into the trees.

He looked around at her approach, and the black, flat-crowned hat came off his head. His dark, wavy hair was plastered to his brow with sweat, and his eyes were gray and curious.

"Good mornin'!" he said. "This is a surprise!"

"Please!" she burst out. "This isn't a social call!

Dan Shute's riding this way with twenty men or more. He's going to wipe you out!"

"You shore?" She could see the quick wonder in his eyes at her warning, then he wheeled his horse and yelled: "Johnny! Johnny Gill! Come a-runnin'!"

Jerking his rifle from his boot, he looked at her again. He put his hand over hers suddenly, and she started at his touch. "Thanks, Ann," he said simply. "You're regular."

Then he was gone, and Johnny Gill was streaking after him. As Gill swept by, he lifted a hand and waved.

There they went, and below were twenty men, all armed. Would they come through alive? She turned the bay and, letting the pony take his own time, started him back over the mountain trail.

Rafe Caradec gave no thought to Ann's reason for warning him. There was no time for that. Tex Brisco and Bo Marsh were at the cabin. They were probably working outside, and their rifles would probably be in the cabin and beyond them. If they were cut off from their guns, the Shute riders would mow them down and kill them one by one at long range with rifle fire.

Rafe heard Gill coming up, and slacked off a little to let the little cowhand draw alongside.

"Shute!" he said. "And about twenty men. I guess this is the pay-off!"

"Yeah!" Gill yelled.

Rifle fire came to them suddenly. A burst of shots, then a shot that might have been from a pistol. Yet that was sheer guesswork, Rafe knew, for distinguishing the two was not easy and especially at this distance.

Their horses rounded the entrance and raced down the main cañon toward the cabin on the Crazy Man, running neck and neck. A column of smoke greeted them, and they could see riders circling and firing.

"The trees on the slope!" Rafe yelled, and raced for them.

He reached the trees with the black at a dead run and hit the ground before the animal had ceased to move. He raced to the rocks at the edge of the trees. His rifle lifted, settled, his breath steadied. Then the rifle spoke.

A man shouted and waved an arm, and at the same moment Gill fired. A horse went down. Two men, or possibly three, lay sprawled in the clearing before the cabin. Were Tex and Bo already down? Rafe steadied himself and squeezed off another shot. A saddle emptied. He saw the fallen man lunge to his feet, then spill over on his face. Coolly then, and taking their time, he and Gill began to fire. Another man went down, and rifles began to smoke in their direction. A bullet clipped the leaves overhead, but too high.

Rafe knocked the hat from a man's head and, as the fellow sprinted for shelter, dropped him.

Suddenly the attack broke, and he saw the horses sweeping away from them in a ragged line. Mounting, Rafe and Gill rode cautiously toward the cabin.

There was no cabin. There was only a roaring inferno of flames. There were five sprawled bodies now, and Rafe ran toward them. A Shute rider—another. Then he saw Bo. The boy was lying on his face with a dark, spreading stain on the back of his shirt. There was no sign of Tex.

Rafe dropped to his knees and put a hand over the young cowhand's heart. It was still beating! Gently, with Johnny lending a hand, he turned the boy over. Then, working with the crude but efficient skill picked up in war and struggle in a half dozen countries, he examined the wounds.

"Four times," he said grimly. He felt something mount and swell within him, a tide of fierce, uncontrollable anger. Around one bullet hole in the stomach the cloth of the cowhand's shirt was still smoldering!

"I seen that!" It was Tex Brisco, his face haggard and smoke-grimed. "I saw it! I know who done it! He walked up where the kid was laying, stuck a gun against his stomach, and shot! He didn't want the kid to go quick. He wanted him to die slow and hard!"

"Who done it?" Gill demanded fiercely. "I'll git him now! Right now!"

Brisco's eyes were red and inflamed. "Nobody

gets him but me. This kid was your pard, but I *seen* it!" He turned abruptly on Rafe. "Boss, let me go to town. I want to kill a man!"

"It won't do, Tex," Caradec said quietly. "I know how you feel, but the town will be full of 'em. They'll be celebratin'. They burned our cabin, ran off some cattle, and they got Bo. It wouldn't do."

"Yeah." Tex spat. "I know. But they won't be expectin' any trouble now. We've been together a long time, boss, and if yuh don't let me go, I'll quit."

Rafe looked up from the wounded man. "All right, Tex. I told you I know how you feel. But if somethin' should happen . . . who did it?"

"Tom Blazer. That big redhead. He always hated the kid. The kid was shot down and left lay. I was out back in the woods, lookin' for a pole to cut. They rode up so fast the kid never had a chance. He was hit twice before he knew what was goin' on. Then, again, when he started toward the house. After the house was afire, Tom Blazer walked up, and the kid was conscious. Tom said somethin' to Bo, shoved the gun against him, and pulled the trigger." He stared miserably at Bo. "I was out of pistol range. Took me a few minutes to get closer, then I got me two men before you rode up."

Wheeling, he headed toward the corral.

Rafe had stopped the flow of blood, and Johnny

had returned with a blanket from a line back of the house.

"Reckon we better get him over in the trees, boss," Gill said.

Easing the cowboy to the blanket with care, Rafe and Johnny carried Bo into the shade in a quiet place under the pines. Caradec glanced up as they put him down. Tex Brisco was riding out of the cañon. Johnny Gill watched him go.

"Boss," Gill said, "I wanted like blazes to go, but I ain't the man Brisco is. Rightly I'm a quiet man, but that Texan is a wolf on the prowl. I'm some glad I'm not Tom Blazer right now." He looked down at Bo Marsh. The young cowhand's face was flushed, his breathing hoarse. "Will he live, Rafe?" Johnny asked softly.

Caradec shrugged. "I don't know," he said hoarsely. "He needs better care than I can give him." He studied the situation thoughtfully. "Johnny," he said, "you stay with him. Better take time to build a lean-to for cover in case of rain or snow. Get some fuel, too."

"What about you?" Johnny asked. "Where you goin'?"

"To the fort. There's an Army doctor there, and I'll go get him."

"Reckon he'll come this far?" Johnny asked doubtingly.

"He'll come."

Rafe Caradec mounted the black and rode

slowly away into the dusk. It was a long ride to the fort, and, even if he got the doctor, it might be too late. That was the chance he would have to take. There was small danger of an attack now. Yet it was not really a return of Dan Shute's riders that disturbed him, but a subtle coolness in the air, a chill that was of more than autumn. Winters in this country could be bitterly cold, and all the signs gave evidence this one would be the worst in years, and they were without a cabin. He rode on toward the fort, with a thought that Tex Brisco now must be nearing town.

XIV

It was growing late, and Painted Rock was swathed in velvety darkness when Tex Brisco walked his horse to the edge of town. He stopped across the bend of the stream from town and planned to leave his horse among the trees there. He would have a better chance of escape from across the stream than from the street, and by leaving town on foot he could create some doubt as to his whereabouts. He was under no misapprehension as to the problem he faced. Painted Rock would be filled to overflowing with Shute and Barkow riders, many of whom knew him by sight. Yet, although he could envision their certainty of victory, their numbers, and was well

233

aware of the reckless task he had chosen, he knew they would not be expecting him, or any riders from Crazy Man.

He tied his horse loosely to a bush among the trees, and crossed the stream on a log. Once across, he thought of his spurs. Kneeling down, he unfastened them from his boots and hung them over a root near the end of the log. He wanted no jingling spurs to give his presence away at an inopportune moment.

Carefully avoiding any dwellings with lights, he made his way through the scattered houses to the back of the row of buildings across the street. He was wearing the gun he usually wore, and for luck he had taken another from his saddlebags and thrust it into his waistband.

Tex Brisco was a man of the frontier. From riding the range in South and West Texas, he had drifted north with trail herds. He had seen some of the days around the beginning of Dodge and Ellsworth, and some hard fighting down in the Nations, and with rustlers along the Mexican border. He was an honest man, a sincere man. He had a quality to be found in many men of his kind and period—a quality of deep-seated loyalty that was his outstanding trait. Hard and reckless in demeanor, he rode with dash and acted with a flair. He had at times been called a hardcase. Yet no man lived long in a dangerous country, if he were reckless. There was a place always for courage, but intelligent courage, not the heedlessness of a harebrained youngster. Tex Brisco was twenty-five years old, but he had been doing a man's work since he was eleven. He had walked with men, ridden with men, fought with men as one of them. He had asked no favors and had been granted none. Now, at twenty-five, he was a seasoned veteran. He was a man who knew the plains and the mountains, knew cattle, horses, and guns. He possessed a fierce loyalty to his outfit and to his friends.

Shanghaied, he had quickly seen that the sea was not his element. He had concealed his resentment and gone to work, realizing that safety lay along that route. He had known his time would come. It had come when Rafe Caradec came aboard, and all his need for friendship, for loyalty, and for a cause had been tied to the big, soft-spoken stranger.

Now Painted Rock was vibrant with danger. The men who did not hate him in Painted Rock were men who would not speak for him, or act for him. It was like Tex Brisco that he did not think in terms of help. He had his job, he knew his problem, and he knew he was the man to do it.

The National Saloon was booming with sound. The tinny jangle of an out-of-tune piano mingled with hoarse laughter, shouts, and the rattle of glasses. The hitching rail was lined with horses.

Tex walked between the buildings to the edge

of the dark and empty street. Then he walked up to the horses and, speaking softly, made his way along the hitching rail, turning every slipknot into a hard knot.

The Emporium was dark, except for a light in Baker's living quarters where he sat with his wife and Ann Rodney. The stage station was lit by a feeble glow of a light over a desk as a station agent worked late over his books.

It was a moonless night, and the stars were bright. Tex lit a cigarette, loosened his guns in his holsters, and studied the situation. The National was full. To step into that saloon was suicide, and Tex had no such idea in mind. It was early, and he would have to wait. Yet might it be the best way, if he stepped in? There would be a moment of confusion. In that instant he could act.

Working his way back to a window, he studied the interior. It took him several minutes to locate Tom Blazer. The big man was standing by the bar with Fats McCabe. Slipping to the other end of the window, Tex could see that no one was between them and the rear door. He stepped back into the darkest shadows and, leaning against the building, finished his cigarette. When it was down to a stub, he threw it on the ground and carefully rubbed it out with the toe of his boot. Then he pulled his hat low, and walked around to the rear of the saloon.

There was some scrap lumber there, and he skirted the rough pile, avoiding some bottles. It was cool out here, and he rubbed his fingers a little, working his hands to keep the circulation going. Then he stepped up to the door and turned the knob. It opened under his hand, and, if it made a sound, it went unheard. Stepping inside, he closed the door after him, pleased that it opened outward.

In the hurly-burly of the interior one more cowhand went unseen. Nobody even glanced his way. He sidled up to the bar, then reached over under Tom Blazer's nose, drew the whisky bottle toward him, and poured a drink into a glass just rinsed by the bartender.

Tom Blazer scarcely glanced at the bottle, for other bottles were being passed back and forth. Fats McCabe stood beside Tom and, without noticing Tex, went on talking.

"That blasted Marsh!" Tom said thickly. "I got him! I been wantin' him a long time! Yuh should have seen the look in his eyes when I shoved that pistol against him and pulled the trigger!"

Tex's lips tightened, and he poured his glass full once more. He left it sitting on the bar in front of him. His eyes swept the room. Bruce Barkow was here, and Pod Gomer. Tex moved over a little closer to McCabe.

"That'll finish 'em off," McCabe was saying. "When Shute took over, I knew they wouldn't last long. If they get out of the country, they'll be lucky. They've no supplies now, and it will be snowin' within a few days. The winter will get 'em, if we don't, or the Injuns."

Tex Brisco smiled grimly. *Not before I get you!* he thought. *That comes first.*

The piano was banging away with "Oh, Susanna!" and a bunch of cowhands were trying to sing it. Joe Benson leaned on his bar talking to Pod Gomer. Barkow sat at a table in the corner, staring morosely into a glass. Joe Gorman and Fritz Handl were watching a poker game.

Tex glanced again at the back door. No one stood between the door and himself. Well, why wait?

Just then Tom Blazer reached for the bottle in front of Tex, and Tex pulled it away from his hand. Tom stared. "Hey, what yuh tryin' to do?" he demanded belligerently.

"I've come for yuh, Blazer," Tex said. "I've come to kill a skunk that shoots a helpless man when he's on his back. How are yuh against standin' men, Blazer?"

"Huh?" Tom Blazer said stupidly. Then he realized what had been said, and he thrust his big face forward for a closer look. The gray eyes he saw were icy, the lantern-jawed Texan's face was chill as death, and Tom Blazer jerked back. Slowly, his face white, Fats McCabe drew aside.

To neither man came the realization that Tex Brisco was alone. All they felt was the shock of his sudden appearance, here, among them. Brisco turned, stepping one pace away from the bar. "Well, Tom," he said quietly, his voice just loud enough to carry over the sound of the music, "I've come for yuh."

Riveted to the spot, Tom Blazer felt an instant of panic. Brisco's presence here had the air of magic, and Tom was half frightened by the sheer unexpectedness of it. Sounds in the saloon seemed to die out, although they still went full blast, and Tom stared across that short space like a man in a trance, trapped and faced with a fight to the death. There would be no escaping this issue, he knew. He might win, and he might lose, but it was here, now, and he had to face it. He realized suddenly that it was a chance he had no desire to make. Wouldn't anyone notice? Why didn't Fats say something? Tex Brisco stood there, staring at him.

"Yuh've had yore chance," Tex said gently. "Now I'm goin' to kill yuh!"

The shock of the word *kill* snapped Tom Blazer out of it. He dropped into a half crouch, and his lips curled in a snarl of mingled rage and fear. His clawed hand swept back for his gun.

In the throbbing and rattle of the room the guns boomed like a crash of thunder. Heads whirled, and liquor-befuddled brains tried to focus eyes. All they saw was Tom Blazer, sagging back against the bar, his shirt darkening with blood, and the strained, foolish expression on his face like that of a man who had been shocked beyond reason.

Facing the room was a lean, broad-shouldered man with two guns, and, as they looked, he swung a gun at Fats McCabe. Instinctively, at the *boom* of guns, McCabe's brain had reacted, but a shade slow. His hand started for his gun. It was an involuntary movement that, had he had but a moment's thought, would never have been made. He had no intention of drawing. All he wanted was out, but the movement of his hand was enough. It was too much.

Tex Brisco's gun *boomed* again, and Fats toppled over on his face. Then Tex opened up, and three shots, blasting into the brightly lit room, brought it to complete darkness. Brisco faded into that darkness, swung the door open, and vanished as a shot clipped the air over his head.

He ran hard for fifty feet, then ducked into the shadow of a barn, threw himself over a low corral fence, and ran across the corral in a low crouch. Shouts and orders, then the *crash* of glass, came from the saloon.

The door burst open again, and he could have got another man, but only by betraying his position. He crawled through the fence and, keeping close to a dark house, ran swiftly to its far corner. He paused there, breathing heavily. So far, so good.

From here on he would be in comparative light,

but the distance was enough now. He ran on swiftly for the river. Behind him he heard curses and yells as men found their knotted bridle reins. At the end of the log, Tex retrieved his spurs. Then, gasping for breath from his hard run, he ran across the log and started for his horse. He saw it suddenly, and then he saw something else.

XV

In the dim light, Tex recognized Joe Gorman by his hat. Joe wore his hat brim rolled to a point in front.

"Hi, Texas!" Gorman said. Tex could see the gun in his hand, waist high and leveled on him.

"Hi, Joe. Looks like yuh smelled somethin'."

"Yeah"—Joe nodded—"I did at that. Happened to see somebody ride up here in the dark, and got curious. When yuh headed for the saloon, I got around yuh and went in. Then I saw yuh come in the back door. I slipped out just before the shootin' started, so's I could beat yuh back here in case yuh got away."

"Too bad yuh missed the fun," Brisco said quietly.

Behind Tex the pursuit seemed to have gained no direction as yet. His mind was on a hair trigger, watching for a break. Which of his guns was still loaded? He had forgotten whether he put the loaded gun in the holster or in his belt.

"Who'd yuh get?" asked Gorman.

"Tom Blazer. Fats McCabe, too."

"I figgered Tom. I told him he shouldn't have shot the kid. That was a low-down trick. But why shoot Fats?"

"He acted like he was reachin' for a gun."

"Huh. Don't take a lot to get a man killed, does it?"

Brisco could see in the dark enough to realize that Gorman was smiling a little.

"How do yuh want it, Tex? Should I let yuh have it now, or save yuh for Shute? He's a bad man, Tex."

"I think yuh'd better slip yore gun in yore holster and go back home, Joe," Tex said. "Yuh're the most decent one of a bad lot."

"Mebbe I want the money I'd get for you, Tex. I can use some."

"Think yuh'd live to collect?"

"Yuh mean Caradec? He's through, Brisco. Through. We got Bo. Now we got you. That leaves only Caradec and Johnny Gill. They won't be so tough."

"Yuh're wrong, Joe," Tex said quietly. "Rafe could take the lot of yuh, and he will. But you bought into my game yoreself. I wouldn't ask for help, Joe. I'd kill yuh myself."

"You?" Gorman chuckled with real humor.

"And me with the drop on yuh? Not a chance! Why, Tex, *one* of these slugs would get yuh, and, if I have to start blastin', I'm goin' to empty the gun before I quit."

"Uhn-huh," Tex agreed, "yuh mean, get me before I could shoot?" He repeated: "Not a chance."

The sounds of pursuit were coming now. The men had a light and had found his tracks.

"Toward the river, I'll be a 'coon!" a voice yelled. "Let's go!"

Here it was! Joe Gorman started to yell, then saw the black figure ahead of him move, and his gun blazed. Tex felt the shocking jolt of a slug, and his knees buckled, but his gun was out, and he triggered two shots, fast. Joe started to fall, and he fired again, but the hammer fell on an empty chamber.

Tex jerked the slipknot in his reins loose and dragged himself into the saddle. He was bleeding badly. His mind felt hazy, but he saw Joe Gorman move on the ground, and heard him say: "Yuh did it, damn yuh! Yuh did it!"

"So long, Joe," Tex whispered hoarsely.

He walked the horse for twenty feet, then started moving faster. His brain was singing with a strange noise, and his blood seemed to drum in his brain. He headed up the tree-covered slope, and the numbness crawled up his legs. He fought like a cornered wolf against the darkness that crept over him. *I can't die . . . I can't!* he kept saying in his brain. *Rafe'll need help! I can't!*

Fighting the blackness and numbness, he tied the bridle reins to the saddle horn, and thrust both feet clear through the stirrups. Sagging in the saddle, he got his handkerchief out and fumbled a knot, tying his wrists to the saddle horn.

The light glowed and died, and the horse walked on, weaving in the awful darkness, weaving through a world of agony and the soft, clutching hands that seemed to be pulling Tex down, pulling him down. The darkness closed in around him, but under him he seemed still to feel the slow plodding of the horse. . . .

Roughly, the distance to the fort was seventy miles, a shade less, perhaps. Rafe Caradec rode steadily into the increasing cold of the wind. There was no mistaking the seriousness of Bo's condition. The young cowhand was badly shot up, weak from loss of blood, and despite the amazing vitality of frontier men, his chance was slight unless his wounds had proper care.

Bowing his head to the wind, Rafe headed the horse down a draw and its partial shelter. There was no use thinking of Tex. Whatever had happened in Painted Rock had happened now, or was happening. Brisco might be dead. He might be alive and safe, even now heading back to the Crazy Man, or he might be wounded and in need of help. Tex Brisco was an uncertainty, but Bo Marsh hung between life and death, hence there was no choice. The friendship and understanding between the lean, hard-faced Texan and Rafe Caradec had grown aboard ship. Rafe was not one to take lightly the Texan's loyalty in joining him in his foray into Wyoming. Now Brisco might be dead, killed in a fight he would never have known but for Rafe. Yet Tex would have had it no other way. His destinies were guided by his loyalties. Those loyalties were his life, his religion, his reason for living.

Yet despite his worries over Marsh and Brisco, Rafe found his thoughts returning again and again to Ann Rodney. Why had she ridden to warn them of the impending attack? Had it not been for that warning the riders would have wiped out Brisco at the same time they got Marsh, and would have followed it up to find Rafe and Johnny back in the cañon. It would have been, or could have been, a clean sweep.

Why had Ann warned them? Was it because of her dislike of violence and killing? Or was there some other, some deeper, feeling? Yet how could that be? What feeling could Ann have for any of them, believing as she seemed to believe that he was a thief, or worse? The fact remained that she had come, that she had warned them. Remembering her, he recalled the flash of her eyes, the proud lift of her chin, the way she walked. He stared grimly into the night and swore softly. Was he in love?

"Who knows?" he demanded viciously of the night. "And what good would it do if I was?"

He had never been to the fort, yet knew it lay between the forks of the Piney and its approximate location. His way led across the billowing hills and through a country marked by small streams lined with cottonwood, box elder, willow, chokeberry, and wild plum. That this was the Indian country, he knew. The unrest of the tribes was about to break into open warfare, and already there had been sporadic attacks on haying or wood-cutting parties, and constant attacks were being made on the Missouri steamboats far to the north.

Red Cloud, most influential chieftain among the Sioux, had tried to hold the tribes together and, despite the continued betrayal of treaties by the white man, had sought to abide by the code he had laid down for his people. With Man-Afraid-Of-His-Horse, the Oglala chief, Red Cloud was the strongest of all the Sioux leaders, or had been. With Custer's march into the Black Hills and the increasing travel over the Laramie and Bozeman Trails, the Sioux were growing restless. The Sioux medicine man, Sitting Bull, was indulging in war talk, and he was aided and abetted by two powerful warriors—Crazy Horse and Gall. No one in the West but understood that an outbreak of serious nature was overdue.

Rafe Caradec was aware of all this. He was aware, too, that it would not be an easy thing to prevail upon the doctor to leave the fort, or upon the commander to allow him to leave. In the face of impending trouble, his place was with the Army. . . .

News of the battle on the Crazy Man, after Ann's warning, reached her that evening. The return of the triumphant Shute riders was enough to tell her what had happened. She heard them ride into the street, heard their yells and their shouts. She heard that Bo Marsh was definitely dead, even though some of the Shute riders were harsh in their criticism of Tom Blazer for that action.

While the Shute outfit had ridden away, following their attack, fearful of the effects of sharpshooting from the timber, they were satisfied. Winter was coming on, and they had destroyed the cabin on the Crazy Man and killed Bo Marsh. Mistakenly they also believed they had killed Brisco and wounded at least one other man.

Sick at heart, Ann had walked back into her room and stood by the window. Suddenly she was overwhelmed by the desire to get away, to escape all this sickening violence, the guns, the killings, the problems of frontier life. Back East there were lovely homes along quiet streets, slow-running streams, men who walked quietly on Sunday mornings. There were parties, theaters, friends, homes.

Her long ride had tired her. The touch of Rafe Caradec's hand, the look in his eyes, had given her a lift. Something had sparked within her, and she felt herself drawn to him, yearning toward him with everything feminine that was in her. Riding away, she had heard the crash of guns, shouts, and yells. Had she been too late?

There had been no turning back. She had known there was nothing she could do. Her natural good sense had told her that she would only complicate matters if she tried to stay. Nor did she know now what she would have done if she had stayed. Where was her sympathy? With Shute's riders, or with this strange, tall young man who had come to claim half her ranch and tell fantastic stories of knowing her father aboard a ship? Every iota of intelligence she had told her the man was all wrong, that his story could not be true. Bruce Barkow's story of her father's death had been the true one. What reason for him to lie? Why would he want to claim her land when there was so much more to be had for the taking? Her father had told her, and Gene Baker agreed, that soon all this country would be open to settlement, and there would be towns and railroads here. Why choose one piece of land, a large section of it worthless, when the hills lay bare for the taking?

Standing by the window and looking out into

the darkness, Ann knew suddenly she was sick of it all. She would get away, go back East. Bruce was right. It was time she left here, and, when he came again, she would tell him she was ready. He had been thoughtful and considerate. He had protected her, been attentive and affectionate. He was a man of intelligence. He was handsome. She could be proud of him.

She stifled her misgivings with a sudden resolution, and hurriedly began to pack.

XVI

Vaguely Ann had sensed Barkow's fear of something, but she believed it was fear of an attack by Indians. Word had come earlier that day that the Oglalas were gathering in the hills, and there was much war talk among them. That it could be Dan Shute whom Barkow feared Ann had no idea.

She had completed the packing of the few items she would need for the trip when she heard the sound of gunfire from the National. The shots brought her to her feet with a start, her face pale. Running into the living room, she found that Gene Baker had caught up his rifle. She ran to Mrs. Baker, and the two women stood together, listening.

Baker looked at them. "Can't be Indians," he

said after a moment. "Mebbe some wild cowhand celebratin'."

They heard excited voices, yells. Baker went to the door, hesitated, then went out. He was gone several minutes before he returned. His face was grave.

"It was that Texas rider from the Crazy Man," he said. "He stepped into the back door of the National and shot it out with Tom Blazer and Fats McCabe. They're both dead."

"Was he alone?" Ann asked quickly.

Baker nodded, looking at her somberly. "They're huntin' him now. He won't get away, I'm afeerd."

"You're *afraid* he won't?"

"Yes, Ann," Baker said, "I am. That Blazer outfit's poison. All of the Shute bunch, far's that goes. Tom killed young Bo Marsh by stickin' a pistol against him whilst he was lyin' down."

The flat bark of a shot cut across the night air, and they went rigid. Two more shots rang out.

"Guess they got him," Baker said. "There's so many of them, I figgered they would."

Before the news reached them of what had actually happened, daylight had come. Ann Rodney was awake after an almost sleepless night. Tex Brisco, she heard, had killed Joe Gorman when Gorman had caught him at his horse. Tex had escaped, but from all the evidence he was badly wounded. They were trailing him by the blood from his wounds. Bo Marsh, now Brisco. Was Johnny Gill alive? Was Rafe? If Rafe were alive, then he must be alone, harried like a rabbit by hounds.

Restless, Ann paced the floor. Shute riders came and went in the store. They were buying supplies and going out in groups of four and five, scouring the hills for Brisco or any of the others of the Crazy Man crowd.

Bruce Barkow came shortly after breakfast. He walked into the store. He looked tired, worried.

"Ann," he said abruptly, "if we're goin', it'll have to be today. This country is goin' to the wolves. All they think about now is killin'. Let's get out."

She hesitated only an instant. Something inside her seemed lost and dead. "All right, Bruce. We've planned it for a long time. It might as well be now."

There was no fire in her, no spark. Barkow scarcely heeded that. She would go, and, once away from here and married, he would have title to the land, and Dan Shute for all his talk and harsh ways would be helpless. "All right," he said. "We'll leave in an hour. Don't tell anybody. We'll take the buckboard like we were goin' for a drive, as we often do."

She was ready, so there was nothing to do after he had gone.

Baker seemed older, worried. Twice riders came in, and each time Ann heard that Tex Brisco was still at large. His horse had been trailed, seemingly wandering without guidance, to a place on a mountain creek. There the horse had walked into the water, and no trail had been found to show where he had left it. He was apparently headed for the high ridges, south by west, nor had anything been found of Marsh or Gill. Shute riders had returned to the Crazy Man, torn down the corral, and hunted through the woods, but no sign had been found beyond a crude lean-to where the wounded man had evidently been sheltered. Marsh, if dead, had been buried, and the grave concealed. Nothing had been found of any of them, although one horse had ridden off to the northeast, mostly east.

One horse had gone east! Ann Rodney's heart gave a queer leap. East would mean toward the fort! Perhaps . . . But she was being foolish. Why should it be Caradec rather than Gill, and why to the fort? She expressed the thought, and Baker looked at her.

"Likely enough one of 'em's gone there. If Marsh ain't dead, and the riders didn't find his body, chances are he's mighty bad off. The only doctor around is at the fort."

The door to the store opened, and Baker went in, leaving the living room. There was a brief altercation, then the curtain was pushed aside, and

Ann looked up. A start of fear went through her.

Dan Shute was standing in the door. For a wonder, he was clean-shaven except for his mustache. He looked at her with his queer, gray-white eyes. "Don't you do nothin' foolish," he said, "like tryin' to leave here. I don't aim to let yuh."

Ann got up, amazed and angry. "You don't aim to let me?" she flared. "What business is it of yours?"

Shute stood there with his big hands on his hips, staring at her insolently. "Because I want to make it my business," he said. "I've told Barkow where he stands with you. If he don't like it, he can say so and die. I ain't particular. I just wanted yuh should know that from here on yuh're my woman."

"Listen here, Shute," Baker flared. "You can't talk to a decent woman that way!"

"Shut yore mouth," Shute said, staring at Baker. "I talk the way I please. I'm tellin' her. If she tries to get away from here, I'll take her out to the ranch now. If she waits . . ."—he looked her up and down coolly—"I may marry her. Don't know why I should." He added, glaring at Baker: "You butt into this and I'll smash yuh. She ain't no woman for a weak sister like Barkow. I guess she'll come to like me all right. Anyway, she'd better." He turned toward the door. "Don't get any ideas. I'm the law here, and the only law."

"I'll appeal to the Army," Baker declared.

"You do," Shute said, "and I'll kill yuh. Anyway, the Army's goin' to be some busy. A bunch of Sioux raided a stage station way south of here last night and killed three men, then ran off the stock. Two men were killed hayin' over on Otter last night. A bunch of soldiers hayin' not far from the Piney were fired on and one man wounded. The Army's too busy to bother with the likes of you. Besides," he added, grinning, "the commandin' officer said that in case of Injun trouble, I was to take command at Painted Rock and make all preparations for defense."

He turned and walked out of the room. They heard the front door slam, and Ann sat down suddenly.

Gene Baker walked to the desk and got out his gun. His face was stiff and old.

"No, not that," Ann said. "I'm leaving, Uncle Gene."

"Leavin'? How?" He turned on her, his eyes alert.

"With Bruce. He's asked me several times. I was going to tell you, but nobody else. I'm all packed."

"Barkow, eh?" Gene Baker stared at her. "Well, why not? He's half a gentleman, anyway. Shute is an animal and a brute."

The back door opened gently. Bruce Barkow stepped in.

"Was Dan here?"

Baker explained quickly. "Better forget that buckboard idea," he said, once Barkow had outlined the plan. "Take the hosses and go by the river trail. Leave at noon when everybody will be eatin'. Take the Bannock Trail, then swing north and east and cut around toward the fort. They'll think yuh're tryin' for the gold fields."

Barkow nodded. He looked stiff and pale, and he was wearing a gun. It was almost noon.

When the streets were empty, Bruce Barkow went out back to the barn and saddled the horses. There was no one in sight. The woods along the creek were only a hundred yards away.

Walking outside, the two got into their saddles and rode at a walk to the trees, the dust muffling the beat of horses' hoofs, then they took the Bannock Trail. Two miles out, Barkow rode into a stream, then led the way north.

Once away from the trail they rode swiftly, keeping the horses at a rapid trot. Barkow was silent, and his eyes kept straying to the back trail. Twice they saw Indian sign, but their escape had evidently been made successfully, for there was no immediate sound of pursuit.

Bruce Barkow kept moving, and, as he rode, his irritation, doubt, and fear began to grow more and more obvious. He rode like a man in the grip of deadly terror. Ann, watching him, wondered. Before, Shute had tolerated Barkow. Now a definite break had been made, and with each mile of their escape Barkow became more frightened. There was no way back now. He would be killed on sight, for Dan Shute was not a man to forgive or tolerate such a thing.

It was only on the girl's insistence that he stopped for a rest, and to give the horses a much needed blow. They took it, while Ann sat on the grass, and Bruce paced the ground, his eyes searching the trail over which they had come. When they were in the saddle again, he seemed to relax, to come to himself. Then he looked at her. "Yuh must think I'm a coward," he said, "but it's just that I'm afraid of what Shute would do if he got his hands on you, and I'm no gunfighter. He'd kill us both."

"I know." She nodded gravely.

This man who was to be her husband impressed her less at every moment. Somehow, his claim that he was thinking of her failed to ring with sincerity. Yet with all his faults, he was probably only a weak man, a man cut out for civilization, and not for the frontier. They rode on, and the miles piled up behind them. . . .

Rafe Caradec awakened with a start to the sound of a bugle. It took him several seconds to realize that he was in bed at the fort. Then he remembered. The commanding officer had refused to allow the surgeon to leave before morning, and then only with an escort. With Lieutenant Bryson and eight men they would form a scouting patrol, would circle around by Crazy Man, then cut back toward the fort.

The party at the fort was small, for the place had been abandoned several years before, and had been utilized only for a few weeks as a base for scouting parties when fear of an Indian outbreak began to grow. It was no longer an established post but merely a camp. Further to the south there was a post at Fort Fetterman, named for the leader of the troops trapped in the Fetterman Massacre. A wagon train had been attacked within a short distance of Fort Phil Kearney, and a group of seventy-nine soldiers and two civilians were to march out to relieve them under command of Major James Powell, a skilled Indian fighter. However, Brevet Lieutenant Colonel Fetterman had used his rank to take over command, and had ridden out. Holding the fighting ability of the Indians in contempt, Fetterman had pursued some of them beyond a ridge. Firing had been heard, and, when other troops were sent out from the fort, they had discovered Fetterman and his entire command wiped out, about halfway down the ridge. The wagon train they had gone to relieve had reached the fort later, unaware of the encounter on the ridge.

Getting into his clothes, Rafe hurried outside. The first person he met was Bryson.

"Good morning, Caradec!" Bryson said, grinning. "Bugle wake you up?"

Caradec nodded. "It isn't the first time."

"You've been in the service, then?" Bryson asked, glancing at him quickly.

"Yes." Rafe glanced around the stockade. "I was with Sully. In Mexico for a while, too, and Guatemala."

Bryson glanced at him. "Then you're *that* Caradec? Man, I've heard of you! Major Skehan will be pleased to know. He's an admirer of yours, sir." He nodded toward two weary, dust-covered horses. "You're not the only arrival from Painted Rock," Bryson said. "Those horses came in last night, almost daylight, in fact, with two riders. A chap named Barkow, and a girl. Pretty, too, the lucky dog."

Rafe turned on him, his eyes sharp. "A woman? A girl?"

Bryson looked surprised. "Why, yes! Her name's Rodney. She . . ."

"Where is she?" Rafe snapped. "Where is she now?"

Bryson smiled slightly. "Why, that's her over there! A friend of yours?"

But Rafe was gone.

Ann was standing in the door of one of the partly reconstructed buildings, and, when she saw him, her eyes widened.

"Rafe! You, here? Then you got away!"

258

"I came after a doctor for Marsh. He's in a bad way." He tossed the remark aside, studying her face. "Ann, what are you doing here with Barkow?"

His tone nettled her. "Why? How does it concern you?"

"Your father asked me to take care of you," he said, "and, if you married Bruce Barkow, I certainly wouldn't be doin' it."

"Oh?" Her voice was icy. "Still claiming you knew my father? Well, Mister Caradec, I think you'd be much better off to forget that story. I don't know where you got the idea, or how, or what made you believe you could get away with it, but it won't do. I've been engaged to Bruce for months. I intend to marry him now. There's a chaplain here. Then we'll go on to the river and down to Saint Louis. There's a steamer on the way up that we can meet."

"I won't let you do it, Ann," Rafe said harshly.

Her weariness, her irritation, and something else brought quick anger to her face and lips. "You won't let me? You have nothing to do with it! It simply isn't any of your business! Now, if you please, I'm waiting for Bruce. Will you go?"

"No," he said violently, "I won't. I'll say again what I said before. I knew your father. He gave me a deed givin' us the ranch. He asked me to care for you. He also gave me the receipt that Bruce Barkow gave him for the mortgage money. I wanted things to be different, Ann. I . . ."

"Caradec!" Bryson called. "We're ready!"

He glanced around. The small column awaited him, and his horse was ready. For an instant he glanced back at the girl. Her jaw was set, her eyes blazing. "Oh, what's the use?" he flared. "Marry who you blasted well please!"

Wheeling, he walked to his horse and swung into the saddle, riding away without a backward glance.

XVII

Lips parted to speak, Ann Rodney stared after the disappearing riders. Suddenly all her anger was gone. She found herself gazing at the closing gate of the stockade and fighting a mounting sense of panic. What had she done? Suppose what Rafe had said was the truth? What had he ever done to make her doubt him?

Confused, puzzled by her own feelings for this stranger of whom she knew so little, yet who stirred her so deeply, she was standing there, one hand partly upraised when she saw two men come around the corner of the building. Both wore the rough clothing of miners. They paused near her, one a stocky, thick-set man with a broad, hard jaw, the other a slender blond young man.

"Miss," the younger man said, "we just come in

from the river. The major was tellin' us you were goin' back that way?"

She nodded dumbly, then forced herself to speak. "Yes, we are going to the river with some of the troops. Or that has been our plan."

"We come up the Powder from the Yellowstone, miss," the young man said, "and, if yuh could tell us where to find yore husband, we might sell him our boats."

She shook her head. "I'm not married yet. You will have to see my fiancé, Bruce Barkow. He's in the mess hall."

The fellow hesitated, turning his hat in his hand. "Miss, they said yuh was from Painted Rock. Ever hear tell of a man named Rafe Caradec over there?"

She stiffened. "Rafe Caradec?" She looked at him quickly. "You know him?"

He nodded, pleased by her sudden interest. "Yes, miss. We were shipmates of his. Me and my partner over there, Rock Mullaney. My name is Penn, miss . . . Roy Penn."

Suddenly her heart was pounding. She looked at him and bit her lip. Then she said carefully: "You were on a ship with him?"

"That's right."

Penn was puzzled, and he was growing wary. After all, there was the manner of their leaving. Of course, that was months ago, and they were far from the sea now, but that still hung over them.

"Was there . . . aboard that ship . . . a man named Rodney?"

Ann couldn't look at them now. She stared at the stockade, almost afraid to hear their reply. Vaguely she realized that Bruce Barkow was approaching.

"Rodney? Shorest thing yuh know! Charles Rodney. Nice feller, too. He died off the California coast after . . ." He hesitated. "Miss, you ain't no relation of his now?"

"I'm Charles Rodney's daughter."

"Oh?" Then Penn's eyes brightened. "Say, then you're the girl Rafe came here to see! You know, Charlie's daughter!"

Bruce Barkow stopped dead still. His dark face was suddenly wary.

"What was that?" he said sharply. "What did yuh say?"

Penn stared at him. "No reason to get excited, mister. Yeah, we knew this young lady's father aboard ship. He was shanghaied out of San Francisco."

Bruce Barkow's face was cold. Here it was, at the last minute. He could see in Ann's face the growing realization of how he had lied, how he had betrayed her, and even—he could see that coming into her eyes, too—the idea that he had killed her father. Veins swelled in his forehead and throat. He glared at Penn, half crouching, like some cornered animal. "Yuh're a liar," he snarled.

262

"Don't call me that," Penn said fiercely. "I'm not wearing a gun, mister."

If Barkow heard the last words, they made no impression. His hand was already sweeping down. Penn stepped back, throwing his arms wide, and Bruce Barkow, his face livid with the fury of frustration, whipped up a gun and shot him twice through the body. Penn staggered back, uncomprehending, staring.

"No . . . gun!" he gasped. "I don't . . . gun."

He staggered into an Army wagon, reeled, and fell headlong.

Bruce Barkow stared at the fallen man, then his contorted face turned upward. On the verge of escape and success he had been trapped, and now he had become a killer. Wheeling, he sprang into saddle. The gate was open for a wood wagon, and he whipped the horse through it, shouting hoarsely.

Men had rushed from everywhere, and Rock Mullaney, staring in shocked surprise, could only fumble at his belt. He wore no gun, either. He looked up at Ann. "We carried rifles," he muttered. "We never figgered on no trouble!" Then he rubbed his face, sense returning to his eyes. "Miss, what did he shoot him for?"

She stared at him, humbled by the grief written on the man's hard, lonely face. "That man, Barkow, killed my father," she said.

"No, miss. If yuh're Charlie Rodney's daughter, Charlie died aboard ship with us."

She nodded. "I know, but Barkow was responsible. Oh, I've been a fool! An awful fool!"

An officer was kneeling over Penn's body. He got up, glanced at Mullaney, then at Ann. "This man is dead," he said.

Resolution came suddenly to Ann. "Major," she said, "I'm going to catch the patrol. Will you lend me a fresh horse? Ours will still be badly worn out after last night."

"It wouldn't be safe, Miss Rodney," he protested. "It wouldn't at all. There's Indians out there. How Caradec got through, or you and Barkow, is beyond me." He gestured to the body. "What you know about this?"

Briefly, concisely she explained, telling all. She made no attempt to spare herself or to leave anything out. She outlined the entire affair, taking only a few minutes.

"I see." He looked thoughtfully at the gate. "If I could give you an escort, I would, but . . ."

"If she knows the way," Mullaney said, "I'll go with her. We came down the river from Fort Benton, then up the Yellowstone and the Powder. We thought we would come and see how Rafe was getting along. If we'd knowed there was trouble, we'd have come before."

"It's as much as your life is worth, man," the major warned.

Mullaney shrugged. "Like as not, but my life has had chances taken with it before. Besides,"—he ran his fingers over his bald head—"there's no scalp here to attract Indians."

Well-mounted, Ann and Mullaney rode swiftly. The patrol would be hurrying because of Bo Marsh's serious condition, but they should overtake them, and following was no immediate problem. Mullaney knew the West and had fought before in his life as a wandering jack-of-all-trades, and he was not upset by the chance they were taking. He glanced from time to time at Ann, then, rambling along, he began to give her an account of their life aboard ship, of the friendship that had grown between her father and Rafe Caradec, and all Rafe had done to spare the older man work and trouble. He told her how Rafe had treated Rodney's wounds when he had been beaten, how he had saved food for him, and how close the two had grown. Twice, noting her grief and shame, he ceased talking, but each time she insisted on his continuing.

"Caradec?" Mullaney said finally. "Well, I'd say he was one of the finest men I've known. A fighter, he is. The lad's a fighter from 'way back. Yuh should have seen the beatin' he gave that Borger! I got only a glimpse, but Penn told me about it. And if it hadn't been for Rafe, none us would have got away. He planned it, and he carried it out. He planned it before yore father's last trouble . . . the trouble that killed him . . . but when he saw yore father would die, he carried on with it."

They rode on in silence. All the time, Ann knew now, she should have trusted her instincts. Always they had warned her about Bruce Barkow, always they had been sure of Rafe Caradec. As she had sat in the jury box and watched him talk, handling his case, it had been his sincerity that had impressed her, even more than his shrewd handling of questions. He had killed men, yes. But what men! Bonaro and Trigger Boyne, both acknowledged and boastful killers of men themselves, men unfit to walk in the tracks of such as Rafe. She had to find him! She must!

The wind was chill, and she glanced at Mullaney. "It's cold!" she said. "It feels like snow!"

He nodded grimly. "It does that," he said. "Early for it, but it's happened before. If we get a norther now . . ." He shook his head.

They made camp while it was still light, and Mullaney built a fire of dry sticks that gave off almost no smoke. Water was heated, and they made coffee. While Ann was fixing the little food they had, he rubbed the horses down with handfuls of dry grass.

"Can yuh find yore way in the dark?" he asked her.

"Yes, I think so. It is fairly easy from here, for we have the mountains. That highest peak will serve as a landmark unless there are too many clouds."

"All right," he said, "we'll try to keep movin'."

She found herself liking the burly seaman and cowhand. He helped her smother the fire and wipe out traces of it.

"If we stick to the trail of the soldiers," he said, "it'll confuse the Injuns. They'll think we're with their party."

They started on. Ann led off, keeping the horses at a fast walk. Dusk came, and with it the wind grew stronger. After an hour of travel, Ann reined in.

Mullaney rode up beside her. "What's the matter?"

She indicated the tracks of a single horse crossing the route of the soldiers.

"Yuh think this is Barkow?" He nodded as an idea came. "It could be. The soldiers don't know what happened back there. He might ride with 'em for protection."

Another thought came to him. He looked at Ann keenly. "Suppose he'd try to kill Caradec?"

Her heart jumped. "Oh, no!" She was saying no to the thought, not to the possibility. She knew it was a possibility. What did Bruce have to lose? He was already a fugitive, and another killing would make it no worse. And Rafe Caradec had been the cause of it all.

"He might," she agreed. "He might, at that. . . ."

$$\bullet \quad \bullet \quad \bullet$$

Miles to the west, Bruce Barkow, his rifle across his saddle, leaned into the wind. He had followed the soldiers for a ways, and the idea of a snipe shot at Caradec stayed in his mind. He could do it, and they would think the Indians had done it. But there was a better way, a way to get at them all. If he could ride on ahead, reach Gill and Marsh before the patrol did, he might kill them, then get Caradec when he approached. If then he could get rid of Shute, Gomer would have to swing with him to save something from the mess. Maybe Dan Shute's idea was right, after all! Maybe killing was the solution.

Absorbed by the possibilities of the idea, Barkow turned off the route followed by the soldiers. There was a way that could make it safer, and somewhat faster. He headed for the old Bozeman Trail, now abandoned.

He gathered his coat around him to protect him from the increasing cold. His mind was fevered with worry, doubt of himself, and mingled with it was hatred of Caradec, Shute, Ann Rodney, and everyone and everything. He drove on into the night.

Twice, he stopped to rest. The second time he started on, it was turning gray with morning, and, as he swung into the saddle, a snowflake touched his cheek. He thought little of it. His horse was uneasy, though, and anxious for the trail. Snow was not a new thing, and Barkow scarcely noticed as the flakes began to come down thicker and faster.

Gill and the wounded man had disappeared, he knew. Shute's searchers had not found them near the house. Bruce Barkow had visited that house many times before the coming of Caradec, and he knew the surrounding hills well. About a half mile back from the house, sheltered by a thick growth of lodgepole pine, was a deep cave among some rocks. If Johnny Gill had found that cave, he might have moved Marsh there. It was, at least, a chance.

Bruce Barkow was not worried about the tracks he was leaving. Few Indians would be moving in this inclement weather, nor would the party from the fort have come this far north. From the route they had taken, he knew they were keeping to the low country. He was nearing the first range of foothills now, the hills that divided Long Valley from the open plain that sloped gradually away to the Powder and the old Bozeman Trail. He rode into the pines and started up the trail, intent upon death. His mind was sharpened like that of a hungry coyote. Cornered and defeated for the prize himself, his only way out, either for victory or revenge, lay in massacre, wholesale killing.

It was like him that having killed once, he did not hesitate to accept the idea of killing again. He did not see the big man on the gray horse who fell in behind him. He did not glance back over his trail, although by now the thickening snow obscured the background so much the rider, gaining slowly on him through the storm, would have been no more than a shadow.

To the right, behind the once bald and now snow-covered dome, was the black smear of seeping oil. Drawing abreast of it, Bruce Barkow reined in and glanced down. Here it was, the cause of it all. The key to wealth, to everything a man could want. Men had killed for less; he could kill for this. He knew where there were four other such seepages, and the oil sold from twenty dollars to thirty dollars a barrel.

He got down and stirred it with a stick. It was thick now, thickened by cold. Well, he still might win. Then he heard a shuffle of hoofs in the snow, and looked up. Dan Shute's figure was gigantic in the heavy coat he wore, sitting astride the big horse. He looked down at Barkow, and his lips parted.

"Tried to get away with her, did yuh? I knew yuh had coyote in yuh, Barkow."

His hand came up, and in the gloved hand was a pistol. In a sort of shocked disbelief, Bruce Barkow saw the gun lift. His own gun was under his short, thick coat.

"No!" he gasped hoarsely. "Not that! *Dan!*"

The last word was a scream, cut sharply off by the hard *bark* of the gun. Bruce Barkow folded slowly and, clutching his stomach, toppled across the black seepage, staining it with a slow shading of red.

For a minute, Dan Shute sat his horse, staring down. Then he turned the horse and moved on. He had an idea of his own. Before the storm began, from a mountain ridge he had picked out the moving patrol. Behind it were two figures. He had a hunch about those two riders, striving to overtake the patrol. He would see.

XVIII

Pushing rapidly ahead through the falling snow, the patrol came up to the ruins of the cabin on the Crazy Man on the morning of the second day out from the fort. Steam rose from the horses, and the breath of horses and men fogged the air. There was no sign of life. Rafe swung down, and stared about. The smooth surface of the snow was unbroken, yet he could see that much had happened since he started his trek to the fort for help. The lean-to, not quite complete, was abandoned.

Lieutenant Bryson surveyed the scene thoughtfully. "Are we too late?" he asked.

Caradec hesitated, staring around. There was no hope in what he saw. "I don't think so," he said. "Johnny Gill was a smart hand. He would figger out somethin', and, besides, I don't see any bodies."

In his mind, he surveyed the cañon. Certainly Gill could not have gone far with the wounded man. Also, it would have to be in the direction of possible shelter. The grove of lodgepoles offered the best chance. Turning, he walked toward them. Bryson dismounted his men, and they started fires.

Milton Waitt, the surgeon, stared after Rafe, then walked in his tracks. When he came up with him, he suggested: "Any caves around?"

Caradec paused, considering that. "There may be. None that I know of, though. Still, Johnny prowled in these rocks a lot and may have found one. Let's have a look." Then a thought occurred to him. "They'd have to have water, Doc. Let's go to the spring."

There was ice over it, but the ice had been broken and had frozen again. Rafe indicated it.

"Somebody drank here after the cold set in."

He knelt and felt of the snow with his fingers, working his way slowly around the spring. Suddenly he stopped.

"Found something?" Waitt watched curiously. This made no sense to him.

"Yes. Whoever got water from the spring splashed some on this side. It froze. I can feel the ice it made. That's a fair indication that whoever got water came from that side of the spring."

Moving around, he kept feeling of the snow. "Here." He felt again. "There's an icy ring where he set the bucket for a minute. Water left on the bottom froze." He straightened, studying the mountain side. "He's up here, somewheres. He's got a bucket, and he's able to come down here for water, but findin' him'll be the devil's own job. He'll need fuel, though. Somewhere he's been breakin' sticks and collectin' wood, but wherever he does, it won't be close to his shelter. Gill's too smart for that."

Studying the hillside, Rafe indicated the nearest clump of trees.

"He wouldn't want to be out in the open on this snow any longer than he had to," he said thoughtfully, "and the chances are he'd head for the shelter of those trees. When he got there, he would probably set the bucket down while he studied the back trail and made shore he hadn't been seen."

Waitt nodded, his interest aroused. "Good reasoning, man. Let's see."

They walked to the clump of trees, and, after a few minutes' search, Waitt found the same icy frozen place just under the thin skimming of snow. "Where do we go from here?" he asked.

Rafe hesitated, studying the trees. A man would automatically follow the line of easiest travel, and there was an opening between the trees. He started on, then stopped. "This is right. See? There's not so much snow on this branch. There's a good chance he brushed it off in passin'."

It was mostly guesswork, he knew. Yet, after they had gone three hundred yards, Rafe looked up and saw the cliff pushing its rocky shoulder in among the trees. At its base was a tumbled cluster of gigantic boulders and broken slabs. He led off for the rocks, and almost the first thing he saw was a fragment of loose bark lying on the snow, and a few crumbs of dust such as is sometimes found between the bark and tree. He pointed it out to Waitt.

"He carried wood this way."

They paused there, and Rafe sniffed the air. There was no smell of wood smoke. Were they dead? Had cold done what rifle bullets couldn't do? No, he decided, Johnny Gill knew too well how to take care of himself.

Rafe walked between the rocks, turning where it felt natural to turn. Suddenly he saw a tipped-up slab of granite leaning against a larger boulder. It looked dry underneath. He stooped and glanced in. It was dark and silent, yet some instinct seemed to tell him it was not so empty as it appeared.

He crouched in the opening, leaving light from outside to come in first along one wall, then another. His keen eyes picked out a damp spot on the leaves. There was no place for a leak, and the wind had been in the wrong direction to blow in here.

"Snow," he said. "Probably fell off a boot."

They moved into the cave, bending over to walk. Yet it was not really a cave at first, merely a slab of rock offering partial shelter. About fifteen feet farther along the slab ended under a thick growth of pine boughs and brush that formed a canopy overhead, offering almost as solid shelter as the stone itself. Then, in the rock face of the cliff, they saw a cave, a place gouged by wind and water long since and completely obscured behind the boulders and brush from any view but from where they stood.

They walked up to the entrance. The overhang of the cliff offered a shelter that was all of fifty feet deep, running along one wall of a diagonal gash in the cliff that was invisible from outside. They stepped in on the dry sand, and had taken only a step when they smelled wood smoke. At almost the same instant, Johnny Gill spoke.

"Hi, Rafe!" He stepped down from behind a heap of débris against one wall of the rock fissure. "I couldn't see who yuh were till now. I had my rifle ready so's if yuh was the wrong one, I could plumb discourage yuh." His face looked drawn and tired. "He's over here, Doc," Gill continued, "and he's been delirious all night."

While Waitt was busy over the wounded man, Gill walked back up the cave with Rafe.

"What's happened," Gill asked. "I thought they'd got yuh."

"No, they haven't, but I don't know much of what's been goin' on. Ann's at the fort with Barkow, says she's goin' to marry him."

"What about Tex?" Gill asked quickly.

Rafe shook his head, scowling. "No sign of him. I don't know what's come off at Painted Rock. I'm leavin' for there as soon as I've told the lieutenant and his patrol where Doc is. You'll have to stick here because the Doc has to get back to the fort."

"You goin' to Painted Rock?"

"Yes. I'm goin' to kill Dan Shute."

"I'd like to see that," Gill said grimly, "but watch yoreself!" The little cowhand looked at him seriously. "Boss, what about that girl?"

Rafe's lips tightened, and he stared at the bare wall of the cave. "I don't know," he said grimly. "I tried to talk her out of it, but I guess I wasn't what you'd call tactful."

Gill stuck his thumbs in his belt. "Tell her yuh're in love with her yoreself?"

Caradec stared at him. "Where'd yuh get that idea?"

"Readin' signs. Yuh ain't been the same since yuh ran into her the first time. She's yore kind of people, boss."

"Mebbe. But looks like she reckoned she wasn't. Never would listen to me give the straight story on her father. Both of us flew off the handle this time."

"Well, I ain't no hand at ridin' herd on women folks, but I've seen a thing or two, boss. The chances are, if yuh'd 'a' told her yuh're in love with her, she'd never have gone with Bruce Barkow."

Rafe was remembering those words when he rode down the trail toward Painted Rock. What lay ahead of him could not be planned. He had no idea when or where he would encounter Dan Shute. He knew only that he must find him.

After reporting to Bryson so he wouldn't worry about the doctor, Rafe had hit the trail for Painted Rock alone. By now he knew that mountain trail well, and even the steady fall of snow failed to make him change his mind about making the ride.

He was burning up inside. The old, driving recklessness was in him, the urge to be in and shooting. His enemies were in the clear, and all the cards were on the table in plain sight. Barkow he discounted. Dan Shute was the man to get, and Pod Gomer the man to watch. What he intended to do was as high-handed in its way as what Shute and Barkow had attempted, but in Rafe's case the cause was just.

Mullaney stopped in a wooded draw short of the hills. The pause was for a short rest just before daybreak on that fatal second morning. The single rider had turned off from the trail and was no longer with the patrol. Both he and the girl needed rest, aside from the horses.

He kicked snow away from the grass, then swept some of it clear with a branch. In most places it was already much too thick for that. After he made coffee, and they had eaten, he got up.

"Get ready," he said, "and I'll get the hosses."

All night he had been thinking of what he would do when he found Barkow. He had seen the man draw on Penn, and he was not fast. That made it an even break, for Mullaney knew that he was not fast himself.

When he found the horses missing, he stopped. Evidently they had pulled their picket pins and wandered off. He started on, keeping in their tracks. He did not see the big man in the heavy coat who stood in the brush and watched him go.

Dan Shute threaded his way down to the campfire. When Ann looked up at his approach, she thought it was Mullaney, and then she saw Shute. Eyes wide, she came to her feet. "Why, hello! What are you doing here?"

He smiled at her, his eyes sleepy and yet wary. "Huntin' you. Reckoned this was you. When I seen Barkow, I reckoned somethin' had gone wrong."

"You saw Bruce? Where?"

"North a ways. He won't bother yuh none." Shute smiled. "Barkow was spineless. Thought he was smart. He never was half as smart as that Caradec, nor as tough as me."

"What happened?" Ann's heart was pounding. Mullaney should be coming now. He would hear their voices and be warned.

"I killed him." Shute was grinning cynically. "He wasn't much good. Don't be wonderin' about that *hombre* with yuh. I led the hosses off and turned his adrift. He'll be hours catchin' it, if he ever does. However, he might come back, so we'd better drift."

"No," Ann said, "I'll wait."

He smiled. "Better come quiet. If he came back, I'd have to kill him. Yuh don't want him killed, do yuh?"

She hesitated only a moment. This man would stop at nothing. He was going to take her if he had to knock her out and tie her. Better anything than that. If she appeared to play along, she might have a chance. "I'll go," she said simply. "You have a horse?"

"I kept yores," he said. "Mount up."

XIX

By the time Rafe Caradec was *en route* to Painted Rock, Dan Shute was riding with his prisoner into the ranch yard of his place near Painted Rock. Far to the south and west, Rock Mullaney long since had come up to the place where Shute had finally turned his horse loose and ridden on, leading the other. Mullaney kept on the trail of the lone horse and came up with it almost a mile farther.

Lost and alone in the thickly falling snow, the animal hesitated at his call, then waited for him to catch up. When he was mounted once more, he turned back to his camp, and the tracks, nearly covered, told him little. The girl, accompanied by another rider, had ridden away. She would never have gone willingly.

Mullaney was worried. During the travel they had talked little, yet Ann had supplied a few of the details, and he knew vaguely about Dan Shute, about Bruce Barkow. He also knew, having heard all about it long before reaching the fort, that an Indian outbreak was feared.

Mullaney knew something about Indians, and doubted any trouble until spring or summer. There might be occasional shootings, but Indians were not as a rule cold-weather fighters. For that, he didn't blame them. Yet any wandering, hunting, or foraging parties must be avoided, and it was probable that any warrior or group of them coming along a fresh trail would fail to follow it and count coup on an enemy if possible.

He knew roughly the direction of Painted Rock, yet instinct told him he'd better stick to the tangible and near, so he swung back to the trail of the Army patrol and headed for the pass into Lone Valley.

Painted Rock lay still under the falling snow when Rafe Caradec drifted down the street in front of the Emporium, and went in. Baker looked up, and his eyes grew alert when he saw Rafe. At Caradec's question, he told him of what had happened to Tex Brisco so far as he knew, of the killing of Blazer, McCabe, and Gorman, and Brisco's escape while apparently wounded. He also told him of Dan Shute's arrival and threat to Ann, and her subsequent escape with Barkow. Baker was relieved to know they were at the fort.

A wind was beginning to moan around the eaves, and they listened a moment.

"Won't be good to be out in that," the store-keeper said gravely. "Sounds like a blizzard comin'. If Brisco's found shelter, he might be all right."

"Not in this cold," Caradec said, scowling. "No man with his resistance lowered by a wound is going to last in this. It's going to be worse before it's better."

Standing there at the counter, letting the warmth of the big potbellied stove work through his system, Rafe assayed his position. Bo Marsh, while in bad shape, had been tended by a doctor and would have Gill's care. There was nothing more to be done there for the time being. Ann had made her choice. She had gone off with Barkow, and in his heart he knew that if there was any choice between the two—Barkow or Shute—she had made the better. Yet there had been another choice. Or had there? Yes, she could at least have listened to him.

The fort was not far away, and all he could do now was trust to Ann's innate good sense to change her mind before it was too late. In any event, he could not get back there in time to do anything about it.

"Where's Shute?" he demanded.

"Ain't seen him," Baker said worriedly. "Ain't seen hide nor hair of him. But I can promise yuh one thing, Caradec. He won't take Barkow's runnin' out with Ann lyin' down. He'll be on their trail."

The door opened in a flurry of snow, and Pat Higley pushed in. He pulled off his mittens and extended stiff fingers toward the red swell of the stove. He glanced at Rafe.

"Hear yuh askin' about Shute?" he asked. "I just seen him, headed for the ranch. He wasn't alone, neither." He rubbed his fingers. "Looked to me like a woman ridin' along."

Rafe looked around. "A woman?" he asked carefully. "Now who would that be?"

"He's found Ann!" Baker exclaimed.

"She was at the fort," Rafe said, "with Barkow. He couldn't take her away from the soldiers."

"No, he couldn't," Baker agreed, "but she might have left on her own. She's a stubborn girl when she takes a notion. After you left, she may have changed her mind."

Rafe pushed the thought away. The chance was too slight. And where was Tex Brisco? "Baker," he suggested, "you and Higley know this country. You know about Tex. Where do you reckon he'd wind up?"

Higley shrugged. "There's no tellin'. It ain't as if he knew the country, too. They trailed him for a while, and they said it looked like his hoss was wanderin' loose without no hand on the bridle. Then the hoss took to the water, so Brisco must have come to his senses somewhat. Anyway, they lost his trail when he was ridin' west along a fork of Clear Creek. If he held to that direction, it would take him over some plumb high, rough country south of the big peak. If he did get across, he'd wind up somewheres down along Tensleep Cañon, mebbe. But that's all guesswork."

"Any shelter that way?"

"Nary a mite. Not if yuh mean human shelter. There's plenty of shelter there, but wolves, too. There's also plenty of shelter in the rocks. The only humans over that way are the Sioux, and they ain't in what yuh'd call a friendly mood. That's where Man-Afraid-Of-His-Hoss has been holed up."

Finding Tex Brisco would be like hunting a needle in a haystack and worse, but it was what Rafe Caradec had to do. He had to make an effort, anyway. Yet the thought of Dan Shute and the girl returned to him. Suppose it was Ann? He shuddered to think of her in Shute's hands. The man was without a spark of decency or mercy. Not even his best friends would deny that.

"No use goin' out in this storm," Baker said. "Yuh can stay with us, Caradec."

"You've changed your tune some, Baker," Rafe suggested grimly.

"A man can be wrong, can't he?" Baker inquired testily. "Mebbe I was. I don't know. Things have gone to perdition around here fast, ever since you came in here with that story about Rodney."

"Well, I'm not stayin'," Rafe told him. "I'm going to look for Tex Brisco."

The door was pushed open, and they looked around. It was Pod Gomer. The sheriff looked even squarer and more bulky in a heavy buffalo coat. He cast a bleak look at Caradec, then walked to the fire, sliding out of his overcoat. "You still here?" he asked, glancing at Rafe out of the corners of his eyes.

"Yes, I'm still here, Gomer, but you're traveling."

"What?"

"You heard me. You can wait till the storm is over, then get out, and keep movin'."

Gomer turned, his square, hard face dark with angry blood. "You . . . tellin' me?" he said furiously. "I'm sheriff here!"

"You were," Caradec said calmly. "Ever since

you've been hand in glove with Barkow and Shute, runnin' their dirty errands for them, pickin' up the scraps they tossed you. Well, the fun's over. You slope out of here when the storm's over. Barkow's gone, and within a few hours Shute will be, too."

"Shute?" Gomer was incredulous. "Yuh'd go up against Dan Shute? Why, man, yuh're insane!"

"Am I?" Rafe shrugged. "That's neither here nor there. I'm talkin' to you. Get out and stay out. You can take your tinhorn judge with you."

Gomer laughed. "You're the one who's through! Marsh dead, Brisco either dead or on the dodge, and Gill mebbe dead. What chance have you got?"

"Gill's in as good a shape as I am," Rafe said calmly, "and Bo Marsh is gettin' Army care, and he'll be out of the woods, too. As for Tex, I don't know. He got away, and I'm bankin' on that Texan to come out walkin'. How much stomach are your boys goin' to have for the fight when Gill and I ride in here? Tom Blazer's gone, and so are a half dozen more. Take your coat"—Rafe picked it up with his left hand—"and get out. If I see you after this storm, I'm shootin' on sight. Now, get!"

He heaved the heavy coat at Gomer, and the sheriff ducked, his face livid. Yet, surprisingly, he did not reach for a gun. He lunged and swung with his fist. A shorter man than Caradec, he was wider and thicker, a powerfully built man who was known in mining and trail camps as a rough-and-tumble fighter.

Caradec turned, catching Gomer's right on the cheekbone, but bringing up a solid punch to Gomer's midsection. The sheriff lunged close and tried to butt, and Rafe stabbed him in the face with a left, then smeared him with a hard right.

It was no match. Pod Gomer had fancied himself as a fighter, but Caradec had too much experience. He knocked Gomer back into a heap of sacks, then walked in on him, and slugged him wickedly in the middle with both hands. Gomer went to his knees.

"All right, Pod," Rafe said, panting, "I told you. Get goin'."

The sheriff stayed on his knees, breathing heavily, blood dripping from his smashed nose. Rafe Caradec slipped on his coat and walked to the door.

Outside, he took the horse to the livery stable, brushed him off, then gave him a rub-down and some oats.

He did not return to the store but, after a meal, saddled his horse and headed for Dan Shute's ranch. He couldn't escape the idea that the rider with Shute may have been Ann, despite the seeming impossibility of her being this far west. If she had left the fort within a short time after the patrol, then it might be, but there was small chance of that. Barkow would never return, having managed to get that far away. There was no one else at the fort to bring her. Scouts had said that a party of travelers was coming up from the river, but there would be small chance that any of them would push on to Painted Rock in this weather.

Dan Shute's ranch lay in a hollow of the hills near a curving stream. Not far away, the timber ran down to the plain's edge and dwindled away into a few scattered groves, blanketed now in snow. A thin trail of smoke lifted from the chimney of the house, and another from the bunkhouse. Rafe Caradec decided on boldness as the best course and his muffled, snow-covered appearance to disguise him until within gun range. He opened a button on the front of his coat so he could get at a gun thrust into his waistband. He removed his right hand from the glove and thrust it deeply in his pocket. There it would be warm and at the same time free to grasp the six-gun when he needed it.

No one showed. It was very cold, and, if there was anyone around and they noticed his approach, their curiosity did not extend to the point where they would come outside to investigate. Rafe strode directly to the house, walked up on the porch, and rapped on the door with his left hand. There was no response. He rapped again, much harder.

All was silence. The mounting wind made

hearing difficult, but he put his ear to the door and listened. There was no sound.

He dropped his left hand to the door and turned the knob. The door opened easily, and he let it swing wide, standing well out of line. The wind howled in, and a few flakes of snow, but there was no sound. He stepped inside and closed the door after him.

His ears tingled with cold, and he resisted a desire to rub them, then let his eyes sweep the wide room. A fire burned on the huge stone fireplace, but there was no one in the long room. Two exits from the room were hung with blankets. There was a table, littered with odds and ends, and one end held some dirty dishes where a hasty meal had been eaten. Beneath that spot was a place showing dampness as though a pair of boots had shed melting snow.

There was no sound in the living room but the crackle of the fire and the low moan of the wind around the eaves. Walking warily, Rafe stepped over a saddle and some bits of harness and walked across to the opposite room. He pushed the blanket aside. Empty. There was an unmade bed of tumbled blankets and a lamp standing on a table by the bed.

Rafe turned and stared at the other door, then looked back into the bedroom. There was a pair of dirty socks lying there, and he stepped over and felt of them. They were damp. Someone, within the last hour or less, had changed socks here. Walking outside, he noticed something he had not seen before. Below a chair near the table was another spot of dampness. Apparently two people had been here.

He stepped back into the shadow of the bedroom door and put his hand in the front of his coat. He hadn't wanted to reach for that gun in case anyone was watching. Now, with his hand on the gun, he stepped out of the bedroom and walked to the other blanket-covered door. He pushed it aside.

A large kitchen. A fire glowed in the huge sheet-metal stove, and there was a coffee pot filled with boiling coffee. Seeing, it, Rafe let go of his gun and picked up a cup. When he had filled it, he looked around the unkempt room. Like the rest of the house it was strongly built, but poorly kept inside. The floor was dirty, and dirty dishes and scraps of food were around.

He lifted the coffee cup, then his eyes saw a bit of white. He put down the cup and stepped over to the end of the woodpile. His heart jumped. It was a woman's handkerchief!

XX

Quickly Rafe Caradec glanced around. Again he looked at the handkerchief in his hand, and lifted it to his nostrils. There was a faint whiff of perfume—a perfume he remembered only too well. She had been here, then. The other rider with Dan Shute had been Ann Rodney. But where was she now? Where could she be? What had happened?

He gulped a mouthful of the hot coffee, and stared around again. The handkerchief had been near the back door. He put down the coffee, and eased the door open. Beyond were the barn and a corral. He walked outside and, pushing through the curtain of blowing snow, reached the corral, and then the barn.

Several horses were there. Hurrying along, he found two with dampness marking the places where their saddles had been. There were no saddles showing any evidence of having been ridden, and the saddles would be sweaty underneath if they had been. Evidently two horses had been saddled and ridden away from this barn.

Scowling, Rafe stared around. In the dust of the floor he found a small track, almost obliterated by a larger one. Had Shute saddled two horses and taken the girl away? If so, where would he take her, and why? He decided suddenly that Shute had not taken Ann from here. She must have slipped away, saddled a horse, and escaped. It was a far-fetched conclusion, but it offered not only the solution he wanted, but one that fitted with the few facts available or, at least, with the logic of the situation. Why would Shute take the girl away from his home ranch? There was no logical reason. Especially in such a storm as this when so far as Shute knew there would be no pursuit? Rafe himself would not have done it. Perhaps he had been overconfident, believing that Ann would rather share the warmth and security of the house than the mounting blizzard.

Only the bunkhouse remained unexplored. There was a chance they had gone there. Turning, Rafe walked to the bunkhouse. Shoving the door open, he stepped inside. Four men sat on bunks, and one, his boots off and his socks propped toward the stove, stared glumly at him from a chair made of a barrel. The faces of all the men were familiar, but he could put a name to none of them. They had seen the right hand in the front of his coat, and they sat quietly appreciating its significance.

"Where's Dan Shute?" he demanded.

"Ain't seen him," said the man in the barrel chair.

"That go for all of you?" Rafe's eyes swung from one to the other.

A lean, hard-faced man with a scar on his jaw-bone grinned, showing yellow teeth. He raised himself on his elbow. "Why, no. It shore don't, pilgrim. I seen him. He rode up here nigh onto an hour ago with that there girl from the store. They went inside. S'pose you want to get killed, you go to the house."

"I've been there. It's empty."

The lean-faced man sat up. "That right? That don't make sense. Why would a man with a filly like that go off into the storm?"

Rafe Caradec studied them coldly. "You men," he said, "had better get out of here when the storm's over. Dan Shute's through."

"Ain't yuh countin' unbranded stock, pardner?" the lean-faced man said, smiling tauntingly. "Dan Shute's able to handle his own troubles. He took care of Barkow."

This was news to Rafe. "He did! How'd you know that?"

"He done told me. Barkow was with this girl, and Shute trailed him. I didn't only see Shute come back, I talked some with him, and I unsaddled his hosses." He picked up a boot and pulled it on. "This here Rodney girl, she left the fort, runnin' away from Barkow and takin' after the Army patrol that rode out with you. Shute, he seen 'em. He also seen Barkow. He hunted Bruce down and shot him near that bare dome in your lower valley, and then he left Barkow and caught up with the girl and this strange *hombre* with her. Shute led their hosses off, then got the girl while this *hombre* was huntin' the hosses."

The explanation cleared up several points for Rafe. He stared thoughtfully around. "You didn't see 'em leave here?"

"Not us," the lean-faced 'puncher said dryly. "None of us hired on for punchin' cows or ridin' herd on women in blizzards. Come a storm, we hole up and set her out. We aim to keep on doin' just that."

Rafe backed to the door and stepped out. The wind tore at his garments, and he backed away from the building. Within twenty feet it was lost behind a curtain of blowing snow. He stumbled back to the house.

More than ever, he was convinced that somehow Ann had escaped. Yet where to look? In this storm there was no direction, nothing. If she headed for town, she might make it. However, safety for her would more likely lie toward the mountains, for there she could improvise shelter, and probably could last the storm out. Knowing the country, she would know how long such storms lasted. It was rarely more than three days.

He had little hope of finding Ann, yet he knew she would never return here. Seated in the ranch house, he coolly ate a hastily picked-up meal and drank more coffee. Then he returned to his horse that he had led to the stable. Mounting, he rode out into the storm on the way to town.

Gene Baker and Pat Higley looked up when Rafe Caradec came in. Baker's face paled when he saw that Rafe was alone. "Did yuh find out?" he asked. "Was it Ann?"

Briefly Rafe explained, telling all he had learned and his own speculations as to what had happened.

"She must have plumb got away," Higley agreed. "Shute would never take her away from his ranch in this storm. But where could she have gone?"

Rafe explained his own theories on that. "She probably took it for granted he would think she would head for town," he suggested, "so she may have taken to the mountains. After all, she would know that Shute would kill anybody who tried to stop him."

Gene Baker nodded miserably. "That's right, and what can a body do?"

"Wait," Higley said. "Just wait."

"I won't wait," Rafe said. "If she shows up here, hold her. Shoot Dan if you have to, dry-gulch him or anything. Get him out of the way. I'm goin' into the mountains. I can at least be lookin', and I might stumble onto some kind of a trail. . . ."

Two hours later, shivering with cold, Rafe Caradec acknowledged how foolhardy he had been. His black horse was walking steadily through a snow-covered avenue among the pines, weaving around fallen logs and clumps of brush. He had found nothing that resembled a trail, and twice he had crossed the stream. This, he knew, was also the direction that had been taken by the wounded Tex Brisco.

No track could last more than a minute in the whirling snow-filled world in which Rafe now rode. The wind howled and tore at his garments, even here, within the partial shelter of the lodgepoles. Yet he rode on, then dismounted, and walked ahead, resting the horse. It was growing worse instead of better, yet he pushed on, taking the line of least resistance, sure that this was what the fleeing Ann would have done.

The icy wind ripped at his clothing, at times faced him like a solid, moving wall. The black stumbled wearily, and Rafe was suddenly contrite. The big horse had taken a brutal beating in these last few days, and even its great strength was weakening.

Squinting his eyes against the blowing snow, he remounted and stared ahead. He could see nothing, but he was aware that the wall of the mountain was on his left. Bearing in that direction, he came up to a thicker stand of trees and some scattered boulders. He rode on, alert for some possible shelter for himself and his horse.

Almost an hour later, he found it, a dry, sandy

place under the overhang of the cliff, sheltered from the wind and protected from the snow by the overhang and by the trees and brush that fronted it. Swinging down, Rafe led the horse into the shelter and hastily built a fire.

From the underside of a log he got some bark, great sheets of it, and some fibrous, rotting wood. Then he broke some low branches on the trees, dead and dry. In a few minutes his fire was burning nicely. Then he stripped the saddle from the horse and rubbed him down with a handful of crushed bark. When that was done, he got out the nosebag and fed the horse some of the oats he had appropriated from Shute's barn.

The next hour he occupied himself in gathering fuel. Luckily there were a number of dead trees close by, débris left from some landslide from up the mountain. He settled down by the fire, made coffee. Dozing against the rock, he fed the blaze intermittently, his mind far away.

Somehow, sometime, he fell asleep. Around the rocks the wind, moaning and whining, sought with icy fingers for a grasp at his shoulder, at his hands. But the log burned well, and the big horse stood close, stamping in the sand and dozing beside the man on the ground.

Once, starting from his sleep, Rafe noticed that the log had burned until it was out of the fire, so he dragged it around, then laid another across it. Soon he was again asleep.

He awakened suddenly. It was daylight, and the storm was still raging. His fire blazed among the charred embers of his logs, and he lifted his eyes. Six Indians faced him beyond the fire, and their rifles and bows covered him. Their faces were hard and unreadable. Two stepped forward and jerked him to his feet, stripped his guns from him, and motioned for him to saddle his horse.

Numb with cold, he could scarcely realize what had happened to him. One of the Indians, wrapped in a worn red blanket, jabbered at the others and kept pointing to the horse, making threatening gestures. Yet when Rafe had the animal saddled, they motioned to him to mount. Two of the Indians rode up then, leading the horses of the others. So this was the way it ended. He was a prisoner.

XXI

Uncomprehending, Rafe Caradec opened his eyes to darkness. He sat up abruptly and stared around. Then, after a long minute, it came to him. He was a prisoner in a village of the Oglala Sioux, and he had just awakened. Two days before they had brought him here, bound him hand and foot, and left him in the teepee he now occupied. Several times squaws had entered the teepee and departed. They had given him food and water.

It was night, and his wrists were swollen from the tightness of the bonds. It was warm in the teepee, for there was a fire, but smoke filled the skin wigwam and filtered out at the top. He had a feeling it was almost morning.

What had happened at Painted Rock? Where was Ann? And where was Tex Brisco? Had Dan Shute returned?

He was rolling over toward the entrance to catch a breath of fresh air when the flap was drawn back and a squaw came in. She spoke rapidly in Sioux, then picked a brand from the fire, and, as it blazed up, held it close to his face. He drew back, thinking she meant to sear his eyes. Then, looking beyond the blaze, he saw that the squaw holding it was the Indian girl he had saved from Trigger Boyne!

With a burst of excited talk, she bent over him. A knife slid under his bonds, and they were cut. Chafing his ankles, he looked up. In the flare of the torchlight he could now see the face of a male Indian.

He spoke, gutturally, but in fair English. "My daughter say you man help her," he said.

"Yes," Rafe replied. "The Sioux are not my enemies, nor am I theirs."

"Your name Caradec." The Indian's statement was flat, not to be contradicted.

"Yes." Rafe stumbled to his feet, rubbing his wrists.

"We know your horse, also the horses of the others."

"Others?" Rafe asked quickly. "There are others here?"

"Yes, a woman and a man. The man is much better. He had been injured."

Ann and Tex! Rafe's heart leaped.

"May I see them?" he asked. "They are my friends."

The Indian nodded. He studied Rafe for a minute. "I think you are good man. My name Man-Afraid-Of-His-Horse."

The Oglala chief! Rafe looked again at the Indian. "I know the name. With Red Cloud you are the greatest of the Sioux."

The chief nodded. "There are others. John Grass, Gall, Crazy Horse, many others. The Sioux have many great men."

The girl led Rafe away to the tent where he found Tex Brisco, lying on a pile of skins and blankets. Tex was pale, but he grinned when Rafe came in.

"Man," he said, "it's good to see yuh! And here's Ann!"

Rafe turned to look at her, and she smiled, then held out her hand. "I have learned how foolish I was. First from Penn, and then from Mullaney and Tex."

"Penn? Mullaney?" Rafe squinted his eyes. "Are they here?"

Quickly Ann explained about Barkow's killing of Penn, and her subsequent attempt to overtake Bruce, guided and helped by Rock Mullaney.

"Barkow's dead," Rafe said. "Shute killed him."

"Ann told me," Tex said. "He had it comin'. Where's Dan Shute now?"

Caradec shrugged. "I don't know, but I'm goin' to find out."

"Please." Ann came to him. "Don't fight with him, Rafe. There has been enough killing. You might be hurt, and I couldn't stand that."

He looked at her. "Does it matter so much?"

Her eyes fell. "Yes," she said simply, "it does. . . ."

Painted Rock lay quietly in a world of white, its shabbiness lost under the purity of freshly fallen snow. Escorted by a band of Oglalas, Ann, Rafe, and Tex rode to the edge of town, then said a quick good-bye to the friendly warriors. The street was empty, and the town seemed to have no word of their coming.

Tex Brisco, still weak from loss of blood and looking pale, brought up the rear. With Ann, he headed right for the Emporium. Rafe Caradec rode ahead until they neared the National Saloon, then swung toward the boardwalk, and waited until they had gone by.

Baker came rushing from the store and, with Ann's help, got Tex down from the horse and inside.

Rafe Caradec led his own horse down the street and tied it to the hitching rail. Then he glanced up and down the street, looking for Shute. Within a matter of minutes Dan would know he was back, and, once he was aware of it, there would be trouble.

Pat Higley was inside the store when Rafe entered. He nodded at Rafe's story of what had taken place.

"Shute's been back in town," Higley said. "I reckon after he lost Ann in the snowstorm he figgered she would circle around and come back here."

"Where's Pod Gomer?" Rafe inquired.

"If yuh mean has he taken out, why I can tell yuh he hasn't," Baker said. "He's been around with Shute, and he's wearin' double hardware right now."

Higley nodded. "They ain't goin' to give up without a fight," he warned. "They're keepin' some men in town, quite a bunch of 'em."

Rafe also nodded. "That will end as soon Shute's out of the way."

He looked up as the door pushed open, and started to his feet when Johnny Gill walked in with Rock Mullaney.

"The soldiers rigged a sled," Gill announced at

once. "They're takin' Bo back to the fort, so we reckoned it might be a good idea to come down here and stand by in case of trouble."

Ann came to the door, and stood there by the curtain, watching them. Her eyes continually strayed to Rafe, and he looked up, meeting their glance. Ann flushed and looked away, then invited him to join her for coffee.

Excusing himself, he got up and went inside. Gravely Ann showed him to a chair, brought him a napkin, then poured coffee for him, and put sugar and cream beside his cup. He took the sugar, then looked up at her.

"Can you ever forgive me?" she asked.

"There's nothin' to forgive," he said. "I couldn't blame you. You were sure your father was dead."

"I didn't know why the property should cause all that trouble until I heard of the oil. Is it really worth so much?"

"Quite a lot. Shippin' is a problem now, but that will be taken care of soon. So it could be worth a great deal of money. I expect they knew more about that end of it than we did." Rafe looked at her. "I never aimed to claim my half of the ranch," he said, "and I don't now. I accepted it just to give me some kind of a legal basis for workin' with you, but now that the trouble is over, I'll give you the deed, the will your father made out, and the other papers."

"Oh, no!" she exclaimed quickly. "You mustn't!

I'll need your help to handle things, and you must accept your part of the ranch and stay on. That is," she added, "if you don't think I'm too awful for the way I acted."

He flushed. "I don't think you're awful, Ann," he said clumsily, getting to his feet. "I think you're wonderful. I guess I always have, ever since that first day when I came into the store and saw you." His eyes strayed, and carried their glance out the window. He came to with a start and got to his feet. "There's Dan Shute," he said. "I got to go."

Ann arose with him, white to the lips. He avoided her glance, then turned abruptly toward the door. The girl made no protest, but as he started through the curtain, she said: "Come back, Rafe. I'll be waiting."

He walked to the street door, and the others saw him go, then something in his manner apprised them of what was about to happen. Mullaney caught up his rifle and started for the door, also, and Baker reached for a scattergun.

Rafe Caradec glanced quickly at the snow-covered street. One wagon had been down the center of the street about daybreak, and there had been no other traffic except for a few passing riders. Horses stood in front of the National and the Emporium and had kicked up the snow, but otherwise it was an even, unbroken expanse of pure white.

Rafe stepped out on the porch of the Emporium. Dan Shute's gray was tied at the National's hitching rail, but Shute was nowhere in sight. Rafe walked to the corner of the store, his feet crunching on the snow. The sun was coming out, and the snow might soon be gone. As he thought of that, a drop fell from the roof overhead and touched him on the neck.

Dan Shute would be in the National. Rafe walked slowly down the walk to the saloon and pushed open the door. Joe Benson looked up from behind his bar, and hastily moved down toward the other end. Pod Gomer, slumped in a chair at a table across the room, sat up abruptly, his eyes shifting to the big man at the bar.

Dan Shute's back was to the room. In his short, thick coat he looked enormous. His hat was off, and his shock of blond hair, coarse and uncombed, glinted in the sunlight.

Rafe stopped inside the door, his gaze sweeping the room in one all-encompassing glance. Then his eyes riveted on the big man at the bar.

"All right, Shute," he said calmly. "Turn around and take it."

Dan Shute turned, and he was grinning. He was grinning widely, but there was a wicked light dancing in his eyes. He stared at Caradec, letting his slow, insolent gaze go over him from head to foot.

"Killin' yuh would be too easy," he said. "I

promised myself that when the time came I would take yuh apart with my hands, and then, if there was anything left, shoot it full of holes. I'm goin' to kill yuh, Caradec."

Out of the tail of his eye, Rafe saw that Johnny Gill was leaning against the jamb of the back door, and that Rock Mullaney was just inside of that same door.

"Take off your guns, Caradec, and I'll kill yuh," Shute said softly.

"It's their fight," Gill said suddenly. "Let 'em have it the way they want it!"

The voice startled Gomer so that he jerked, and he glanced over his shoulder, his face white. Then the front door pushed open, and Higley came in with Baker. Pod Gomer touched his lips with his tongue and shot a sidelong glance at Benson. The saloonkeeper looked unhappy.

Carefully Dan Shute reached for his belt buckle and unbuckled the twin belts, laying the big guns on the bar, butts toward him. At the opposite end of the bar, Rafe Caradec did the same. Then, as one man, they shed their coats.

Lithe and broad-shouldered, Rafe was an inch shorter and forty pounds lighter than the other man. Narrow-hipped and lean as a greyhound, he was built for speed, but the powerful shoulders and powerful hands and arms spoke of years of training as well as hard work with a double jack, axe, or heaving at heavy, wet lines of a ship.

Dan Shute's neck was thick, his chest broad and massive. His stomach was flat and hard. His hands were big, and he reeked of sheer animal strength and power. Licking his lips like a hungry wolf, he started forward. He was grinning, and the light was dancing in his hard gray-white eyes. He did not rush or leap. He walked right up to Rafe, with that grin on his lips, and Caradec stood flat-footed, waiting for him. But as Shute stepped in close, Rafe suddenly whipped up a left to the wind that beat the man to the punch. Shute winced at the blow, and his eyes narrowed. Then he smashed forward with his hard skull, trying for a butt. Rafe clipped him with an elbow and swung away, keeping out of the corner.

XXII

Still grinning, Dan Shute moved in. The big man was deceptively fast, and, as he moved in, suddenly he left his feet and hurled himself feet foremost at Rafe. Caradec sprang back, but too slowly. The legs jack-knifed around him, and Rafe staggered and went to the floor. He hit hard, and Dan was the first to move. Throwing himself over, he caught his weight on his left hand and swung with his right. It was a wicked, half-arm blow, and it caught Rafe on the chin. Lights exploded in his brain, and he felt himself go down. Then Shute sprang for him.

Rafe rolled his head more by instinct than knowledge, and the blow clipped his ear. He threw his feet high, and tipped Dan over on his head and off his body. Both men came to their feet like cats and hurled themselves at each other. They struck like two charging bulls with an impact that shook the room.

Rafe slugged a right to the wind and took a smashing blow to the head. They backed off, then charged together, and both men started pitching them—short, wicked hooks thrown from the hips with everything they had in the world in every punch. Rafe's head was roaring, and he felt the smashing blows rocking his head from side to side. He smashed an inside right to the face, and saw a thin streak of blood on Shute's cheek. He fired his right down the same groove, and it might well have been on a track. The split in the skin widened, and a trickle of blood started. Rafe let go another one to the same spot, then whipped a wicked left uppercut to the wind.

Shute took it coming in and never lost stride. He ducked and lunged, knocking Rafe off balance with his shoulder, then swinging an overhand punch that caught Rafe on the cheekbone. Rafe tried to sidestep and failed, slipping on a wet spot on the floor. As he went down, Dan Shute aimed a terrific kick at his head that would have ended the fight right there but, half off balance, Rafe hurled himself at the pivot leg and knocked Dan sprawling.

Both men came up and walked into each other, slugging. Rafe evaded a kick aimed for his stomach and slapped a palm under the man's heel, lifting it high. Shute went over on his back, and Rafe left the floor in a dive and lit right in the middle of Dan Shute and knocked the wind out of him, but not enough so that Dan's thumb failed to stab him in the eye.

Blinded by pain, Rafe jerked his head away from that stabbing thumb and felt it rip along his cheek. Then he slammed two blows to the head before Shute heaved him off. They came up together.

Dan Shute was bleeding from the cut on his cheek, but he was still smiling. His gray shirt was torn, revealing bulging white muscles. He was not even breathing hard, and he walked into Rafe with a queer little bounce in his step. Rafe weaved right to left, then straightened suddenly and left-handed a stiff one into Shute's mouth. Dan went under a duplicate punch and slammed a right to the wind that lifted Rafe off the floor. They went into a clinch then, and Rafe was the faster, throwing Dan with a rolling hillock. He came off the floor fast, and the two went over like a pinwheel, gouging, slugging, ripping, and tearing at each other with fists, thumbs, and elbows.

Shute was up first, and Rafe followed, lunging in, but Dan stepped back and whipped a right uppercut that smashed every bit of sense in Rafe's head into a blinding pinwheel of white light. But he was moving fast and went on in with the impetus of his rush, and both men crashed to the floor.

Up again and swinging, they stood toe to toe and slugged viciously, wickedly, each punch a killing blow. Jaws set, they lashed at each other like madmen. Then Rafe let his right go down the groove to the cut cheek. He sidestepped and let go again, then again and again. Five times straight he hit that split cheek. It was cut deeply now and streaming blood.

Dan rushed and grabbed Rafe around the knees, heaving him clear of the floor. He brought him down with a thunderous crash that would have killed a lesser man. Rafe got up, panting, and was set for Shute as he rushed. He split Dan's lips with another left, then threw a right that missed and caught a punch in the middle that jerked his mouth open and brought his breath out of his lungs in one great gasp.

All reason gone, the two men fought like animals, yet worse than animals for in each man was the experience of years of accumulated brawling and slugging in the hard, tough, wild places of the world. They lived by their strength and their hands and the fierce animal drive that was within them, the drive of the fight for survival.

Rafe stepped in, punching Shute with a wicked, cutting, stabbing left, and his right went down the line again, and blood streamed from the cut cheek. They stood then, facing each other, shirts in ribbons, blood-streaked, with arms a-swing. They started to circle, and suddenly Shute lunged. Rafe took one step back and let go a kick from the hips. An inch or so lower down and he would have caught the bigger man in the solar plexus. As it was, the kick struck him on the chest and lifted him clear of the floor. He came down hard, but his powerful arms grabbed Rafe's leg as they swung down, and both men hit the floor together.

Shute sank his teeth into Rafe's leg, and Rafe stabbed at his eye with a thumb. Shute let go and got up, grabbing a chair. Rafe went under it, heard the chair splinter, and scarcely realized in the heat of battle that his back had taken the force of the blow. He shoved Dan back and smashed both hands into the big man's body, then rolled aside and spilled him with a rolling hillock.

Dan Shute came up, and Rafe walked in. He stabbed a left to the face, and Shute's teeth showed through his lip, broken and ugly. Rafe set himself and whipped an uppercut that stood Shute on his toes.

Tottering and punch-drunk, the light of battle still flamed in Shute's eyes. He grabbed at a bottle and lunged at Rafe, smashing it down on his shoulders. Rafe rolled with the blow and felt the bottle shatter over the compact mass of the deltoid at the end of his shoulder, then he hooked a left with that same numb arm, and felt the fist sink into Shute's body.

The strong muscles of that rock-ribbed stomach were yielding now. Rafe set himself and threw a right from the hip to the same place, and Shute staggered, his face greenish-white. Rafe walked in and stabbed three times with a powerful, cutting left that left Shute's lips in shreds. Then, suddenly calling on some hidden well of strength, Dan dived for Rafe's legs, got him around the knees, and jerked back. Rafe hit the floor on the side of his head, and his world splintered into fragments of broken glass and light, flickering and exploding in a flaming chain reaction. He rolled over, took a kick on the chest, then staggered up as Shute stepped in, drunk with a chance of victory. Heavy, brutal punches smashed him to his knees, but Rafe staggered up. A powerful blow brought him down again, and he lunged to his feet.

Again he went to his knees, and again, he came up. Then he uncorked one of his own, and Dan Shute staggered. But Dan had shot his bolt. Head ringing, Rafe Caradec walked in, grabbed the bigger man by the shirt collar and belt, right hand at the belt, then turned his back on him and jerked down with his left hand at the collar and heaved up with the right. He got his back under him, and then hurled the big man like a sack of wheat.

Dan Shute hit the table beside which Gene Baker was standing, and both went down in a heap. Suddenly Shute rolled over and came to his knees, his eyes blazing. Blood streamed from the gash in his cheek, open now from mouth to ear, his lips were shreds, and a huge blue lump concealed one eye. His face was scarcely human, yet in the remaining eye gleamed a wild, killing, insane light. And in his hands he held Gene Baker's double-barreled shotgun! He did not speak—just swept the gun up and squeezed down on both triggers.

Yet at the very instant that he squeezed those triggers, Rafe's left hand had dropped to the table near him, and with one terrific heave he spun it toward the kneeling man. The gun belched flame and thunder as Rafe hit the floor flat on his stomach, and rolled over to see an awful sight.

Joe Benson, crouched over the bar, took the full blast of buckshot in the face and went over backward with a queer, choking scream.

Rafe heaved himself erect, and suddenly the room was deathly still. Pod Gomer's face was a blank sheet of white horror as he stared at the spot where Benson had vanished.

Staggering, Caradec walked toward Dan Shute. The man lay on his back, arms outflung, head lying at a queer angle.

Mullaney pointed. "The table," he said. "It busted his neck."

Rafe turned and staggered toward the door. Johnny Gill caught him there. He slid an arm under Rafe's shoulders and strapped his guns to his waist.

"What about Gomer?" he asked.

Caradec shook his head. Pod Gomer was getting up to face him, and he lifted a hand. "Don't start anything. I've had enough. I'll go."

Somebody brought a bucket of water, and Rafe fell on his knees and began splashing the ice-cold water over his head and face. When he had dried himself on a towel someone had handed him, he started for a coat. Baker had come in with a clean shirt from the store.

"I'm sorry about that shotgun," he said. "It happened so fast I didn't know."

Rafe tried to smile, and couldn't. His face was stiff and swollen. "Forget it," he said. "Let's get out of here."

"Yuh ain't goin' to leave, are yuh?" Baker asked. "Ann said that she . . ."

"Leave? Shucks, no! We've got an oil business here, and there's a ranch. While I was at the fort, I had a wire sent to the C Bar down in Texas for some more cattle."

Ann was waiting for him, wide-eyed when she saw his face. He walked past her toward the bed and fell across it. "Don't let it get you, honey," he said. "We'll talk about it when I wake up next week."

She stared at him, started to speak, and a snore sounded in the room. Ma Baker smiled. "When a man wants to sleep, let him sleep, and I'd say he'd earned it."

About the Author

Louis Dearborn LaMoore (1908-1988) was born in Jamestown, North Dakota. He left home at fifteen and subsequently held a wide variety of jobs although he worked mostly as a merchant seaman. From his earliest youth, L'Amour had a love of verse. His first published work was a poem, "The Chap Worth While," appearing when he was eighteen years old in his former hometown's newspaper, the *Jamestown Sun*. L'Amour wrote poems and articles for a number of small circulation arts magazines all through the early 1930s and, after hundreds of rejection slips, finally had his first story accepted, "Anything for a Pal" in *True Gang Life* (10/35). He returned in 1938 to live with his family where they had settled in Choctaw, Oklahoma, determined to make writing his career. He wrote a fight story bought by Standard Magazines that year and became acquainted with editor Leo Margulies who was to play an important rôle later in L'Amour's life. "The Town No Guns Could Tame" in *New Western* (3/40) was his first published Western story.

During the Second World War L'Amour was drafted and ultimately served with the U.S. Army Transportation Corps in Europe. However, in the two years before he was shipped out, he managed to write a great many adventure stories for Standard Magazines. The first story he published in 1946, the year of his discharge, was a Western, "Law of the Desert Born" in *Dime Western* (4/46). A call to Leo Margulies resulted in L'Amour's agreeing to write Western stories for the various Western pulp magazines published by Standard Magazines, a third of which appeared under the byline Jim Mayo, the name of a character in L'Amour's earlier adventure fiction.

L'Amour's first Western novel under his own byline was *Westward the Tide* (World's Work, 1950). L'Amour sold his first Western short story to a slick magazine two years later, "The Gift of Cochise" in *Collier's* (7/5/52). Robert Fellows and John Wayne purchased screen rights to this story from L'Amour for $4,000 and James Edward Grant, one of Wayne's favorite screenwriters, developed a script from it. L'Amour retained the right to novelize Grant's screenplay, which differs substantially from his short story. *Hondo* (Fawcett Gold Medal, 1953) by Louis L'Amour was released on the same day as the film, *Hondo* (Warner, 1953), with a first printing of 320,000 copies.

With *Showdown at Yellow Butte* (Ace, 1953) by Jim Mayo, L'Amour began a series of short Western novels for Don Wollheim that could be doubled with other short novels by other authors in Ace Publishing's paperback two-fers. Advances on these were $800 and usually the author earned few royalties. *Heller with a Gun* (Fawcett Gold Medal, 1955) was the first of a series of original Westerns L'Amour had agreed to write under his own name following the success for Fawcett of *Hondo*.

The great turn in L'Amour's fortunes came about when he was signed by Bantam Books. By 1962 he was writing three original paperback novels a year. *All* of his Bantam Western titles came to be continuously kept in print. Independent distributors were required to buy titles in lots of 10,000 copies if they wanted access to other Bantam titles at significantly discounted prices. L'Amour himself comprised the other half of this successful strategy. He dressed up in cowboy outfits, traveled about the country in a motor home visiting with independent distributors, taking them to dinner and charming them, making them personal friends. He promoted himself at every available opportunity, insisting he was telling the stories of the people who had made America a great nation and he appealed to patriotism as much as to commercialism in his rhetoric. There are also several characteristics in purest form that, no matter how diluted they ultimately would become, account in largest measure for the loyal following Louis L'Amour won from his readers: the young male narrator who is in the process of growing into manhood and who is evaluating other human beings and his own experiences; a resourceful frontier woman who has beauty as well as fortitude; a strong male character who is single and hence marriageable; and the powerful, romantic, strangely compelling vision of the American West which invests L'Amour's Western fiction and makes it such a delightful escape from the cares of a later time—in this author's words that "big country needing big men and women to live in it" and where there was no place for "the frightened or the mean."

Center Point Large Print
600 Brooks Road / PO Box 1
Thorndike, ME 04986-0001 USA

(207) 568-3717

US & Canada:
1 800 929-9108
www.centerpointlargeprint.com